Praise for Walk with

Annie Wald reminds us that a wedding is more of a jour
marriage is more of a story than a to-do list. There is no
a creative guide.

—JOHN ORTBERG, senior pastor of Menlo Park Presbyteria... ......, and author of
Who Is This Man?

Annie has given couples a glimpse of hope with an amazing story through *Walk with Me!* Using *Pilgrim's Progress* as a foundation for her story was the perfect plan. **Every couple should read this book** to get a different perspective of what it takes to succeed in marriage through the power of the Holy Spirit!

—DR. GARY SMALLEY, author of *The DNA of Relationships*

In marriage, "two become one flesh" and travel together on a journey full of great troubles and joys. **Wald's allegory provides** *Pilgrim's Progress* realism about how daunting the troubles and ultimately joyous the journey when two lovers set out in faith for the King's city.

—Harold Myra, author and former CEO of Christianity Today International

Annie Wald has written a classic. It's a classic not just because Annie is a skilled writer, but because she will touch the depth of your soul. She really gets love. Not everyone does. Annie does this by combining two genres—a marriage book and an allegorical pilgrimage—that no one has combined before. It works beautifully because marriage is a pilgrimage; in fact, all long-term love is a pilgrimage. The allegory form allows Annie to say hard things about love easily and lightly, allowing her to get in close to your heart and do surgery before you know it is happening.
It is an excellent book. I teared up several times in the last twenty pages.

—PAUL MILLER, author of *A Praying Life* and *Love Walked Among Us*

Walk with Me lights up married life in fresh ways on virtually every page. Its insights are simultaneously fascinating, instructive, encouraging, sobering, and transforming. And all of this comes in the form of a story **that reads like a good mystery novel; you can't put it down!** Above all, Annie Wald shapes her compelling allegory around the singular passion that assures fulfillment for any couple: the King's Highlands, the King's City— the King, Jesus. Ultimately, *Walk with Me* is about for whom and to whom we're walking together. That's why it overflows with great hope for anyone seeking God's best for their marriage.

—DAVID BRYANT, founder, Proclaim Hope!; author, *Christ Is All!*

Walk with Me is the kind of story that **hits to the heart of every couple's journey** toward healing and restoration! We will make this a must-read for every couple before they come to our Smalley Intensive program!

—MICHAEL AND AMY SMALLEY, founders of SmalleyCenter.com

Walk with Me

an allegory

To Charlie
Blessings
as you
journey on!
Annie
Wald

ANNIE WALD

Foreword by Eugene H. Peterson

MOODY PUBLISHERS

CHICAGO

All Scripture quotations, unless otherwise indicated, are taken from the *Holy Bible: New International Version®*, NIV®. Copyright ©1973, 1978, 1984 by Biblica, Inc.™ Used by permission of Zondervan. All rights reserved worldwide. www.zondervan.com

Scripture quotations marked NLT are taken from the *Holy Bible, New Living Translation*, copyright © 1996, 2004. Used by permission of Tyndale House Publishers, Inc., Wheaton, Illinois 60189, U.S.A. All rights reserved.

Scripture quotations marked THE MESSAGE are from *The Message*, copyright © by Eugene H. Peterson 1993, 1994, 1995. Used by permission of NavPress Publishing Group.

Scripture quotations marked ESV are taken from *The Holy Bible, English Standard Version*. Copyright © 2000, 2001 by Crossway Bibles, a division of Good News Publishers. Used by permission. All rights reserved.

Edited by Andy Scheer
Interior design: Ragont Design
Cover and illustration design: Maralynn Jacoby
Author photo: Jack Wald

Library of Congress Cataloging-in-Publication Data

Wald, Annie.
Walk with me : pilgrim's progress for married couples / Annie Wald.
    p. cm.
ISBN 978-0-8024-0593-7
1. Man-woman relationships—Fiction. 2. Married people—Fiction. I. Title.
PS3623.A35665W35 2012
813'.6—dc23
                                    2012020939

We hope you enjoy this book from River North Fiction by Moody Publishers. Our goal is to provide high-quality, thought-provoking books and products that connect truth to your real needs and challenges. For more information on other books and products written and produced from a biblical perspective, go to www.moodypublishers.com or write to:

River North Fiction
Imprint of Moody Publishers
820 N. LaSalle Boulevard
Chicago, IL 60610

1 3 5 7 9 10 8 6 4 2

Printed in the United States of America

This book is dedicated to Jack
who walks the pilgrim way with me
and to Elizabeth & Matt, Caitlin & John:
Happy trails . . .

"How blessed all those in whom you live,
whose lives become roads you travel;
They wind through lonesome valleys,
come upon brooks, discover cool springs and pools,
brimming with rain!
God-traveled, these roads curve up the mountain
and at the last turn—Zion! God in full view!"

—Psalm 84:5–7 The Message

Contents

the great garden

slouching city

gathering hut

upright villiage

With many similar parables Jesus spoke
the word to them, as much as they could understand.
He did not say anything to them without using a parable.

—MARK 4:33–34

Foreword

. . . .

Celeste grew up in Slouching City. Peter grew up in Upright Village. Both on their way to the King's City, they meet at a gathering hut, fall in love, and become partners in the journey. Using John Bunyan's pioneering allegory of *Pilgrim's Progress* as a model, Annie Wald tells a *Pilgrim's Progress* story for married couples.

Marriage is wonderful. Marriage is difficult. Most of us know that without really thinking about it. But few of us have an imagination capable of comprehending both the dazzling days and the dark nights that lie ahead. Annie Wald brings her considerable skills as a writer of fiction to explore the intricacies involved in both the ecstasies and the difficulties encountered in the country of marriage. Her use of John Bunyan's *Pilgrim's Progress* as an allegory of the complexities involved in the Christian life provides images and circumstances that prevent us from turning the subject of marriage into a laundry list of things to be done and avoided.

Such laundry lists are a drug on the market: do this; don't do that—accompanied by promises of a better life if we are just determined and persistent enough to keep the rules. But the results are not very impressive. The fact is, we need a story if we are going to understand our marriages as a living, inter-relational, creative exploration in the ways of love—God's perfect love and our imperfect loves. For love cannot be explained or defined. It is the deepest, most complex partici-pation in the human condition and requires grace and crea-tivity—not rules and principles. A story is precisely the kind of language designed to deal with the unique conditions of married love—not a handbook, not a therapeutic technique, but a story that integrates God's love and ours in the mar-riage covenant.

It is significant that stories are given such a prominent role in revealing God and God's ways to us. In both the Old and New Testaments of our Christian Scriptures, stories are the major verbal means of bringing God's Word to us. For that we can be grateful, for story is our most accessible form of speech. Young and old love stories; literate and illiterate alike tell and listen to stories. Neither stupidity nor sophistication puts us outside the magnetic field of story. The only serious rival to story in terms of accessibility and attraction is song, and there are plenty of those in the Bible too.

But there is another reason for the appropriateness of story as a major means of bringing God's Word into our lives. Story doesn't just tell us something and leave it there—it invites our participation. A good storyteller gathers us into the story. We feel the emotions, get caught up in the drama, identify with the characters, see into nooks and crannies of life that we had overlooked, and realize there is more to this business of being human than we had yet explored. If the storyteller is good, doors and windows open. Annie Wald and John Bunyan are good storytellers, good in both the artistic and moral sense.

One characteristic of Scripture stories is a certain reticence. They don't tell us too much. They leave a lot of blanks in the narration, an implicit invitation to enter the stories, just as we are, and find how we fit into it. *Walk with Me* is a story like that. It respects our freedom; it doesn't manipulate us, doesn't force us. It shows us a spacious world in which God creates and saves and blesses. First through our imaginations and then through our faith—imagination and faith are close kin here—we are offered a place in the story, invited into this large story that takes place under the broad skies of God's purposes, in contrast to the gossipy anecdotes that we cook up in the stuffy closet of the self.

The form in which language comes to us is as important as its content. If we mistake its form, we will almost certainly respond wrongly to its content. If we mistake a recipe for lamb stew for a set of clues for finding buried treasure, no matter how carefully we read it, we will end up as poor as ever and hungry besides. Ordinarily, we learn these discriminations early and well and give equal weight to both form and content in determining meaning.

But sometimes when we are faced with the task of Christian living, and in this case, the task of Christian marriage, we don't do that. We pick out rules or advice or "principles"— *de-story* them from the story of God—then apply what we read apart from the story of God. We try to dress the story, this marriage pilgrimage story, in the latest Paris silk gown of theology or outfit it in a sturdy three-piece suit of ethics, so we can deal with it on our terms, not God's. The simple story is soon, like David under Saul's armor, so encumbered with moral admonitions, theological constructs, and scholarly debates that it can hardly move. One of the tasks of this book, quite brilliantly executed, is to keep the story out in front.

A major consequence of learning to "read" our lives in the pilgrimage allegory of Celeste and Peter is a sense of affirmation and freedom. We don't have to fit into prefabricated moral or mental or religious boxes before we are admitted into the company of God—we are taken seriously just as we are and given a place in God's story, for it is, after all, *God's* story; none of us are the leading characters in the story of our marriage.

Parents preparing their children for marriage, pastors preparing their parishioners for marriage, and married couples who need a "story" for their marriage will find this book a treasure.

EUGENE H. PETERSON
Professor Emeritus of Spiritual Theology
Regent College
Vancouver, B.C.

On the King's Way

LEAVING SLOUCHING CITY
AND UPRIGHT VILLAGE

I dreamed a dream of love, and in my dream I saw a lonely traveler, Celeste, and another lonely traveler, Peter. Each was walking on the way to the King's City, for they wanted to live life as it was meant to be, whole and holy in a world set right.

Celeste had just started on the journey, for she had grown up in Slouching City where no one ever talked about the King of Love or the rule of His realm. The inhabitants there were clever and cunning, and they were always inventing new machines to do the work of living. But in recent generations the once-magnificent city had begun to sink into a slow and dismal ruin. When it rained, the old drains overflowed with sewage and left a perpetual odor in the air. The outer ramparts were crumbling, and the fences were in dreadful condition. Still, people liked to boast about how wonderful it was to live in a place where they could do whatever they pleased.

As a child, Celeste had often walked among the broken ramparts. If she pushed away the ivy and scraped off the moss, she found, chiseled into the stones, fragments of ancient songs that told of a King's love for the torn world and His Son who came as the Servant to mend the tear. Like almost everyone else in Slouching City, Celeste's parents thought the songs were nonsense. But Celeste's grandfather still knew the old melodies. Every time he sang songs of the Servant's selfless love and the restored wholeness He wanted to give, Celeste felt a deep ache in her soul.

After her grandfather died, she tried to hold on to the promise of the beautiful songs. But her friends teased her when she mentioned the King or the hope of His city. So she grew up and learned the ways of the world: how to push to get ahead and how to grab all she could. Most of the time, she thought she was happy enough, but there were moments when she realized that deep down she felt very lonely. Although life in Slouching City was full of comfort and ease, there was no machine that could create love or keep it alive when it began to fade. As the years went by, she yearned to find a love that would never change or die.

Then one day she found the King's guidebook her grandfather had left. She went back to the broken ramparts to read it. Captivated by the poems and history and visions and stories, she hummed along as she read, for she could hear the echo of her grandfather's songs. Soon tears began to stream down her cheeks; to her grownup heart the old songs sounded even more hopeful than before.

Every afternoon Celeste returned to the ramparts to study the guidebook and learn more about the King. Just as the songs had said, He loved every person in the world. He had sent His Son, the Servant, not to condemn men and women, but to bring them back home to His city where they would be part of His family forever. For He loved them enough to give them His life, first by dying for them and then by giving them His very Breath.

The more Celeste read the guidebook, the more she longed to experience the love of the King and to make her way to His city. But every time she thought about starting the journey, she gave up the idea. All of her outfits were stained and ripped from years of playing in the back lanes of Slouching City. She didn't see how she would be allowed into the King's City wearing such shabby clothes. The doorkeeper would think she was an imposter—not a daughter of the King—and turn her out.

But one day when she came to the ramparts, she found a spotless cloak of fine white linen. "This is My robe of righteousness to cover the stains of your guilt," she heard the King say to her. "Come and take it, because I want you to be My beloved daughter."

Celeste gazed at the bright, radiant robe which was perfect in every way. She could hardly believe that the King would let her wear it. Then she became very sad. "But I have no money to buy such a wonderful robe."

"You cannot pay for it. It is a free gift," the King said. "My Son purchased it for you."

Celeste hesitated a moment, then she took the robe and put it on. The transformation was instantaneous: she had become a member of the King's family. She beamed with delight. Now she could start her journey to His city. "Thank you, thank you," she told the King.

"As you follow the trail I have blazed to My city, go with joy and remain always in My love. Your great adventure begins!"

Like a powerful wind pouring through her being, the Breath of the King filled Celeste—never had she felt so light and free. Then, on the other side of the ramparts, a path opened before her. Hurrying to it, she started on her way. As soon as she stepped out of Slouching City, a glorious country appeared before her, and it seemed that she was looking at the world for the very first time. The sky was bluer than she had ever seen, and there were so many birds singing, it sounded like a symphony. The air held a fragrance whose sweet-smelling bouquet was deeper and fuller than any perfume made in Slouching City. She took one last look at its tumbled-down walls. Now in the bright sunlight, she could see what a small, dark place the city was. Then she turned. Grateful to leave it behind, she set her gaze on the far horizon, and headed to the King's City.

That first day of Celeste's journey the path was straight and flat, bordered with soft ferns. She swung her arms as she walked, singing the King's songs out loud and smiling at the beauty she saw all around. She expected the journey would be smooth and easy the entire way. However the next day, the trail became studded with tree roots and stubby stones. The years she had spent pacing the dead-end alleys of Slouching City had left her legs weak. By early afternoon, she was exhausted. But she pressed on, working to strengthen her flabby muscles.

In the days that followed, she discovered she was not the

only one going to the King's City. There were other travelers on
the path and she became friends with many of them. She enjoyed
walking with them and learning more about the journey. They told
her it was always good to ask other travelers which direction to
go, for some trails through the King's country had been taken
over by people who no longer cared about reaching the King's
City. They encouraged her to stop regularly at the gathering huts
along the way, where travelers shared meals and encouraged each
other, for the long journey to the King's City was not meant to be
taken alone. If she walked with other travelers, it would be easier
to avoid the difficulties and dangers that lay ahead.

One day when Celeste's legs were strong enough, she climbed
to the top of an overlook. As she gazed at the towering peaks, the
thick forests, and the vast, spacious sea, she thought of the great-
ness of the King's love for her, how wide and long and high and
deep it was. She knew that no matter what happened to her or
how hard the journey was, she would never go back to Slouching City. She was headed for a better kingdom, and she couldn't
wait to get there.

She continued on her journey, sometimes walking with other
travelers, sometimes going by herself. Before long, she began to
wish she had someone to walk with the whole way. During the
day, as she enjoyed the scenery and chatted with her new friends,
she didn't mind it so much. But at night as she ate her supper, she
felt a deep yearning for a partner. It was not a thirst that could be
filled in one swallow, but a hunger that could be satisfied only in
a long banquet. Celeste often spent the evening thinking about the
kind of husband she hoped to find. She wanted someone who was

handsome, but witty and brilliant too. Most of all, she wanted a man who would love her with a strong and tender love. As the months went on and she still walked alone, she tried to be patient. For she knew it was better to be single than to join with the wrong partner, even if he was also going to the King's City.

Now in my dream, I saw the other traveler, Peter, as he made his way to the King's City. Unlike Celeste, he had come from an established family of travelers. As a child in Upright Village, his parents had faithfully taken him to the gathering hut every week, where the King's songs were sung, though always off-tune and painfully slow. They dutifully read the guidebook to Peter so he could learn how important it was to obey all the King's rules, in order that when the time came, he would be allowed into the King's City. Peter's parents never ventured on the King's path themselves, for like the other residents in Upright Village they were certain it was more prudent to stay where they were and avoid the dangerous journey.

Because the village had been built as a temporary outpost for travelers and not as a permanent settlement, it was cramped and there was little to do for entertainment. Still, people kept busy guarding the village from attack and cleaning it scrupulously according to the King's guidelines. Not a speck of dirt nor a single weed was allowed to remain, especially in their neighbor's yards. The only real hardship was the lack of water. When the springs had dried up, many residents had moved to Slouching City. But the hardy travelers who remained took great pride in what they suffered for the King.

When Peter was old enough to read the guidebook for himself, he became confused. There was much about the Servant King that he had never heard in all his years in Upright Village. He learned in the guidebook that the Servant had not come to punish people who failed to obey the King. Instead the Servant had come to give those who followed Him life to the full. The Servant promised that if someone believed in Him, streams of living water would flow from within. Peter's heart began to burn with the hope that there was more to life than dour rule keeping. If he really belonged to the Servant, his true life was on the Servant's path to the King's City.

When he told his parents what he aimed to do, they were completely opposed.

"You can keep the King's rules perfectly well here," his father said.

"And you know the way to the King's City is unsafe," his mother said. "The roaring lion prowls around, looking for unsuspecting travelers to devour."

"Don't worry," Peter said. "I've been lifting the weights of decrees and regulations to build my strength. I'm sure I will be able to fight off any dangers on the way."

Peter packed his bag and started on the King's path. But he soon realized the journey would be much more strenuous than he had anticipated because around his waist he wore heavy chains of debt. In the confines of Upright Village, the chains had never bothered him. But now as he crossed streams and climbed hills, it was very taxing to carry the weight. After three months, when he stopped to see how far he had gone, he was discouraged to see that for all his effort, Upright Village was still not far behind.

Peter was no longer confident he could reach the King's City. He could never pay what he owed the King and be freed of his chains. Desperate to go on, he searched in his pack for something to cut through his chains. However, he had left his tools behind. The only thing he could find was a file of good works. He sat down and started to file the chains, but after a week he had filed off just one chain. And by then, two more had been added to the length. Still he was determined to be free of his chains, and he doubled his efforts. If only he could work hard enough, he was sure he could get rid of them. He was still filing away when a wise old guide came upon him.

"Dear friend," Freedom said to Peter. "You can file your chains until the world ends, but you'll never get them off by your own effort. Don't you know the song from the guidebook that tells how the Servant died to free the prisoners from their chains?"

"We never sang that in Upright Village."

"From Upright Village, are you? Now I understand why you're attempting such an impossible task. Only the knife of grace can cut through your chains." Freedom held up a gleaming knife, and before Peter could say anything, he cut through one of Peter's chains as if it was warm butter.

Peter stared in amazement at the broken chain at his feet. Then he fell to his knees and told the King he was sorry for every debt he owed. Freedom helped him cut through the rest of his chains and gave him the knife so he could use it on the journey.

"You mean my chains aren't gone for good?"

"Until you reach the King's City, new links will appear. But when they do, simply tell the King you are sorry and cut them off with His grace."

Freed at last of his heavy chains, Peter was so elated, he started trotting down the path, shouting and kicking pebbles as he went.

THE GREAT QUESTION

As Peter walked on through the Low Country, he stopped at gathering huts and learned many new songs about the King. He also made friends with other travelers who also liked to take long hikes. Together they would go to the highest overlooks where they could look out at the way that lay ahead. However, one by one his friends began to find partners and then had little travelers, and they no longer had time to go exploring with him.

Peter had always thought it would be better to travel to the King's City by himself because he was afraid he might choose the wrong person. Peter knew his parents had started out happy together, for there was a picture hanging in their living room that showed them looking lovingly at each other on their weaving day. But Peter could not remember a single occasion when he had seen them exchange smiles. Peter could also see that his friends had to wait for their partners to get ready every morning, a disagreeable thing for Peter since he liked to start walking as soon as the sun rose. Other friends couldn't go as fast as they used to because now they were carrying their partner's burdens. Peter didn't want to be slowed down like that.

However, in spite of his qualms about having a partner, he became very lonely as he kept walking on the King's path. He went to talk with a guide for advice on how to choose a good partner.

"The journey is very long," Discernment said, "so look for someone you can be friends with, who walks with a similar pace and a similar stride. Don't worry about how pretty she is, for most of the journey you will be walking side by side, not looking at each other. When you find someone you like, take time to see if your attraction will mature into a deeper love or whether it will remain a pleasant friendship. And don't forget that love is a choice, not a feeling. It's important to choose your partner wisely, but it's even more important to choose to love her every day."

The night after he talked to Discernment, Peter sat alone by the campfire. As he looked up at the vast number of stars, he thought what a miracle it would be to find someone who matched him.

He continued his journey and consoled himself that he was free to come and go as he pleased; he didn't have to worry about anyone else. But his loneliness remained. When he heard of a gathering for travelers in the Low Country, with amusements and singing and guides to teach about the King's way, he decided to go. As he drew near, he could hear the sound of chatting and laughing, but when he arrived and saw the grove filled with travelers, he almost turned away, for he much preferred small, quiet gatherings. Then he noticed another traveler halfway across the grove, tilting her head as if trying to hear a song. He was about to walk over and introduce himself when she went up to the front of the gathering and began to sing a song about the Servant. Peter had never heard anyone sing so beautifully. He asked another traveler if he knew anything about the singer. "Her name is

Celeste," the man said. "Fits her well with such a heavenly voice, doesn't it?"

The next day the sun rose bright in the grove, and the travelers woke to the joyful racket of birds proclaiming the King's glory. After a morning of talks and singing, the travelers broke into small groups in the afternoon, according to what they wanted to do. Some were going fishing in the river that flowed beyond the grove, some were going berry picking, and others were climbing to the top of the nearby peak that on a clear day gave a glimpse of the King's City. Normally Peter would have gone on the hike, but he had climbed the peak on his way to the grove and when he saw Celeste join a group of travelers who were going to a nearby meadow to pick berries, he went too. Peter managed to end up walking beside Celeste, and as they went along he began to stare at her, for he saw she was swerving a bit as she walked.

When Celeste realized he was staring at her, she stopped and blushed.

"What are you doing?" he asked. "It looks like you are curving in and out instead of walking a straight line."

Celeste hesitated. She had been mocked by other travelers for her habit of kicking pebbles, but something in Peter's voice made her feel at ease. "I know, I can't help it. Well, I suppose I could help it, but I'd rather not. I like to kick pebbles as I walk. I know it's silly but that's the way I am."

When Peter said nothing, Celeste began to feel uncomfortable. "I'm sorry if it bothers you." She started to walk away.

"No, wait. I am not irritated. I'm just amazed."

"Amazed?"

"Yes, I do the same thing when I am walking by myself."

"Don't make fun of me." Celeste turned red again.

"No, I am telling the truth. Look, here are my pebbles. I've collected some nice ones along the way." He dug into his pocket and took out a handful. He threw the biggest pebble onto the ground and, with the tip of his right shoe, made it skitter across the dirt. Then his left foot stopped it and kicked it ahead to his right foot. "Let's see you do it."

Celeste had no rhyme or reason to the way she kicked pebbles, and she didn't want him to laugh at her. "No, I don't feel like it."

"Don't be embarrassed. I liked the way you were kicking."

Celeste looked at his kind expression. She had never met a person who was so reassuring. "Really?"

"Really. I won't laugh."

She kicked her pebble along, then Peter came beside her, kicking his. On they walked, kicking their pebbles while they hunted for berries. Once when her stone went off into the grass, Peter raced for it and started to kick both his stone and hers at the same time, making her burst out laughing as he twisted around like a top. When they got back to the grove, Peter told Celeste how much he had enjoyed their time.

"So did I," Celeste said.

"I was wondering," he said, "would you like to walk with me tomorrow?"

"I'd love to."

The next afternoon they went with a group who were exploring the paths that wandered in and out of the grove. Peter and Celeste quickly discovered they not only enjoyed kicking pebbles, but they also liked to identify flowers they saw in the woods. They found spearmint and Jack-in-the-Pulpit, lady slippers and violets, and Queen Anne's Lace. As they walked, they talked and talked. Neither had imagined they would ever have so much to talk about with another person—or be so eager to listen. When they returned to the grove, Peter again asked Celeste if she would walk with him the next day.

"Of course," she said.

Before she went to bed that night, she got her pack and took out the collection of postcards she had brought with her. These postcards were not like the ones people buy on vacation to remind them of all the places they visited. These postcards were larger and much more brilliant, each with a scene that revealed a person's deepest yearnings. They were so vivid that if Celeste looked at one long enough, say of a young woman enjoying a honeysuckle flower, she could almost smell the fragrance and imagine that if she reached out she could feel the soft petal and pull out the pistil and taste a drop of sweetness.

One card showed a man and a woman holding hands as they walked in a lush meadow of flowers. Another showed a couple surfing on the waves in front of an expanse of golden sand. There was not a single flaw in her postcards. In card after card, there was not a single flaw to be seen.

When Celeste started on the King's way, some travelers warned her to leave her postcards behind because the desires in them might lead her away from the King; His gifts were always better than what she could imagine. But Celeste cherished her visions of beauty and tenderness and adventure. She didn't see what was wrong about thinking of a sailboat on a turquoise sea or drinking from a jeweled chalice filled with the sweetest pleasures of earthly love or strolling through a garden of roses. Celeste was convinced that if the King loved her, He would give her the desire that was represented in each scene.

After she took out her postcards, she sorted through them until she found her favorite, the vision of romantic love. The scene showed a couple gazing at each other with a gauzy veil between them. Celeste tilted the card to one side. Then a light came down on the couple and the veil came up so they could see each other face-to-face, filled with adoring love until it seemed they were fused into a single being. She stared at the card a long time, imagining the deep oneness of being chosen and loved. Finally she put all her cards away and fell asleep, dreaming of Peter.

In the days that followed at the grove, Peter and Celeste continued spending time together. They meandered while they kicked their pebbles, and they talked about the different flowers they saw alongside the road. Celeste taught Peter duets, and Peter showed Celeste how to climb rock trails. Soon Peter asked Celeste to sit at his table for breakfast. When it was time for a guide to give the morning talk, they always found seats together. Every time Peter took a turn chopping wood and came back tired, Celeste would put warm cloths on his arms to soothe his muscles. Some days Celeste was in charge of singing, then Peter would sit in the front row and watch her with pride. When Celeste was alone with her friends, she couldn't stop talking about Peter—how solid and dependable he was, how knowledgeable and diligent and eager to serve the King.

But the best time each day was when they could go walking

together. They told each other stories about their families and growing up and how they first heard about the King. They found they agreed on almost everything, and the things they didn't, they simply put to one side. When they tired of talking, they kicked pebbles, and when they grew tired of that, they made up songs. Their time together seemed like water flowing down a stream. Just as it was impossible to think of the water flowing in the opposite direction, neither Peter nor Celeste could imagine doing anything but walking and talking together.

Before long they were going into the Meadows of Intimacy to share their deepest secrets. Sometimes they stopped and looked into each other's eyes, and Celeste thought of the couple in her favorite postcard. As she looked at Peter, she felt she was melting into a deep pool, yet at the same time she felt she was being filled.

One week, then another, rushed by. One night Peter stayed up late by the campfire, unable to sleep, poking the coals with a stick. In a few more weeks it would be time to take up his journey again, but he didn't want to leave Celeste. He loved the way she laughed with lightness, how beautifully she sang, and how she could talk with the shyest person. He felt so happy when they walked together, always relaxed and not worrying what she thought. He remembered how she looked at him with admiration when he had skipped a stone across a small pond they discovered. He thought of how much fun they had kicking pebbles together.

The next day, Peter and Celeste volunteered to help collect more berries. They walked through the higher meadow, plinking the berries into their buckets until they came to an overgrown field and sat on a log.

"I could do this forever," Peter said.

"Me, too," Celeste said. "I never get tired of walking in the meadows."

"No, that's not what I meant. I never get tired of walking with you."

"Oh." She smiled. "It's the same for me."

Peter took Celeste's hand and looked into her eyes.

"Will you be my partner? Will you walk with me until we reach the King's City?"

Celeste blushed and took a deep breath. Her vision of romance was finally becoming real; she was chosen and loved by the perfect partner. "Yes," she said. "A hundred yeses. Yes."

THE CORDS OF COMMITMENT

As soon as Peter and Celeste returned to the grove, they began to prepare for their weaving day and send-off party. There were decorations to get, music to find, food to order. When Peter started to tally all the expenses, he suggested they skip the send-off party and just have only a small, private dinner. But Celeste said that was impossible. All her relatives from Slouching City were coming. And besides, she had always wanted to have a fancy send-off celebration.

One day they took a break from their planning and visited a guide named Devotion so they could pick out their Cords of Commitment. When they became partners forever, three strands would be woven around their wrists to make a single bracelet. The first strand represented the strengths they brought to their partnership and the things they shared in common. The second strand symbolized the love that would bind them forever and their willingness to lay down their lives for each other. The last strand stood for the promise they would make to never let go but stay with each other to the very end. Even if the first two strands became frayed, nothing could rip the third strand apart.

There were so many patterns and materials and colors that it took Peter and Celeste a long time to make their decision. They finally chose a royal blue silk for the first strand and a soft, red sheep's wool for the second. For the third, they chose a durable, thick gold.

"This is so exciting," Celeste said as Devotion measured their wrists.

"It is," Devotion said. "But never forget that this braided bracelet is not just something pretty to wear. Your cords will be extremely sensitive to the state of your partnership. They will match the invisible threads that will intertwine through your hearts when you become one. Once the cords are on your wrists, they will cause painful wounds if they are ever cut off. So I trust you have considered well your decision to become partners."

"We're absolutely sure." Peter looked at Celeste with a loving smile.

Celeste smiled back. "There is no one else I want for a partner but Peter."

"I have seen many who became partners while they were still traveling in the Low Country," Devotion said. "But when they set out for the Mountains of Maturity, as everyone must, they came to challenging routes they never knew existed. Soon the excitement of being partners disappeared, and they discovered their partner had flaws and limitations they had never seen before. Their cords began to chafe, and sometimes in desperation they wished to take them off."

"You don't have to worry about us doing that," Celeste said.

"We agree with the guidebook," Peter said. "Anyone who cuts the cords, except for unfaithfulness, and joins with another partner breaks the King's rule."

"That is a good start, but I still want to caution you. You will be traveling together longer than you have already lived, and on a path harder than you have ever walked. You may suffer burrs of unkind words. You may go through the Swamp of Selfishness, the Plains of Distance, or even the Way of Winter. You may doubt that your partner really is the right one for you. You may begin to feel like a prisoner, and your braided cords will feel like handcuffs."

"You make it sound so gloomy!" Celeste said. "Don't you have any encouragement for us?"

Devotion chuckled. "You're right. Although there is no partnership in the King's City, He created the first partners in the Great Garden. Having a partner can double your joys and divide your griefs. You will lose some freedom walking together, but you will also gain many benefits. You will share the greater strength of two halves made into one whole. You will find pleasant paths and warm mineral springs. When you experience the glory of drinking from the chalice together, you will find your most intimate desires satisfied. You may be blessed with the joy of little travelers—and with them will come many new ways to show how much you love each other.

"Whatever comes," Devotion continued, "your love can protect you and help you to persevere. I'm sorry if I sounded too pessimistic. These days so many partners are separating and cutting their cords." He went to a cabinet and took out two pairs of scissors.

The young travelers shrank away. "We don't want those," Peter said.

"We will never need them," Celeste said.

Devotion rolled up each pair of scissors in a thick cloth. "I'll put them in the bottoms of your packs. You will do well to leave them there."

"But do we have to take them at all?" Celeste said.

"Remember the King has set you free. You are no longer slaves. You always have the choice to do good or to do harm, even when you take on a partner."

"Wouldn't it be better if there weren't any scissors?"

"There have been times when scissors have been hard to find, but the scissors are not the real problem. The King intended partnership to make you stronger—and to make you shine more brightly together than alone. But to do this you must love each other with a deep, selfless love. Many partners who have not cut their cords believe they are still following the King's way, but their partnership is only an empty shell of the King's design. It's only a duty for them, or worse, a prison. So don't be fooled into thinking that if you wear your cords with a cold heart, you are fulfilling the law of love."

Finally the day came for Peter and Celeste to be joined. The sky was crisp and blue, as beautiful as any postcard. Celeste trembled as she put on her white dress. She felt like a princess, and her mother said she had never looked more lovely. Peter wore a new suit, and his mother began crying when she saw him in it. She said it seemed only yesterday when he had been a little boy and refused to wear one.

Peter and Celeste walked together through the gathering and stood before Faithfulness. Before the guide wove the cords on their wrists, he gave them some counsel. "Peter and Celeste, each of you has been greatly blessed with gifts. Peter, you are a serious follower of the King. Your faith is so strong that you could move a mountain if you had to. But remember this gift is worthless if you are not loving. Strength used without love is the worst power in the world. You could put every mountain into the ocean, and you would be nothing if you did it without love.

"And Celeste, you have a wonderful gift of words—you speak with such expressiveness, and when you sing the King's songs, it sounds like an angel. But your songs will sound like rusty hinges if you sing without love.

"Now listen to the description of love that the guidebook gives—and keep it close to your hearts.

Love is patient and kind;
love does not envy or boast;
it is not arrogant or rude.
It does not insist on its own way;
it is not irritable or resentful;
it does not rejoice at wrongdoing,
but rejoices with the truth.

"This is the love of the King, which He has given to you—and now you can give this love to each other. Remember, the King's love never gives up and never loses faith. His love is always hopeful. His love endures through every circumstance."

Then Faithfulness took the three strands and began to weave them around Peter's and Celeste's wrists as they sang their pledge together:

> *"I take you as my partner, to live in the covenant of love.*
> *Heart of my heart, flesh of my flesh, bone of my bone.*
> *Whom the King has joined together with me, let no person*
>   *pull apart."*

The cords became strong and bright as they sang on:

> *"I will love you, I will honor you,*
> *I will give you my affections.*
> *I will walk with no other partner,*
> *and no matter how dark or how cold the way,*
> *no matter how weak you become,*
> *I will love you always and walk together with you*
> *until we reach the King's City."*

Faithfulness had Peter and Celeste join hands and raise them high so all the crowd could see the cords. "Peter and Celeste, husband and wife, partners forever."

A great cheer went up through the gathering. As Peter and Celeste stood there, glowing with love for each other, some people thought they were seeing a glimpse of what it would be like to stand before the King, fully loved by Him.

Afterward the new partners were greeted by the guests. An unfamiliar couple approached, and Celeste whispered to Peter, "Do you know who they are?"

"I'm not sure. I think it's the couple who lived next door to us when I was growing up. But they've changed so much, I hardly recognize them. The woman was a nasty gossip, and the man was stingy and mean. Look at how joyful they are now."

Indeed, the couple looked radiant, as if their journey together had transformed them into a source of light.

"Lord Will and Lady Sophia." The man extended his hand to Peter. "Congratulations. We're so happy for you."

"We didn't bring our gifts today," Lady Sophia said. "But we hope you can come visit us soon so we can give them to you."

"We'd love to," Celeste said, happy at the thought of getting more presents.

"They're not too heavy, are they?" Peter said, thinking of the extra clothes Celeste wanted to add to their bags.

"Oh no," Lord Will said. "These special kingly gifts are very light."

"And they will make your journey together easier—" Lady Sophia said.

"So you'll be able to reach the Highlands," Lord Will said.

"The Highlands?" Peter and Celeste asked in unison.

"The King's Highlands—"

"As close as you can get to His city without crossing over—"

"A wonderful region of blessing and joy—"

"Where the view is so much better," Lady Sophia said. "You

can see out over the entire land of the King and wander in the high meadows—"

"And the chalice is sweeter and richer and thicker, like milk and honey mixed together."

"But milk is an ordinary drink," Celeste said.

"Not this milk," Lord Will said. "You've never tasted such milk. It gives you energy and strength and joy, long after you have finished drinking."

"If we follow the King's path, will we be sure to get there?" Peter asked.

"No, not every traveler reaches the Highlands. That's why we want to give you our gifts. They will help you on the climb."

Peter and Celeste promised they would come for their gifts soon.

When night came, Peter and Celeste said goodbye to everyone and set off for the moon of honey. They held hands and followed a path lit by a golden moon that brought them to a small, private meadow. The air was warm and scented with roses. In the center of the meadow was a beautiful chalice of gold and silver, ringed with sparkling diamonds. They walked to the chalice. Each taking a handle, they lifted it and drank. It was the sweetest, most refreshing liquid they had ever tasted, revealing their innermost selves and binding them into one. Then they sang a song of the King:

> *Place me like a seal over your heart,*
> *like a seal on your arm;*
> *for love is as strong as death,*

its jealousy unyielding as the grave.
It burns like blazing fire,
like a mighty flame.
Many waters cannot quench love;
rivers cannot wash it away.
If one were to give
all the wealth of his house for love,
it would be utterly scorned.

"Oh Peter, I have never been so happy," Celeste said.

"It's the same for me," Peter said. "And it all began with a simple walk."

But in my dream as I looked ahead, I saw that Peter and Celeste did not walk happily ever after.

In the Low Country

THE FORBIDDEN MEADOW

few days later, Celeste reminded Peter about picking up Lord Will and Lady Sophia's gifts, but he didn't want to take a detour. "I'm not sure it's a good idea to stop just after we've started out together."

"Maybe you're right," Celeste said. "As much as I enjoy getting gifts, I think our love for the King will be enough for us."

"And we have our supplies and the guidebook to the King's City."

"And the chalice." Celeste smiled.

"Exactly," Peter said.

They decided they would follow the moon of honey for as long as they could. The path was straight and flat, wide enough to walk side by side. Broad shade trees sheltered them from the noonday sun. They joined often to drink from the chalice. But for all their drinking, they never tired of the sweet liquid of love. They watched sunrises and sunsets and stopped for long picnics whenever they came to a meadow. Their happiness was just as Faithfulness had described, so they were quite sure he had exaggerated the dangers of being partners. They had seen no mountain ranges in the distance, or swamps or plains, only woods and lowlands dotted with lakes.

Then one day they came to a side path that turned sharply off the main road. When they stopped to look where it led, they could see an inviting forest dell in the distance—and beyond that, the tiniest glimpse of the King's City. As they got closer, they could hear a brook gurgling. Clusters of butterflies flitted through the air. Over the next rise, they came to a large meadow covered with white clover like a carpet, its edge trimmed with rows of lavender. The path led straight through the meadow.

"What a beautiful path. Oh Peter, let's take it. We must." One of Celeste's postcards bore a striking resemblance to the scene. She was so happy, she was ready to push Peter down the path.

But Peter stopped short. "Wait." He pointed to an ancient sign planted at the entrance. Printed in large letters were the words, "Verboten. Interdit. Forbidden. Prohibido. Terlarang. Haramu. Yasak . . ." The word was written in 623 other languages, and there was a button to push that played the sign's message in any language that was spoken but not written. Every traveler who came that way would know what the sign meant.

"It doesn't make any sense," Celeste said. "This is the nicest path we've come to. I can't imagine why we wouldn't be allowed to take it."

"Well, not everything that looks pleasant is always good for us," Peter said.

"True, but I don't see any harm in taking this way. Check the map. I'm sure there's some mistake."

Peter found the path on the map. "You're right. It looks like a very direct way to the King's City."

"So there you are." Celeste felt pleased with herself. "How ridiculous to tell us not to take a path that goes to the King's City. Besides, if this path really was forbidden, the sign would have explained why."

"I don't know." Peter hesitated. "On the map there's a hatched line through the path, as if it has been blocked off. Maybe we should turn back."

"Come on, Peter, you don't live in Upright Village anymore. We're free to do whatever we want." Celeste didn't realize she was beginning to sound like her relatives back in Slouching City. "And the path is so well-worn—how can it be the wrong way? Besides, it looks like it would be a wonderful place to drink from the chalice."

Peter gave up trying to persuade Celeste to turn away, and together they went down the path.

"Look," Celeste said. "I've never seen so many tulips in different shades of white and pink and red and orange and yellow. And there's a flowering orange tree." She stopped and pulled a branch down so she could inhale the fragrance.

"Come on," Peter said, wanting to hurry her along.

"But we'll never come by this way again."

"I'm sure we'll see flowers like this from time to time." He took her hand and gave it a tug.

Celeste held her ground. "Maybe next year there will be a drought and the flowers won't be so pretty. Please, let's stop and rest for just a bit. I'm getting a little tired. You're walking too fast."

"We don't have time, dear, if we're going to drink from the chalice," Peter said.

"Yes, we do," Celeste said. "And don't speak to me like I was a child."

"No, we don't, and I'm not speaking to you like a child."

"Yes, we do—and you are."

"No, we don't."

They argued as they walked, concentrating so hard on gaining the upper hand that neither noticed a humming noise that grew louder as they went up the hill.

Then Celeste looked up and noticed a dark cloud forming at the hill's crest. The humming sounded like a thousand doors being buzzed. "Peter, look. What is it?"

"Bees. Run!"

They turned and sprinted as fast as they could, but suddenly bees were everywhere. Peter was the first to get stung, then Celeste was stung twice. Each time she screamed.

They kept running, trying to dodge them. But if Peter leaped to avoid a swarm on the left, another swarm would mass to the right. So he flapped his arms and legs as he ran, but several bees found their way under his shirt and pants.

Celeste tried to run bent over, to keep the bees from flying into her face. But they came up from the clover and stung her under the chin and on her arms.

Finally Peter and Celeste escaped from the meadow. Back on the main path, they stopped to catch their breath.

"Where did those bees come from?" Celeste asked between gulps of air.

"The sign said 'forbidden.'"

"But it didn't say why."

"I shouldn't have listened to you."

"Listened to me? We went down the path together. I didn't force you."

"I wouldn't have taken it except you were so eager."

"If you knew better, why didn't you stop me?"

"Oh, be quiet."

"We're in this together—" Celeste began.

"Shut up." Peter scowled.

Celeste had never seen Peter so angry. Her lip began to quiver. She felt tricked that such a wonderful-looking path could turn into a disaster. For the first time, she doubted her postcards. What if some of her other cards had also deceived her? "It's not my fault," she said. "We didn't have any signs in Slouching City. How was I supposed to know it was serious?"

They treated their bites with balm, but that took a long time, especially since they refused to help each other with the ones on their backs.

Peter finished first, and he started stomping down the path without Celeste.

"Wait, don't leave me," Celeste said. "The stings hurt so much."

Peter turned around. "You can still walk."

"I can't." She whimpered in her most pitiful voice, but Peter refused to wait.

"You are so heartless," Celeste yelled after him.

"You're driving me mad, so we're even."

Celeste dragged herself after Peter—and comforted herself that it was all his fault. If she had gone down the path with another partner, the day wouldn't have turned out so badly. Another man would have agreed to stop and smell the flowers. Another man would have been nice enough to walk slowly. Another man would have waited for her. Another man would have asked her what she wanted to do. For the first time since becoming partners with Peter, she wept.

When they stopped for lunch, they ate in silence, each blaming the other for what they had suffered. They were still eating when they saw a guide coming down the path toward them. Ashamed to be seen covered with bee stings from the forbidden meadow, they quickly hid behind some trees.

Kingly Obedience walked to where they were hiding. "What happened? Did you find trouble?"

Celeste stepped from behind the tree. "Something has to be done about that sign at the entrance. It's not explicit enough."

The guide just stood quietly.

"This area is part of the King's country like every other part," Celeste said, "and we're free to go wherever we want. So why are there any forbidden paths at all, especially a path that goes directly to the King's City?"

Kingly Obedience looked at Peter, peeking out from his tree. "What are you looking at me for?" Peter said. "She's the one who wanted to go down the path in the first place."

Kingly Obedience sighed. "No matter how many people read the sign, no one ever believes it. There used to be a lengthy explanation, but it didn't do any good. People would try to find a loophole to worm their way through, so the sign was put back to the original, one-word command."

"So we weren't the only ones to make that mistake?" The thought made Celeste feel a little better.

"I'm sure you've read in the guidebook how the first partners disobeyed the King and suffered the consequences. Adam went from being Eve's mate to being her master—from being her lover to being her lord. Eve's desire for Adam grew so strong, she was no longer willing to risk losing his love. She avoided conflict with him and turned to scheming and manipulating to get what she wanted. The King's perfect plan for partnership was ruined."

Celeste bit her lip, thinking of her beautiful postcards.

"Today, you too have experienced the consequences of ignoring the King's commands." Kingly Obedience shook his head. "I sometimes wonder why He puts up with such flagrant disobedience."

"Why does He?" Celeste said. Suddenly it seemed the King's fault that her postcard scene had been ruined by the bees. If He had built a barrier across the path to block their way, it would have been impossible to take a wrong turn—and she would still have her perfect postcard vision.

"Because He loves you, pure and simple. Still, He does not force you, and you are free to go where you like. But if you do whatever you want, you will end up destroying the very freedom He bought for you with His life. Instead, you can use your freedom to serve one another in love. That's real freedom."

Peter pointed a finger at Celeste. "Well, I wouldn't have taken the path if it hadn't been for her."

"Don't be so quick, my friend. If you have never disobeyed a sign, go ahead and judge her." Kingly Obedience gave Peter a chance to reflect. "As I suspected. None of us has obeyed perfectly, except the Servant, and He does not condemn you. Go now, and don't disobey any more signs."

AT LADY SOPHIA AND LORD WILL'S

The next morning Peter woke up and saw Celeste sleeping beside him, her face and arms covered with red welts from the bee stings. His heart again filled with tenderness for her. He told the King he was sorry he had been harsh to Celeste, and he vowed to be more careful in choosing their paths. To make it up to Celeste, he brought her breakfast and knelt beside her. "I'm so sorry for the way I behaved and all those terrible things I said yesterday. Will you still walk with me?"

"Oh yes, Peter. I'm sorry too. I don't ever want us to have another day like that."

"You know, our journey together may be more difficult than we thought. Perhaps this is a good time to visit Lady Sophia and Lord Will and pick up the gifts they said would help us."

"Peter, you are such a wise traveler."

The old couple was very happy to see them. "So you've been in a swarm of bees." Lord Will pointed to their stings.

"Yes, we went down a forbidden path."

"I'm afraid that happened to us on more than one occasion too," Lord Will said. "Many times we made a foolish decision and ended up harming ourselves."

Peter noticed for the first time that both Lord Will and Lady Sophia bore horrible scars. A deep gash marked Lord Will's cheek, and Lady Sophia had a spread of ugly burns on her arms. But somehow over time these scars had softened, and now they looked almost beautiful.

"It was so bad, we almost cut our cords," Lady Sophia said. "That's why we're so eager to help you. The journey together can bring such happiness, but it can also be very taxing. The King's gifts can make it easier for you. Could you show us what gifts you have already received, so we don't give you any duplicates?"

Peter and Celeste took out all their kingly gifts and put them on the table. They had sheepskins of humility to remind them of the Servant's sacrifice, their robes of righteousness and knives of grace, and their garments of praise—capes of fine silver mesh.

"Very good, very good," Lord Will said when he saw the capes. "Those can be quite helpful when you feel a spirit of heaviness, for singing to the King can lift your burdens. Now, along with what you have, I'd suggest a basket of remembrance. What do you think, Lady Sophia?"

"That's just what I was going to propose." She brought out a simple woven basket. "The guidebook talks often about how we are to remember what the King has done for us, the love He has given, His gifts, His grace. Take this basket and store in it the good memories of your partnership—and then stop often and look at your treasures. I think you already have many mementos you can put in it: things from your first days walking together, your weaving day, souvenirs of how the King has provided for you along the way. During your difficulties, these tokens will help remind you that the King has been faithful in the past—and He will be faithful in the future."

Peter took from his pocket a few stones he had collected under the moon of honey. Celeste put in some confetti from their weaving celebration and dried berries from their first walks together in the grove.

Then Lady Sophia lifted up a small hourglass that was attached to the basket's handle. Peter and Celeste exchanged glances. Neither could figure out how it might help them on their journey.

"I know it looks like a strange gift," Lady Sophia said, "but time is precious on the King's path and this hourglass of today will remind you to encourage each other daily, and not to let the sun set on your anger. Make sure your accounts with each other are put right before you go to sleep, for you never know when the King will call one of you home to His city."

The next gift was even more puzzling. It was nothing but a plain, humble rag, gray and frayed around the edges.

Celeste shook her head. "I think you brought this out by mistake."

"Oh no, it's no mistake," Lord Will said.

"But what is it?"

"Why, it's a rag."

"Yes," Peter said, "but what is it for?"

"For when you suffer wounds along the way," Lord Will said.

Peter and Celeste looked at each other and thought of their bee stings.

"We have seen partners become so battered and bruised on their journey together," Lady Sophia said. "Sometimes they wander off the path and fall down a ravine. Sometimes they pick up clubs to defend themselves against dangers on the trail, but when they start to fight, they hit each other with the clubs. It is shocking to watch two adults attack each other. Sometimes they suffer horrible burns from eruptions of fiery anger. If you receive any hurts on your journey, use this rag of compassion to wash them."

Celeste reached out and touched the rag. "Amazing. It's so soft."

"It has been soaked with the tears of the Servant Himself. But if you ever suffer wounds that are very deep, you will need to go to the Healing Springs and soak them there."

Peter carefully folded the rag and put it into his pocket.

"We have saved the best for last." Lady Sophia took out a bundle of sticks. "You will have many companions on your journey, but it is essential to get away by yourselves so you can talk and laugh and share together. If you ever find this hard to do, rub this kindling of affection together and create a warm fire for yourselves."

"Thank you so much." Celeste put the kindling in her bag.

"Oh, we almost forgot the most important gift of all." Lord Will handed them a guidebook.

"We don't need that," Peter said. "We each already have our own."

"Perhaps we could exchange it for a special guidebook for how to be partners." Celeste paused as if explaining a great discovery. "That's really what we need because being partners is so much different than traveling alone. We'd be happy to have the King's guidance for that."

Lady Sophia shook her head. "I think, dear friends, that you are mistaken. Yes, this is the guidebook you received when you started your journey. But the wisdom it contains is for everyone—travelers with partners and travelers walking alone, friends, little travelers, parents—for the King is the source of all love. In fact, we think you'll find you need the guidebook more than ever."

"We've underlined a few of the passages we've found especially helpful," Lord Will said. "'Make allowance for each other's faults, and forgive anyone who offends you. Remember, the King forgave you, so you must forgive others.'"

"That is good to remember," Peter said.

"And here's another: 'Do everything without complaining or arguing.'"

"I already know that," Celeste said.

"Yes, but don't you see how these instructions will help your partnership?" Lady Sophia turned to another passage, 'Do not let any unwholesome talk come out of your mouths, but only what is helpful for building others up according to their needs, that it may benefit those who listen.' Can you think of any better guidance for what to say to each other?"

"We'll be sure to bring it." Peter realized the hard, flat book would make an excellent support at the bottom of his bag.

"Along with these gifts," Lord Will said, "we advise you to take time now to develop good walking patterns together. Though Lady Sophia and I had each been walking to the King's City since we were young, we discovered that traveling with a partner requires a different gait. It took us a while to adjust our stride—especially when we went through Echo Gap where it is easy for partners to get separated from one another."

"And always pay attention to each other's weaknesses and troubles," Lady Sophia said. "If you feel a little twinge, take care of it right away. Otherwise it may develop into a much more serious problem and make it difficult to reach the Highlands."

"How can we be sure we will get there?" Celeste asked.

"Don't cut your cords no matter what happens—that is the first and the most important task," Lord Will said. "Second, don't avoid the path to Skull Hill when you come to it. Many travelers steer away from it, thinking it is too steep to climb, and they never make it to the Highlands."

"Keep your love for the King strong," Lady Sophia said. "Serve Him with all your heart and with all your soul—and be careful not to turn away from His path. It is a dangerous journey to His city, and there have even been guides who have lost their way, and some travelers have been tortured and stoned."

"We are ready to die for the King," Peter said.

"That is good," Lord Will said. "But sometimes it takes even more courage to live for Him. There was another traveler named Peter who had courage to walk on water, but was not brave enough to acknowledge the Servant. You will need much strength and resolve to avoid the Valley of Cut Cords."

Lady Sophia shivered. "It is such a terrible sight of destruction. I pray that you will not see it. Listen to the guides you meet along the way and visit the gathering huts every chance you have to share with other travelers. They may be able to steer you away from some of the hardest sections of the path. And most of all, persevere, for in the end it will be worth it when you reach the Highlands."

Peter and Celeste thanked the old couple for the gifts and said goodbye. They started off again on the path, their hearts lighter and filled with hope. Soon they were singing and kicking pebbles together. Although it was not quite like their time under the moon of honey, it was close enough.

THROUGH ECHO GAP

As they walked through the flourishing woodlands of the Low Country, they tried out their new kingly gifts. At first, Peter found it uncomfortable to use the kindling of affection and the hourglass of today, but Celeste showed him how they could make drinking from the chalice even more enjoyable. They weren't walking as fast as they had before, but Peter found himself appreciating the journey more.

The path through the woodland soon brought them to a tall rock gap with high ridges on either side. As they approached the entrance, they were met by two guides, Leave and Cleave.

"Welcome to Echo Gap," said Leave.

Celeste turned to Peter. "This is the place Lord Will and Lady Sophia told us about. They said couples can get separated going through it."

"Yes, it can be a tricky journey," Cleave said. "The rock walls have an echo effect. If you're not careful, one of you might get pulled off the path. But I'm afraid there's really no way around the gap."

"Good echoes or bad ones?" Celeste asked.

"Could be either, could be both," Leave said. "It depends on what your families were like. In the gap, travelers hear echoes and whispers of everyone who ever cared for them, and told them where they should go and what they should do."

"Sometimes parents miss their grown-up children so much, they come right down into the gap and follow alongside the partners, giving them advice," Cleave said. "The couple can become thoroughly confused with four parents talking to them, along with the echoes and the whispers. They don't know who to listen to, and if they let themselves become pulled every which way, they don't learn properly how to walk together. But if your parents stay above on the ridge road, they can help cheer you on and warn you of dangers ahead on the path. You can have a much easier time going through the gap because of their encouragement and advice."

At that moment, a couple came running out of the gap with their hands over their ears.

"Oh dear," Leave said. "Echo Gap has done it again."

The couple went straight to Leave and Cleave. "It was so awful, we turned around and came back here," the wife said. "We have to find a way to get through the gap without being tormented by all the echoes. They were so loud and insistent, we thought we would go crazy."

"At first it didn't bother me," the man said. "But one morning we were packing our bags and she put the food in first, rather than putting it on top. I never did it that way when I was growing up. Without thinking, I started criticizing her. The strange thing was, it sounded so much like my father, I stopped and looked to see if he was there. It was uncanny how I used the exact words and the same tone, even the same pauses."

"The same thing happened to me," the wife said. "I started saying, 'Dinner at 7, dinner at 7' all the time—even at breakfast."

"When I asked her what she was talking about, she'd say she hadn't said anything. Then a little while later, she'd start up again, saying it louder and more insistently, until she was almost screaming at me."

"Finally I realized that was what my mother always said to my father, 'Dinner at 7, we have to have dinner at 7.' I don't think I would have minded that so much, but after that I started hearing accusing whispers."

"I could tell something was wrong," the husband said, "because she started looking so sad and saying to herself, 'You'll never amount to anything, you'll never amount to anything.' And then she began to hit herself. So we came back here to find out what to do. We just couldn't go on anymore."

"The secret," Leave said, "is to whisper in your wife's other ear."

"Sweet, loving phrases," Cleave said.

"Yes, that might work." The man nodded. "I did that once, and a little smile came on her face."

"It may take some time," Leave said.

"But eventually," Cleave said, "she'll barely be able to hear the whispers in her other ear."

Peter and Celeste started through the gap, determined not to be pulled off course by the echoes. But they quickly discovered it was not just the echoes that made the journey difficult. The echoes Peter heard always contradicted the ones that Celeste heard, and before long they were disagreeing about everything. Celeste liked to take a long rest for lunch like her family always did. But in Upright Village there was never time for leisurely meals, so Peter liked to eat as they went. Celeste wanted to buy new walking shoes every season, as she had done in Slouching City. But Peter wanted to repair his and save the money, as his parents had taught him.

Celeste became homesick listening to the echoes. It wasn't that she didn't like walking with Peter, but he didn't pay attention to her like he had when they were first walking in the grove or under the moon of honey. She remembered how her mother and father were always eager to listen to her; they never yawned when she talked. She started nagging Peter to visit her family, but Peter insisted they keep going on. After a while they gave up arguing and started to slowly drift apart. They might not have noticed except their new cords were very sensitive. The farther away from each other they got, the tighter the cords squeezed their wrists.

"Wait a minute," Peter finally yelled to Celeste. "This is no good. We can't go in two directions—my cords are hurting too much."

Celeste rubbed her wrists. "Can't we just loosen them?"

"Celeste, don't you want to walk with me?"

"Peter, what a silly question. Of course I want to walk with you; I'm your partner. But I don't think it will hurt to go our own ways for a little bit, especially since you won't come to visit my family."

Peter sat down on his side of the path and got out the guide-book Lord Will and Lady Sophia had given them. "I think they underlined some instructions about this. Yes, here it is: 'For this reason a man will leave his father and mother and be united to his wife, and the two will become one flesh. So they are no longer two, but one.'"

Celeste grew quiet and Peter decided it might be wise not to press his point.

"It's true," Celeste finally said from her side of the path. "I left my parents and chose to make the journey with you."

Peter suggested they put cotton in their ears to block out the echoes, and they agreed to work harder at walking together. Peter tried to play with Celeste more, and Celeste tried to listen more attentively when Peter talked about the different paths they could take once they had gone through the gap. But one day Celeste heard such a loud echo, she asked Peter to stop so they could find where it was coming from. They followed the sound down a small side canyon and discovered Celeste's entire family camped at the end.

"How did you get here?" Celeste asked.

"We all missed you so much," Celeste's father said, "we left Slouching City and found you."

Her mother waved a sack. "We didn't want you to go off without your childhood treasures."

"Oh Peter, isn't this wonderful? There's no harm stopping

now, since they came all this way just to see us."

Peter knew it would be rude not to stop. "All right, we'll stay for a day."

Celeste was so happy to be with her parents again, she convinced Peter they should spend at least a week visiting. Her mother cooked all of Celeste's favorite meals, and her father took her aside and asked her if she was having enough fun. "Not to criticize Peter, but he has always struck me as a bit of a stuffed shirt. And look at your shoes—I don't think he's been providing properly for you. But don't worry, we'll get you some nice new things."

Every night Celeste stayed up late with her brothers and sisters, telling family stories and playing games. Peter joined in as best he could, but he felt like a stranger, even with Celeste. She seemed a different person around her family. And whenever he mentioned resuming their journey, Celeste pretended not to hear. By the end of the week he worried that if they stayed much longer, Celeste would never want to return to the King's path. It seemed as if her family was tying strings over her Cords of Commitment. But when he told Celeste this, she laughed.

The next day Celeste's parents put on a big party for Peter and Celeste. They gave Celeste a complete new wardrobe and gave Peter a set of woodworking tools. "For your new place," Celeste's father said with a wink.

"You see," Celeste's mother said, "we've been discussing it, and we've decided it's time to stop your silly journey."

"We've got everything all set," Celeste's father said. "We've built you a house right next to us in Slouching City. Big enough for all the children you'll have."

"You don't want your children growing up with strange ideas about some mythical King," her mother said. "They'll become poorly adjusted."

Celeste frowned. It was one thing to stay with her family for a visit, but it was quite another thing to give up her journey.

"Of course, you can always head out on this path later," Celeste's father said, "but for now it would be better for you to come back home."

Peter and Celeste had no chance to talk by themselves until everyone was asleep. They took a little stroll through the side canyon, and Peter asked Celeste what she thought about her parents' offer.

"Think? There's nothing to think about," Celeste said. "Of course we are going to keep going. I want to see more vistas; I want to get to the King's City. Besides, the idea of raising a little traveler where people laugh if you talk about the Servant—no, that's not the life I want."

"Oh, good." Peter sighed.

"Did you think I wanted to go with my family?"

"You seem so happy with them. And I admire how generous they are with both of us—I know they can give you everything you want."

"That's true, but walking with you I've begun to realize I don't really need all those things. I want to store up my treasures in the King's City."

In the morning, Celeste told her parents that she and Peter were going their own way. She pointed to the path that led back to the gap.

"But we don't want to go that way," her mother said. "Won't you be lonely without us?"

"Peter and I will take good care of each other." Celeste looked at her parents. "Besides, as wonderful as Slouching City is, the King's City is a hundred times nicer. Won't you come with us?"

"Don't be ridiculous," her father said. "We can't leave Slouching City. How would we survive without all our comforts?"

"Your father is right, Celeste. And I've never understood why you allow yourself to take orders from this King."

"But I gave up my citizenship to the Slouching City. I'm an alien now."

"Don't worry," her father said. "With my connections, it will be easy to get your residency back."

"No, we're going to the King's City." Celeste was glad Peter was right next to her, for she was very sad to leave her family behind. She might not have had the courage to go on without him.

For a good while after Celeste left her family, accusing whispers tormented her for being so selfish and abandoning her family. Peter and Celeste both began to look up to the ridge, hoping they would see Peter's parents encouraging them on. But one day, to their surprise, they bumped into his parents sitting right in the middle of the path.

"What are you doing here?" Peter said.

"We thought we would come and see how you are doing," his father said.

"And I brought all your cleaning supplies." Peter's mother handed him a bag. "Spot remover, a dustpan and brush, and a strong disinfectant."

The four of them spent a quiet day together. Peter told his parents how much they were enjoying their journey and what they had seen along the way. Peter's father argued with him, saying the way to the King's City was too hard. If Peter and Celeste ever had little travelers, they would have to come back right away to Upright Village, where they could be protected from the storms and thieves and all the other dangers they would encounter.

While Peter's father badgered him, Peter's mother cornered Celeste. She began pointing out what Celeste needed to change: her clothes were too fancy, her hair was too long, the songs she sang were too sprightly. Poor Celeste stood listening, too polite to plug her ears. When Peter came in and found his mother lecturing Celeste, he stepped in front of Celeste. "Mother, when you criticize Celeste, you are criticizing me."

"I don't know where you learned to be so unkind," his mother said. "You should be more respectful. I'm your mother."

"Yes, you are my mother, but Celeste is my wife. We are going to leave if you keep scolding her."

"I see. Well, if that's the way you want it . . ."

"No, I would prefer that you would honor my choice and accept Celeste for who she is. You might even compliment her. But if you refuse to care for her—"

"Oh, I do care about her, very much. That is why I am pointing out her errors. How else will she be corrected?"

"The logs, dear mother, the logs," Peter said.

"What logs?"

"The ones in your eyes."

At that his mother went off in a huff.

That night, Peter and Celeste talked about what to do. "It's too bad," Celeste said. "Your parents are so conscientious about following the King's rule. I'm sure they're only acting this way because they miss you so much."

"Telling me to stop going to the King's City? Criticizing you for the way you sing? If we stay here any longer, I'm afraid it will harm us. I can't put their happiness above our partnership. We'll have to leave tomorrow."

In the morning, they packed their bags. Peter's parents wept, for they were convinced Peter and Celeste would be killed before they reached the King's City.

As they started on the path, Peter took Celeste by the hand. "Will you walk on with me?"

"Certainly," she said, smiling.

And they traveled on through Echo Gap, listening carefully for each other's whispers until they came out on the other side.

IN THE BURR PATCH OF UNKIND WORDS

The path became smooth and grassy as it had been at the beginning of their journey together. They collected things for their basket of remembrance, and every morning before they set off, they read the guidebook together. They stopped whenever they met other travelers, so Celeste could talk with them and find out their news. Peter didn't mind because they were making such good progress. But one night Celeste stayed up quite late talking with some travelers. In the morning Peter woke her up early, as he always did, then set out on their usual brisk pace. Celeste started to fall behind, but Peter just kept hiking. Celeste started to feel cross that he never looked back to see if she was all right. Finally she ran and caught up with him.

"Please stop," she said, sounding a little more cross than she intended. "You got so far ahead I couldn't see you anymore."

"Sometimes I think you just want to play all the time." Peter sounded just as cross. "We have a journey to make."

"Do you always have to go so fast?"

"Why don't you ever keep up? Why do you always drag behind? Sometimes I wonder if you really want to walk with me. If you did you'd go faster, instead of being so lazy."

A patch of burr bushes began to border the path.

"You're always in such a hurry."

"If you were more disciplined and focused, you could keep up," Peter said.

"If you weren't so rigid about reaching a certain spot," Celeste said, "you would slow down."

As their voices grew heated, the burr bushes started to crowd them on both sides of the path.

"We'd never get to the nice campsites."

"When we keep your pace, I'm too tired to enjoy them when we get there."

By then, the burr bushes had surrounded them completely. Each time one of them said something unkind, a burr jumped and stuck to their clothes.

"If you didn't talk so much, you could concentrate on keeping up."

"If you would slow down, I could sing better."

They kept throwing barbs at each other.

"You're too slow."

"You don't know how to enjoy life."

"You dawdle."

"You're sour."

Soon they were covered with burrs from head to toe.

"Stop it!" Celeste said. "You're pinching me."

"No, I'm not—you're pinching me."

"It's all these burrs."

"Well, where did they come from? We were fine until you started to complain about how fast I was going."

"No, it's all your fault." But as she spoke these words, three burrs blew onto Peter's pant leg.

"You started it," Peter said, not caring that two more burrs stuck onto Celeste.

"What does it matter? The path is so thick with burr bushes, we can't go any farther."

"We can keep on."

"Just because you are thick-skinned—"

"What do you mean?" Peter said. "Just because I don't cry at the smallest bit of pain?"

Celeste was already feeling sorry for herself. When he said this, she stopped. She couldn't sit because her backside was covered with burrs, so she just stood, arms and legs apart, and tried to think what she should do. "Look at us —" she said. "We're both covered with burrs. We have to find a way to get them off. Will any of our gifts help us?"

"We weren't given tweezers," Peter said.

Celeste tried to pull the burrs off herself, but they clung as if they were fastened on with glue.

Peter started to walk on, but Celeste refused. "I'm not going any farther until we find how to get these off. They are not just pinching me, they are digging in like they have teeth." She pulled up her sleeve and showed Peter the marks the burrs had made.

He felt a twinge of sympathy. "Let's look in the guidebook. Maybe it talks about a remedy for burrs."

They searched the guidebook and came to the passage Lady Sophia had read to them about speaking to encourage other. Then they read, "Get rid of all bitterness, rage and anger, brawling and slander, along with every form of malice. Be kind and compassionate to one another."

Peter closed the book. He thought about how free he had felt when his chains of debt had been cut with the knife of grace.

Finally Celeste said, "I'm sorry, Peter. I shouldn't have been cross." As soon as she said this, a burr fell off him.

"Oh, I was wrong too," he said, and a burr fell off her.

"Look, that's how to do it," Celeste said. "Every time I speak a kind word, a burr comes off you. You are such a good walker, strong and steadfast." Another fistful dropped from Peter.

"And you remind me to enjoy the world, not just work," Peter said, and a handful detached from Celeste. "It's amazing. The power of words—I had no idea."

They laughed and turned it into a game to see who could say the nicest words and get the burrs off the other person first. Finally they managed to free themselves.

"Whew. That was unpleasant. Let's not do that again," Celeste said.

"And it's not very efficient either. We wasted an entire morning."

"But we learned how to avoid getting burrs."

Later that day, they came upon a couple covered with burrs. "So you got trapped in the burr patch too," Peter said.

"Yes, sticky business," the husband said.

"But you still are covered with burrs," Celeste said. "How did you get out?"

"It wasn't easy," the wife said. "We finally just closed our eyes and pushed ahead."

"Didn't it hurt?" Celeste said.

"Of course," the husband said. He turned to Peter and whispered, "Women are so soft sometimes. My wife complained at first, but I told her she just had to buck up and get through it."

Peter noticed streaks of blood coming through the woman's sleeves. "But she's bleeding."

"Just a flesh wound. On this journey, you have to take a little bit of pain. Can't worry about every little burr that sticks to you."

"But they're still on you. Your backs are covered with them. What happens when you lie down?"

"We sleep on our stomachs."

"Isn't that rather uncomfortable?"

"Better than feeling the sharp pain when we lie on our backs."

"You know," Peter said, "if you spoke kind words to each other, they would fall off. That's how we removed our burrs."

The man shook his head. "I don't go in for all that coddling stuff. And she has to learn to get tough sooner or later."

"What am I supposed to do?" The woman shrugged. "I don't

think he would even notice if I managed to take all the burrs off him."

As Celeste watched the couple walk away, she felt sorry that they would rather suffer than learn to speak kindly to each other.

Around the Mountains of Maturity

INTO THE SAND DUNES OF FOOLISHNESS

*I*n my dream I saw that the path for Peter and Celeste became rockier and started to rise. Soon they came to the Mountains of Maturity that ranged all the way to the King's City. Celeste felt her heart sag when she saw the first one, Virtue Peak, soaring in front of them. She was convinced she could never attempt such a rugged climb. Even Peter, who always loved a challenge, was daunted by the steep slope. In places it looked like the trail took them up an almost sheer rock face. That would be hard enough for him alone, but he'd also have to help Celeste and he wasn't sure he had the strength. "There has to be another way around this mountain, don't you think?" Peter asked.

"We could try this way." Celeste pointed to the side where a comfortable sandy path led away from the mountain. She remembered her postcard of a couple surfing. "There is no sign saying it is forbidden, and it looks like it might lead to a beach. I don't think it would hurt to take a little rest and enjoy the sun and the sea. It would be like our time under the moon of honey."

Peter would have never agreed to rest before. But he was discovering that what he had observed before he met Celeste was true: it was much more difficult to make the journey with a partner than alone, and he was often very tired at the end of the day. "I always wanted to go to the beach, but the leaders in Upright Village didn't think it was a wise place to visit."

"How can there be anything wrong with going to the beach? A little fun never hurt anyone. We'll just stay for a short while and when we're ready, we'll leave."

"They also warned about the roaring lion who roamed through the King's country looking for travelers to devour. It favors the lower, sandy regions where travelers haven't learned to be on guard."

"A lion." Celeste shook her head. "Have you ever seen one? I'm sure that was just a folktale they used to scare people from leaving the village. And even if this lion does exist, I'm sure the King would never allow it to run free in His country."

Peter didn't want to argue, especially since the sandy path looked so inviting. "You're probably right, and we could use a little break from our journey."

As soon as the path turned away from Virtue Peak, it opened onto a broad area of sand dotted with tufts of grass. At first the sand was firm. Sometimes Peter and Celeste heard the distant rumble of waves, though they couldn't see the ocean. They passed by several trails that split off from the beach path: the Course of

Testing, the Course of Discipline, and the Course of Suffering.
Each looked too rocky or climbed right back up toward the Mountains of Maturity. So Peter and Celeste continued their pleasant
meander through the soft warm sand. Peter wondered why the
leaders of Upright Village had been so adamant about avoiding the
beach.

Soon the path gently descended into a section of low mounds
of sand. The sun was hot, and they wished for the shady trees they
had walked under in the Low Country. Even the forested slopes
on the mountains behind them looked appealing. But Peter and
Celeste pushed on, sweaty and sticky, drawn by the sound of the
ocean that seemed always just around the next dune. They thought
of how refreshing it would be to plunge into the cool water and
swim in the waves. Finally they came to the beach. A crystal blue
sky matched the vast ocean that sparkled in the sun. Seabirds
swooped down and scavenged bits of food and dead fish that had
washed up.

Other travelers had come to the beach too, walking down
the long stretch of soft sand or playing in the surf. Some travelers had assembled shelters with scraps of driftwood to shade
themselves from the relentless sun. Peter asked one traveler if
the flimsy shack could withstand a storm. The traveler assured
Peter he had carefully followed the instructions he had been given
by a man wearing a sheepskin of humility.

Peter frowned. He remembered the Servant's warning about
guides disguised as harmless sheep but who really were vicious
wolves.

"Well, this shelter is better than getting grilled to a crisp," the traveler said. "You'll soon be building your own."

"Come on, Peter." Celeste tugged at his hand. "Let's go swimming."

They left their packs on the beach and dashed into the waves. But they didn't swim for long. The water was so salty, it stung their eyes and pinched their skin. They asked another traveler if there was fresh water near the beach so they could wash off.

The traveler said there wasn't, but that was for the best. "It's fine to come and take a rest at the beach. After all, the Sabbath is one of the King's rules. But I'm only going to stay for a short while and then continue my journey to the King's City."

Peter was ready to go back to the path, but Celeste convinced him to stay a few more hours. While they rested on the beach, a powerful wind came driving down the coast and stirred up a sandstorm. They could do nothing but close their eyes and wait. The sand stung their faces and arms and legs, and whipped into their hair. When the wind finally died and they opened their eyes again, the mounds of sand behind them had turned into a field of tall, sharp dunes. There was no sign of a trail to lead them out.

"How are we going to find our way back to the path?" Peter asked.

"Doesn't matter." Celeste shook her head, still determined to live her postcard of the couple riding the waves. "We're at the beach, and that's all that matters."

"Except we have no fresh water."

"Don't be so negative. You just need to look at this as an adventure."

It sounded like wishful thinking to Peter, but he was too tired to say anything. He hoped the wind would shift the dunes during the night and make a clear path for them.

Then Celeste thought of her favorite postcard of the couple gazing at each other. "I know, let's imagine we're under the moon of honey again."

They drank quickly from the chalice and soon fell asleep under the stars, with the sound of the ocean lapping with its endless thirst. When they woke up the next morning, nothing had changed. The wind was still hot, they were still sticky, the dunes were still tall and pathless, and the sand had turned even softer. They wandered around trying to find a way out, but with each step they sunk deep in the sand.

Peter was worried, but Celeste said that sooner or later the wind would blow the dunes away. She decided that if they had to stay in the dunes, she was going to have fun. She climbed one of the dunes as high as she could, then slid down with a whoop. "If you can't beat them, join them," Celeste called to Peter. She spent the entire day sliding down one dune after another, never stopping to see how Peter was getting on. If she had, she would have seen he was quite miserable. He was pale-skinned, and without any shade he was getting a punishing sunburn.

The next day Celeste continued playing on the dunes while Peter, now painfully pink, managed to scrounge enough driftwood to build a little shack to shelter them. That night they ate the last biscuits from their packs. "I'm worried about finding more supplies," Peter said.

Celeste drank the last of the juice they had brought. "I'm sure something will work out."

As the days went on, their muscles grew weaker in the soft sand until Celeste could no longer climb the dunes. Occasionally they found puddles of brackish water that collected in low spots between the dunes. Although the water was not very refreshing, at least it took the edge off their growing thirst. They also were becoming thin, for their diet of stewed beach grass was not very nourishing. It was impossible to kick pebbles, and Celeste's throat was too dry for her to sing. Then one day storm clouds massed on the horizon. Some travelers laid out makeshift basins to catch the fresh rainwater the storm would bring. But Peter and Celeste had stayed up late yet again and were sound asleep. By the time they awoke, the brief shower had passed.

"I am so thirsty," Celeste said.

"You're the one who wanted to go to the beach."

"But it wasn't supposed to be like this."

"I liked it better when you sang."

"There's nothing to sing about."

"Then I'd appreciate it if you would keep your comments to yourself."

Celeste turned her back on Peter. "I can complain if I want."

They went on bickering, thinking only about their own comfort. Sand got under their Cords of Commitment and began to rub at the threads.

There was no gathering hut at the beach, but other travelers sometimes stopped by Peter and Celeste's shack and told them dreadful stories about travelers who had set up camp in the dunes and had slowly starved. Others had been carried off by the roaring lion and never seen again. Then a traveler warned them that hurricane season was coming; their shack could not withstand the fierce winds. But Peter was proud of the shack he had built and thought it could survive any storm until one day it started to rain, and the wind began to howl. All day, the rain poured down and streams rushed through the sand. The wind beat relentlessly against their shack. Then with one strong gust, it collapsed.

After the storm died, Peter and Celeste huddled together and looked at what was left of their shelter. Peter stood up, as if waking from a dream. "We can't stay here; we have to get back on the path to the King's City. There's no decent water, no shelter, no solid food. I want to walk again on a firm path of righteousness and peace—and not give up until we get to the King's City. No matter how painful or difficult, we need to press on."

Celeste knew Peter was right. The emptiness in her life had begun to remind her of Slouching City. Together they called to the King for help, and the Breath of the King strengthened them as they started tramping through the maze of dunes. The dunes had become so tall, they could see nothing but walls of sand. With their weakened legs, they struggled to make their way. In the distance they could hear the roaring lion growling for prey. When they heard a traveler give an agonizing scream, Celeste became terrified the lion would find them. "We're never going to get out of here. It's too hard."

Peter decided to encourage her with songs from the guidebook, and he sang to the King:

Turn Your ear to listen to me;
rescue me quickly.

Be my rock of protection,
a fortress where I will be safe.
You are my rock and my fortress.
For the honor of Your name, lead me out of this danger.

Then he sang:

Oh, that my steps might be steady,
keeping to the course You set;
Then I'd never have any regrets
in comparing my life with Your counsel.

Peter took Celeste by the hand and pulled her along. Their progress was slow, and a few times they slid back to the bottom of a dune.

"It's hopeless, Peter. We'll never get out of here."

Peter opened up the guidebook again and sang another song to the King:

My sad life's dilapidated, a falling-down barn;
build me up again by your Word.
Barricade the road that goes Nowhere;
grace me with your clear revelation.
I choose the true road to Somewhere,
I post your road signs at every curve and corner.

They started up again, singing the song as they went until together they reached firmer ground. Soon they were back on the

King's path, with the Mountains of Maturity looming, for their detour along the beach had taken them far south of Virtue Peak. They headed north, and after a few days they came to a boulder-filled path. A guide named Persistence stood by a sign that said, "To Mount Self-Control, Elevation: 16,583 feet."

"Can you tell us the best way to get around this mountain?" Peter asked.

"I always encourage travelers to go up every peak they come to."

"The first one we saw looked much too steep," Peter said, "and this one looks even harder."

"You'll find that avoiding the mountains in the beginning will make your journey harder, not easier. I can see you're still covered with grit from the Sand Dunes of Foolishness. You're fortunate the roaring lion didn't get you. Please trust me when I say that while these peaks may look difficult to climb, going up them is superior to all the other ways."

Peter and Celeste looked doubtful.

"You're suggesting we go up that?" Celeste said.

Persistence nodded.

"Are you sure?" Peter said. In all his travels, he had never attempted such a difficult path.

"The path doesn't go straight up," Persistence said. "The King knows your weakness and has mercy on you."

"I suppose we could at least try it," Peter said, not wanting to repeat their disaster in the sand dunes.

So they started up the mountain. Though the path rose steadily, the way was shaded by thick green trees. In the open stretches, bushes were bursting with berries. They finally came to what they thought was their first peak and stopped for a rest. But it wasn't a peak at all, just a small hill not even a quarter of the way up. But they could see Slouching City and Echo Gap behind them, and they were encouraged by how far they had come. Ahead, the Mountains of Maturity went on, peak after peak after peak: Self-Control in front, followed by Patient Endurance, Godliness, Kindness, and finally Love.

"It's daunting to see so many peaks to climb," Celeste said. "Why can't we just climb one and be done with it?"

Peter sighed. "I wish I knew."

UP TO PIGEON HOLE PASS

A little farther up the path, they came upon a fork and a sign that pointed to the left and said, "Best view of the King's City" in gold lettering with curlicue flourishes and a border of painted daisies. The path looked quite promising. The ground was smooth and had only a gentle incline. Celeste agreed with Peter that it would be good to take it. But they hadn't gotten far when they came to another fork with another sign, not nearly as fancy as the first. This time the lettering was bigger and darker and proclaimed, "Right way, this way." Since they wanted to stay on the right path, they also took the second fork.

The path became narrower, and the trees along the way grew shorter. Peter told Celeste that was a good sign; it showed they were gaining altitude A little while later, there was another sign, "Only way to the King's City." Though the sign was very plain with a white background and large black letters, they couldn't argue with the message and they continued. The next sign looked ominous. It said, "Death if you turn back" with a skull and cross bones underneath. Since Peter and Celeste knew that death awaited those who did not reach the King's City, they didn't hesitate to keep going up the path.

They followed along the path for some time. Celeste said it was odd that the trail to the best overlook was in such poor condition. Branches had fallen across the path from winter storms, and rocks had tumbled from above. They came to another sign, smaller than the others. In a heavy, foreboding script, it declared, "All travelers, this way." The path now scaled a series of sharp ravines connected by narrow ledges.

"At least we'll have a great view." Peter began climbing yet another ravine.

Celeste gasped for breath. "You go on ahead." She knew Peter was anxious to get to the top.

He pushed on until the path reached a high, slender gap where there should have been a spectacular vista toward the King's City. But the view was blocked by a tall rock wall that had been built across the gap. The wall was covered with neatly carved alcoves that looked like pigeon holes. A thin walkway led from one alcove to another, and a long ladder at the end of each row provided a way to reach the next level. There were six levels, and it seemed to Peter the wall had been built little by little over a long period. The shorter, lower levels were more crudely built and seemed to be sinking under the weight of the upper levels.

"There isn't any view of the King's City from here," Celeste said when she finally caught up with Peter. She felt disappointed that she had made the hard climb for nothing. "How are we going to go any farther? Even if we made it to the top on those rickety ladders, we can't be sure there is any way over and down the other side."

"It looks like a nice place to stop for a bit," Peter said. "Everything is so neat and tidy." The paths were well-swept, and the brass doors to the alcove rooms gleamed with polish. Even the dirt on the ground looked like it had been bleached clean.

A pale man in an elaborately embroidered coat stood guard at the entrance. "Reverend Strict, at your service. Would you like a tour?" He had small piercing eyes and a long pointed chin, and his fingernails were so long, they curved like claws. For a moment Celeste thought he looked like a wolf.

"We'd love to," Peter said. "I'm quite intrigued by your set-up. You keep it so clean."

"We're very proud of this place," the guard said. He pushed out his chest, raised his nose into the air, and led them across the yard. "We plan to expand into other regions as well. Our vision is that one day every view of the King's City in the entire land will be developed like this."

"Very smart," Peter said.

Celeste shivered. "But you've built the compound so the sun never shines directly."

"We don't think the sun is a good thing. It makes you hot, and when you're hot, you're thirsty, and when you get thirsty, you want to drink, and that leads to all kinds of temptations."

"You mean with the chalice?" Celeste said.

Reverend Strict looked offended. "Young lady, we do not say filthy words here. I kindly ask you to respect our rules." He lowered his voice. "Partners drink from the chalice only when absolutely necessary." He shook himself. "It's not just that temptation, but all the other enticements of the world that create havoc in poor travelers. We've decided that since the flesh is too weak to resist temptation, it is best to give up the journey and stay here where you can be safe. That's why our cells look so nice. It's better not to walk than to be tempted to break one of the King's rules."

Celeste stopped following the guard. She suddenly realized the grass was brown, the bushes were brown, even the pine trees were brown. "Where's the river of life?" She remembered what the King had promised her when she first started the journey.

"We believe it's better if travelers don't have access to a rushing stream. Who knows where it would take them? Instead we haul water from the other side of the wall. We have to ration it, but that is a good discipline for our associates."

"Still, there should be a stream of living water." Peter considered how dry it had been in Upright Village.

"Once travelers become acclimated to our way of life, they find they are able to do without water for long periods. They know if they are patient and follow the rules, one day the King might come to visit—just think how wonderful it would be to watch the King admire our compound." Reverend Strict put his hand to his chest and looked away in rapturous contemplation. "I'm sorry. I get carried away whenever I think that. Now let me show you the rules."

He led Peter and Celeste to the base of the high wall where all the rules from the guidebook had been carefully cut and plastered, as neat as everything else in the place. "A full set, you'll find. Not one missing."

"But this isn't the complete guidebook." Celeste glanced over the rules. "Where are the parts about joy and love and freedom? Where's the part about the knife of grace?"

"If something has been left off, it's for one of two reasons. Either the section isn't necessary or it's been misused by travelers. Most people, if you give them freedom, will do all sorts of awful things the King specifically forbids. So we make it easier for them by keeping them on a short leash, as it were."

"They're not dogs!" Celeste said.

"Well, some of them are beastly, not like our most exalted saints." He pointed to a sign by the wall that said "The Top Saints," with pictures of the most dour people.

Peter recognized several from Upright Village.

"Wait a minute." Celeste was still at the wall reading the rules. "Not only are you missing some things from the guidebook, there are a lot of extra rules. Here's a list of holidays to be celebrated, with rules on how to do it. And lists of foods you can eat, clothes you can wear and what kinds of clothes you can't wear, what colors your Cords of Commitment have to be, how often you can look out your window at the King's City, how many times a day you have to polish your door . . . This is ridiculous."

"We have found over the years that the guidebook isn't as specific in some areas as we think it should be. After careful deliberation, we came up with these additional rules. Everyone here has appreciated the extra guidance."

Peter nodded. Many times he had read the guidebook and wished it was more specific.

But Celeste remembered something she had read in the guidebook: "These people come near to me with their mouth and honor me with their lips, but their hearts are far from me. Their worship of me is made up only of rules taught by men."

"I'd also like to show you our library," Reverend Strict said. He led them to a place that had once been a gathering hut, but the walls had been dismantled and the wood used to make a book-case. He took the largest book, which was titled, "Dues Paid." "Look." He opened the volume and showed it to them. "The most careful account you will ever find, and not a cent missing. We are very careful to pay everything we owe the King. The standard ten percent."

Celeste took another book, labeled "Accounts of Fairness." It was very dusty. When she opened it, the pages were blank. She checked the book beside it, "Acts of Compassion," and found it too was blank. She put them back without saying anything. But she was beginning to suspect that the travelers who lived in Pigeon Hole neglected the more important matters of the King's law, ignoring justice, mercy, and faithful-ness—even love itself. Perhaps they would also strain out a gnat from their cup while swallowing a horse whole.

"I'll leave you to study the rules. It's time to do my obligations." Without offering them anything to eat or drink or showing them where they might rest, Reverend Strict went off.

"Isn't this great?" Peter said. "Just think, a room of our own, guaranteed safety, a view of the King's City. What more do we need?"

"Didn't you notice he only talked about the King's rules and never talked about the King Himself? I think he cares more about the regulations than the One who gave them."

"But you heard what he said. If we stay here and follow all the rules, the King is bound to come here for a visit. We won't have to worry about making any more wrong turns, falling into any traps, or being devoured by the roaring lion."

"But the Servant walked the path to free us from this," Celeste said. "Don't you remember the heavy chains you had to carry?"

"This is different. No one is forcing us to come here. We're free to stay."

"But there is so little water, and they don't even have a regular guidebook, just the snippets pasted on the rule wall. And where's the view of the King's City?"

Another guard appeared, looking like a twin of the first one. "I'm Reverend Severe, the brother of Reverend Strict. Come with me, and I'll show you the view."

They followed him to the second level. At one of the doors, he took a key from his pocket.

"Are all the doors locked?" Celeste asked.

Reverend Severe gave a little laugh. "You think it's strange that the traveler is locked in the room? Yes, people wonder about that. But you can see how high up we are, so we keep the doors locked to protect the travelers inside."

"But why doesn't it lock from the inside? Then the person could get out when they want to."

"No one has ever asked," Reverend Severe said. "They are so afraid that they may sleepwalk during the night and fall down and be killed, they prefer to let me have the keys."

When he opened the door, Celeste and Peter were so surprised, they stepped back and almost fell off the ledge behind them. The inside was as dirty as the outside was clean. It had no furniture, but was littered with piles of bones and garbage. A man sat on the floor with his eyes closed. There was a strong odor of decay, and Celeste noticed a white mass moving in the corner. When she realized it was a heap of maggots, she almost screamed.

Reverend Severe seemed oblivious to the stench and the filth. "The thing to notice is what an excellent view this traveler has of the King's City."

Celeste refused to enter, but Peter stepped in gingerly. He went to the back wall, where there was a hole the size of a dinner plate. "He's right, there is a view of the King's City. But it's a shame the window is too small to see the full panorama. It's such a beautiful sight."

"The traveler doesn't mind," Reverend Severe said. "He's learned not to be greedy and to be content with what he has."

"Does every room have a window?" Peter asked.

"Yes." Reverend Severe seemed to swell. "Every single one. The ones on the top level are the best, though they are a little smaller and the air is much colder at the top. But all the same they give a very nice view of what there is to see."

"How small exactly are the windows on the top level?" Celeste asked from the doorway.

"Oh, big enough."

She supposed that meant the windows were tiny. "The size of a coin?"

"Yes, that sounds about right."

The traveler had gotten up off the floor and began bowing in front of Reverend Severe. "Oh, pure one," he said.

Reverend Severe puffed out his chest. "Thank you, traveler," he said. "Please, sit down. No need to stand." But the traveler remained standing, as if he was afraid of Reverend Severe.

Reverend Severe led Peter out and locked the door.

"Who lives on the top level?" Peter asked.

"The most obedient have earned the rooms on the top level. As I said, it's colder up there, but by the time saints get there, they've learned not to mind suffering."

"And which room is yours?" Celeste asked.

"It's on the top level, the one in the very middle."

It was the most prominent alcove and jutted out with a little veranda. The door was silver instead of brass, engraved with an ornate design.

"I see you're admiring my door—it's one of my small pleasures," Reverend Severe said.

Celeste shuddered, thinking how much filthier his room would be than the one they had just seen.

Reverend Severe led Peter and Celeste back down to the ground and left them alone until it was time for dinner.

"I'm curious to see how couples manage to live here," Celeste said.

"What do you mean?" Peter asked her.

"Being so preoccupied with following the rules, it seems there would be no time to love the others around you. It makes me wonder if the travelers listen to the rules but don't put them into practice. And have you noticed how dry it is? If we ever dared to use the kindling of affection, we'd probably burn the place down."

They walked back toward the bookshelves and passed a handful of residents whispering to each other, and then past another murmuring group. Several feet away, another group was talking vigorously, but it was the most hideous noise—like clanging gongs, screeching hinges, and annoying drips.

"Doesn't it strike you that no one here is speaking the truth in love?" Celeste said. "It's all malicious mumblings and gossip. I don't see any fruit here. There's no evidence of love or joy or peace or patience. Where is kindness and goodness? And look there."

Two residents were walking across the compound. One carried a guidebook, and every few steps he whacked the other person with it.

"I'm sure he has a good reason for doing that," Peter said.

After a meal of thin soup, Reverend Strict showed them to a room on the ground floor. Fortunately, since it was for newcomers, it was relatively clean.

"It's time to turn in for the night," Reverend Strict said.

"But it's just after sunset," Celeste said.

"We find that an early curfew works best—and may I remind you that female travelers are not allowed to express any opinions."

"Come on, Celeste," Peter whispered. "Don't make a scene on our first night."

As soon as they were inside their room, Celeste turned to Peter. "Have you noticed there's no place to kick pebbles anywhere on the grounds?"

"I think one of the rules talked about that. Something about it being frivolous."

"Doesn't that bother you?" Worried that Peter might want to stay, she started to sing one of the King's songs.

"Be quiet!" Reverend Strict's voice roared down from the top level.

Celeste stuck her head out of the back window. "Where is the rule that says you shouldn't sing? In fact, there's a rule that says you should sing."

There was a pause. "All right," Reverend Strict said, "you can sing—but don't be happy. How can you be happy if you are aware of how many rules you have broken?"

"How can you not be happy?" she asked. "The Servant came and set us free and oh—" She broke into song, trilling like a bird.

"Silence! The King is holy."

"Sir, the King is holy, but the King is also love and joy." Celeste turned to Peter. "I can't stay here any longer; it will rob all my joy and destroy all my love, not only for the King, but also for you. I'm going down."

"But you can't leave. It's against the rules."

"Then I'll have to break them. I'll wait for you at the bottom."

"But there's no view of the King's City down there."

"Frankly, a hole that size isn't much to boast of." Celeste pointed to the little window. "And this looks more like a cell than a room."

"But how are you going to get out? The guard locked us in, remember?"

"The King's truth will set me free." Celeste went to the door, turned the handle, and pushed the door open.

"What about the darkness? How will you find the path?"

"I have my guidebook to light my way."

Peter listened to her make her way across the compound, and then the silence returned. He thought how empty the night was going to be without Celeste singing, and he began to hum to himself quite softly. Reverend Strict roared again, sounding almost as ferocious as the roaring lion. "Be quiet! I can't hear myself think."

Peter stopped humming, but he put his face to the peephole and looked out at the night. He could hear Celeste's singing coming from below. It was a beautiful song of the King's love—how the Servant had healed the lame and opened the eyes of the blind and fed the hungry. But when Peter thought about the rules on the walls and how much he'd like to study them, he could not bring himself to leave.

In the morning, Reverend Severe was extremely displeased to hear that Celeste had left in the night, and without permission. "Well, it's for the best." He put his arm around Peter. "She obviously is rebellious and disobedient, and she would have caused a lot of trouble here."

"But she's my partner. I need to stay with her."

"Trust me, the best thing you can do is forget her—unless you want to call out and command her to come back. It will take her several days to walk out of range since the wall we built gives a tremendous echo in the surrounding region. For now, come with me and I'll give you a private lesson on how to look out of your window."

Peter was eager to see the view of the King's City, and he soon forgot all about Celeste. He spent the whole day with Reverend

Severe who taught Peter how to squint so he wouldn't be blinded by the sight of the King's City. Then he taught Peter how to count to fifty and then turn away, because one had to learn not to be too distracted by the view since there was much work to be done in the compound. It wouldn't do at all, Reverend Severe said, for travelers to stay all day in their cells admiring the view.

In the afternoon, Peter joined a group of travelers who were picking up heavy stones and carrying them across the yard to build another section of the wall. The stones were so heavy, Peter thought his back might break. But every time he slowed down or stumbled, Reverend Strict was right beside him, berating him for his weakness and his carelessness.

By the time curfew came, Peter was exhausted. As he lay on the cold hard floor of his room, he remembered Celeste had said the place looked like a cell. Then in the silence, a soft song came up on the breeze. It was not loud, but neither was it far away. Celeste had been true to her word and was waiting for him. Peter stayed awake, his ear to the door. As the night grew darker and the guards fell asleep, she sang louder. Peter listened and remembered how much he wanted to walk to the King's City—and to walk there with Celeste. He got up, opened the door, and walked out into the night to rejoin his partner.

When he saw Celeste, he gave her a big hug and kiss. Then he put his arms in hers and walked on with her. "Oh, Celeste, how thankful I am that you're my partner and that you didn't leave me. I don't think I would have—could have—left if it hadn't been for your singing. I would have been locked up there forever."

"Oh Peter, it was the least I could do. I couldn't leave you behind in that prison. Have you noticed how much fresher the air is here?"

Peter took a deep breath. "You're right. It is so good to be free again and walking with you on the King's path."

They hiked all night to get far away from Pigeon Hole as quickly as they could. By dawn, they had reached the bottom of the valley. Ahead they could see velvet green hills that stretched all the way to the King's City. The sign on the way to Pigeon Hole had once been true. Before the wall was put up, there had indeed been a wonderful view of what lay ahead.

"Look at this scenery," Celeste said. "Have you ever seen anything so beautiful? This is why I wanted to walk with you, to see sights like this."

"It is a nice path here," Peter said. Walking with Celeste had changed him. He now paid more attention to the landscape, and he appreciated how Celeste always stopped to pick a few flowers and put them in her hat or his button hole. He found it pleasant to smell the flowers and to see a bit of color, especially when the path turned dull.

As for Celeste, she had gotten used to Peter's walking rhythm and was content now to take fewer stops. When they overtook travelers with slow, ungainly strides, she was pleased Peter was such an expert walker.

But they didn't stop to enjoy the scenery for they were still in the range of Pigeon Hole, and they could hear the guards' voices booming through the valley, warning all travelers to return to their rooms. They kept on, and though the glorious vista toward the King's City was no longer visible, Peter and Celeste were sure they would see it again.

ON THE SPLIT PATH

Now in my dream, Peter and Celeste came to the edge of the region ruled by the Pigeon Hole guards where a gigantic tree had fallen and split the path in two. Many years had passed since its fall, for the trunk was half buried in the dirt, and the branches had been sawed off for firewood. All the bark had been taken off, so Peter and Celeste could see it had started as two separate trees that had grown together to create a single magnificent one. As they wondered what could have caused such a mighty tree to topple, Peter noticed the statement a traveler had scrawled on the trunk: "The Tree of Oneness, felled by the upheaval in the Great Garden."

"Too bad we didn't see the tree when it was standing strong and whole as the King meant it to be," Peter said. "It must have been the tallest in the forest."

"And imagine what a broad canopy the branches made. There would have been enough shade for dozens of travelers."

Because the tree had fallen right in the middle of the way to the King's City, they had to choose whether to go down one side or the other. Two small signs marked the choices: "headship" or "co-heirs." Both footpaths were well-trampled.

The sun was sinking. Soon it would be too dark to continue, so they decided to set up camp near the tree. Peter gathered firewood, Celeste gathered some nuts and berries, and they had a delicious meal by the fire. After they had eaten, Peter stretched back. "Tomorrow we'll take the side marked 'headship.'"

Celeste was startled because he said this like a commandment. "I thought we were going to discuss which side to take."

"That might have worked earlier in our journey, but the walking is getting more complicated. Remember, you haven't walked as much as I have. Besides, you're a woman, so you aren't as good at figuring out where to go."

Celeste jumped up with her hands on her hips. "But, but, but—" She was so upset, she couldn't think of anything to say.

"See, you don't even have any good arguments. You know this is the way it is supposed to be."

"No!" she said. "It's true I was thinking we should try the headship path, but if you're going to be such a tyrant, I think it would be better to take the side marked 'co-heirs.'"

"Of course you would."

"What do you mean by that?"

"Growing up in the Slouching City, your head was filled with all sorts of ideas that aren't anywhere in the King's guidebook. So of course you might think that co-heirs is the way to go."

"And why are you so sure that headship is the right way?"

"Because I'm the head, and I know what is best." He lifted his head. "And if you had examined the two sides as I did, you would have seen that the headship side is clearly better worn and wider, so obviously it is the preferred way."

"To me," Celeste said, "both sides looked equally well traveled."

"That doesn't matter, because I've decided—and I'm in charge."

"You are not; we are taking this journey together."

"Maybe, but I lead and you follow."

"That's not what I read in the guidebook."

"You only read the things you agree with."

"As if you're perfect?"

"I'm the man. I was created first, and you have to obey me." Peter raised his voice. "That's what the King wants." Then he bellowed, "You will obey me."

He sounded so much like the guards at Pigeon Hole, Celeste became frightened and ran into the woods.

Peter didn't bother to go after her. Truthfully, he was glad to see her leave. She was being altogether stubborn and irrational; she needed to come to her senses. Spending a night alone in the cold, dark woods would do her good. When he woke up in the morning, refreshed and warmed by the coals of the fire, he looked around for Celeste. Then he remembered she had run off. "Well, it serves her right for being so stubborn."

Celeste had spent the night shivering and miserable in the hollow of a tree. She woke up stiff and achy—and troubled by Peter's attitude, especially his insistence and hardness. It wasn't that she didn't want to follow; often she didn't have a strong preference one way or another. At the beginning of their journey together, he had often asked her what she had thought. Sometimes they had gone the way she wanted to without any problem. Now he seemed so intent on his plans, she didn't think he would notice if she got into trouble. She had made a vow to honor and love and serve him, but did it mean following him when he ignored her?

"Celeste?" Peter was calling.

"I'm here," she said, weak and tired.

"Oh, there you are," Peter said. "I found someone who can help you."

Celeste looked at the man standing beside Peter. He was

dressed all in black and carried the largest guidebook she had ever seen. And he stared at her with an expression that reminded her of Reverend Strict and Reverend Severe.

"His name is Mr. One Verse," Peter said. "He has all the arguments to change your mind."

With great ceremony, Mr. One Verse cleared his throat and opened the guidebook. "Wives, submit to your husbands as to the King. For the husband is the head of the wife as the Servant is head of all whom He saved. Now as you submit to the Servant, so also wives should submit to their husbands in everything."

Peter looked at Celeste in triumph. "There, you've heard it straight from the guidebook. I'm the head and you have to follow me, and I say we're going down the side marked 'headship.'"

Celeste thought if Peter was the head, he was a very stuffed head.

"Come," he commanded, and strode briskly back to the path.

Celeste was so tired and cold that she didn't know what else to do, so she started shuffling behind Peter.

"Now don't you feel better?" he said back to her.

"No, I don't," she said. She felt miserable, but she was afraid to tell Peter that. "And what happened to Mr. One Verse?"

"He had to go proclaim that verse to other couples. He told me that is his special calling."

"I don't think that is right." Celeste had not yet lost her spirit. "The guidebook is very big, and it's wrong to focus on one part and ignore the rest. It reminds me of Pigeon Hole."

"Yes, well, that's what you would say. When you don't like what it says, you simply pretend it's not there."

They were almost back at the great fallen tree. "When we get to the tree," Celeste said, "can we rest for a moment?"

"No. I'm in charge and I don't want to."

But as they approached the tree, a flood of travelers came down the path, and Peter and Celeste had to stand to one side to let the group pass. They watched in amazement as the couples went on without stopping to discuss which way to take. Clearly most were in agreement about which way to go. Some went down one side and some went down the other, and though Peter tried to predict which couples would go where, he couldn't. At the end of the group, an old guide trailed behind.

"Dear friends," Sacrificial Love said to Peter and Celeste. "I'm sorry for your wait. You can go now. Take your course."

"All right," Peter said. "We're going down the side marked 'headship.' I know it is the right way to go."

"Are you so sure?" the guide asked.

"Yes."

"And Celeste, what do you think?"

"Her opinion doesn't matter. I've just met Mr. One Verse, who read from the guidebook. It's clear what Celeste has to do. She is going to follow me. We were only waiting for everyone else to go by."

"She doesn't look very happy," Sacrificial Love said.

"She's being obstinate. She just needs to follow the King's law and she'll recover her joy."

"Yes, joy," Sacrificial Love said. "Dear sister, you look tired. Why don't you sit here on the bench and drink this." The guide handed Celeste a warm mug of sympathy, then took his sheepskin of humility and put it around her shoulders.

Grateful for his care, Celeste gladly sat down and started sipping from the mug.

"Now, my dear brother." Sacrificial Love put his hand on Peter's shoulder. "While your partner is recovering from spending a night alone in these woods, you and I should take a little stroll."

"Oh, I can't leave her," Peter said.

"You did last night."

"She went off herself."

"Did you go after her?"

"She was the one who left."

"Yes, just like the one-hundredth sheep."

"What do you mean?"

"How does the King deal with us when we stray? He searches us out, like the shepherd seeking the one lost sheep. Now I'm not saying you are the King. In fact, anyone who drags his partner down the way of headship needs to be reminded of that."

"But lots of couples went down that side," Peter said.

"Yes, I'll get to that. But first I'd like to read you something." Sacrificial Love took out his guidebook, which was covered with stains from tears and blood. Then he read the passage Mr. One Verse had read.

"Exactly!" Peter said.

"Oh, I'm not finished." The guide continued reading. "Husbands, love your wives as the Servant loved you and gave Himself for you, to make you pure and clean as a radiant crown, without stain or wrinkle or any other blemish. In this same way, a husband ought to love his wife as he loves his own body. He who loves his wife loves himself. After all, no one ever hated his own body, but he feeds and cares for it, just as the Servant does for us, for we belong to Him." He slowly closed the book. "So which path should you take?"

Peter looked at Sacrificial Love and wondered if the guide was trying to trick him. "The path of headship," he said.

"Could you tell me just on this verse alone—which is addressed to you, not the earlier one that was addressed to Celeste—what it says husbands are to do?"

Peter reread the section and said, "To love his wife as his own body."

"Very good. And could you tell me what the Servant did when He walked on this earth? How did He show His love for the travelers?"

Peter thought for a moment and then spoke slowly, because it was a little painful for him to say. "The Servant washed His followers' feet, He healed, He gave His life."

"And what did the Servant demand before He gave His life in love?"

"Nothing," Peter said.

"Nothing, that's right." Sacrificial Love put his hand on Peter's shoulder, and they started walking back to the bench where Celeste was waiting. "I have gone down both sides, and I can tell you they both lead to the King's City. Before the Tree of Oneness fell, there was a single path and it was never the King's design to split it in two. In some places the tree trunk has sunk so low in the ground that you can barely make out any distinction in the two sides. But in other places the trunk is quite thick and tall, and you can't even see the other side.

"Travelers struggle down both of these ways," the guide said, "but it is not which side they take that causes their difficulties; it's their stubbornness. I have seen people go down the co-heirs side and take off their cords, that is true. And I have also seen people go down the headship side, and by the time they get to the end their cords are also cut. But I have also seen travelers come out of both sides more willing to love their partner.

"Here is another passage I would like you to learn by heart," he said to Peter. "You know that the rulers in this world lord it over their people, and officials flaunt their authority over those under them. But among you it will be different. Whoever wants to be a leader among you must be your servant, and whoever wants to be first among you must be the slave of everyone else. For even the Servant came not to be served but to serve others and to give His life as a ransom for many."

Sacrificial Love looked at Peter. "Put this into practice with your dear wife and you will begin to understand the burden and challenge that will be yours. Can you bear the Servant's cross as you love Celeste?"

"Yes," Peter said, "but—"

"Yes, but what about her? That is what the men who are so keen on being heads always want to know. All I will say is that you are called to do your part, and your part alone. You know that the second greatest commandment is to love your neighbor as yourself. And you know that when the Servant was asked what this meant, He told a story of mercy and compassion and then said the questioner should go and do the same. Love Celeste as you love yourself, and then you will be ready to take the way of headship." Sacrificial Love gave Peter a little push. "Now, go to her and make amends."

Peter returned to the Tree of Oneness. The color had returned to Celeste's cheeks, and she looked much stronger. As he approached, Celeste said nothing, but she bowed her head a little.

He extended his hand to hers and pulled her up from where she was sitting. "Will you walk with me?" His voice barely a whisper, for he feared her answer. He had been pompous, and he wouldn't have blamed her if she didn't want to go on with him.

"Of course. You are my husband whom I love."

"I thought that we might try the side marked 'co-heirs.'"

"As you wish," Celeste said.

To Peter's surprise, the way of co-heirs was not as treacherous as he thought. For a stretch it passed through a delightful meadow, much like the one where they had first drunk from the chalice. As Sacrificial Love had said, some couples they met were very happy while others were squabbling back and forth, saying, "My rights," "No, my rights."

After some distance they passed the end of the fallen Tree of Oneness, and the two sides joined once more. Peter could see that the couples coming out of the headship side seemed to argue less. But some were very quiet and the women were so burdened, carrying both their bags and their partner's, they looked like slaves. He could hear them muttering, "He's the head, he's the head," while the men walked on, paying no attention to their partners except to turn occasionally and bark, "Do as I say, do as I say." Peter understood then that what Sacrificial Love had said was true.

Now in my dream, I pondered the lesson of the split path, for it seemed the struggle had been hard only for Peter. But I suspected that later on Celeste might have to face her own choice on the way to the King's City, one equally difficult.

Across the Swamp of Selfishness

LOST IN THE QUAGMIRES

*P*eter and Celeste walked in harmony for many days after the split path, and they often enjoyed the company of other travelers. But eventually the trail through the Low Country brought them to the vast Swamp of Selfishness. The swamp had been formed after the Tree of the Knowledge of Good and Evil— a tree even more majestic than the Tree of Oneness—had been uprooted in the Great Garden. When it had crashed to the ground, the whole world had been shaken, creating havoc and destruction throughout the King's country. The fallen branches had dammed many streams. With the flow of water blocked, the lowlands soon became a swamp. Treacherous quagmires were created, filled with all kinds of evil: envy, pride, greed, self-indulgence, ingratitude, slander, jealousy, and fits of rage.

Peter and Celeste considered finding a path around the swamp, but it reached as far as they could see. The only other way was to head west, where the Mountains of Maturity towered over the swamp, looking even steeper and more forbidding.

Peter sighed. "I wish we had gone up the first mountain we came to. It looked like such a difficult climb. But compared to the ones we see now, I think it would have been easy. I don't think we can scale these mountains; we'll have to take a longer route across the swamp."

"Do you really think it will be hard to go through the swamp?" Celeste said. "You are always so careful about picking the best way to go."

With that encouragement, Peter began to plot out the route they would take through the gloomy place. The trees that had once given shade and shelter were now reduced to drowned skeletons with bare branch stubs, sometimes draped in gray moss that looked like giant spider webs. Flies and mosquitoes swarmed over the murky water, and a dank odor reminded Celeste of Peter's dirty socks. But in places, the swamp gave way to tracts of firmer marsh grass and Peter thought if they paid close attention, they might get across without too much difficulty.

As they started through the swamp, they found guidebooks, walking sticks, and sheepskins that had been thrown aside. They couldn't understand why travelers would discard their kingly gifts. Then they stepped into the first quagmire and quickly began to sink into the foul mud. "Now I understand why the travelers tried to lighten their loads," Peter said.

"Do you think we should take something out of our packs too?"

"No. Whatever we do, we'll keep everything we've been given, because the King's gifts aren't heavy. But I wonder if we should turn back and try to find a firmer way. The King will show us a way out so we don't give in to the temptation to take an easy path that leads nowhere."

Celeste pointed out that there were many travelers in the swamp ahead of them. "This must be a good way to go, and if we get into trouble, we have the King's gifts to help us." With that, Peter was persuaded and they set off through the swamp.

However, they had to concentrate so hard on making their way and gathering whatever meager food they could find, they soon forgot their gifts. As night fell, they searched for solid ground where they could set up camp. They finally settled for a soggy patch of dirt where they rolled out their sleeping bags. As soon as they lay down, the water soaked through and they spent a miserable night, damp and cold. Celeste minded it most of all, but because she had convinced Peter to take the swamp route, she kept quiet, afraid that he might become angry with her. In the morning, they surveyed the swamp. It looked much wider and longer than it had the day before. They were so discouraged at the thought of going through it, they didn't start off until noon.

The days that followed brought no change. Their progress was tedious as they tried to avoid the quagmires and find the driest sections of marsh grass. The sky became pasted with dark clouds that never moved.

"We haven't seen the sun in such a long time." Celeste thought of all the sunlit scenes in her postcards. "I never thought we would have to go through such a dismal place on our journey to the King's City."

"Don't blame me. It's not my fault."

"Oh, no? You were so keen on being the leader," Celeste said, "but you're doing a pretty bad job if you ask me."

"Well, I didn't ask you."

"Of course not. That's just like you, to go off without bothering to ask what I think."

"Oh, shut up."

"Maybe I don't feel like it."

"No, you love to talk; that's for sure."

"If you would say something once in awhile, I wouldn't have to listen to the sound of my voice all the time. We could actually have a conversation—you know, the kind where I say something and then you say something to respond."

"If we did that, you would be even slower than you are now. Talking distracts you."

"Unlike you, I can do two things at once. And talking makes the time go faster."

"Not to me," Peter said. To prove his point he began to walk faster through the marsh grass.

"I think you would rather go your own way than go together with me," Celeste shouted ahead to him. "I don't think you love me."

Peter stopped. "Don't be stupid. All right, we'll stay together. But if you fall behind again, I'm not going to wait."

THE SNAPPING TURTLES

They continued to struggle through the swamp. They hardly had energy to talk and when they did, it was usually to quarrel over their dwindling provisions. After their experience of running out of food and water in the Sand Dunes of Foolishness, Peter wanted to limit what they used each day. Celeste thought it was better to eat what they had, because the extra weight in their packs made walking harder. Besides, she was positive there was plenty ahead for Peter to find.

He said she didn't know what she was talking about. It wasn't that easy to look for provisions. Celeste said it had never been difficult when she had walked alone. The real problem was that Peter wanted to save more than they needed.

One day when they stopped for lunch, they again began to fight over how much they would eat. They squabbled back and forth, their voices becoming louder and more angry.

Another couple came over and they warned them to be careful. "We heard you arguing," the husband said, "and we want you to know that we used to argue like that until we were attacked by an army of snapping turtles."

"An army?" Celeste imagined thousands of snapping turtles on the path. "How horrible!"

"Where do they live?" Peter asked. Maybe they could avoid them.

"Generally you find them in wet places, watered by stormy arguments—though some have been seen in the dry washes nipping at travelers' heels. They came after us when we had been walking together so long, we thought we knew exactly what our partner was going to say. We gave up being patient with each other. One of us would snap, and then the other would snap back."

"It was the most frightful time of our journey," the woman said. "I suppose we were more tired than usual because we had spent the night in a particularly swampy area. There were so many mosquitoes buzzing around us all night, we couldn't sleep. Then my husband decided we just had to get to a certain spot for lunch, and he set the fastest pace we had taken so far, even though we had gotten no sleep."

Celeste felt a little comforted to hear that Peter wasn't the only one who sometimes walked too fast for his partner.

"But after that night in the swamp," the man said, "I just wanted to get to firm, dry land."

"When we finally stopped . . . oh I don't know." The woman looked embarrassed. "He was tired and lay down to rest before lunch. But I was hungry after walking so fast. 'There you go again,' I said."

The husband broke in. "The tone had much more of a bite than that—"

"Yes, maybe it did, but then he snapped back, 'What's wrong?' I told him I knew he was going to fall asleep and leave all the cooking to me. He said he was just going to rest for five minutes. But I told him, 'Hah! I bet.' And then he yelled, 'Will you stop it?' 'Stop what?' I asked him. 'You just harp on me all the time,' he said. I started to tell him I wouldn't if he would do what he was supposed to, but he interrupted and told me to relax. 'Stop interrupting me,' I told him. And he said, 'It takes you forever to think of what you're going to say.'"

"So we snapped back and forth at each other," the husband said, "each of us being quick to speak but not quick to listen. We never gave each other the benefit of the doubt—or any grace. Then the turtles came up out of the water—on the left and on the right, from behind, and coming straight toward us—chomping their huge jaws."

"I got bitten in three places." The woman lifted her pant leg to show Peter and Celeste three unsightly bites the color of plums. "But I'm more fortunate than others. We heard about one couple whose Cords of Commitment were almost ripped apart by the turtles." She shook her head. "It is sad because I'm much more civil with people I hardly know or care about. With my husband I let my irritation spring to anger at the smallest spark. We can tame a tiger, but we can't tame the tongue. Out of the same mouth comes blessing for the King and curses for our partner, the most precious person to us."

"Since then," the man said, "we've been working on listening rather than getting angry first. We are trying to be patient with each other and put aside the little irritations and grievances. It isn't easy, but it's better than getting to the King's City without any arms or legs."

Peter and Celeste thanked them for the advice and went on their way. But they didn't take the warning to heart. For all their arguing in the swamp, they had never seen a single turtle. They assumed the couple had made up the story to shock them, so they kept quarreling. The next afternoon while they were arguing about where to set up camp, three large turtles lumbered up out of the water and began snapping at them. At first Peter and Celeste did nothing, thinking they could outpace the turtles. But the turtles were surprisingly nimble and caught up to the travelers in a flash. Peter picked up a stick to club them away, without bothering to get one for Celeste. Although he managed to fend off two of the turtles, the third saw that Celeste had nothing to protect herself with and bit her in the leg.

Peter wasn't very sympathetic to her ugly wound or to her crying. "There's no need to carry on like that. It's just a flesh wound."

"But it hurts!" Celeste wailed. When Peter said it was time for them to start walking again, she insisted that they wait until her bite was healed before they went on.

Peter fumed for two days. Then in exasperation, he went off and found a stick that Celeste could use as a crutch. "Here, now you can walk," he said, throwing it down at her feet. However, Celeste refused to go until he showed her how to club the turtles. It was a good thing he did, for they were plagued by the snapping turtles for several days, and without their clubs, they might have been eaten alive.

SINKING IN THE QUAGMIRE OF SELF-PITY

If this was not enough—oh, how I wished it was another dream—Peter was becoming more distant from Celeste. He was usually so wrapped up in his own thoughts that when Celeste talked, he didn't hear a word she said. And Celeste became more inconsiderate of Peter. She would often go off and talk with other travelers, then get back to camp so late that she slept in, always too tired to make breakfast or pack the bags, leaving all the work to Peter. Then she decided they should have a party to celebrate the first anniversary of their weaving day.

Peter said they were still working hard to find enough food; it would be irresponsible to waste their provisions.

"Who said anything about wasting?" Celeste said. "I just want to have a little party."

"Frivolous." Peter harrumphed. "I'm not going to let you use up all our food for that. And I suppose you'll want a new outfit for the party—"

"As a matter of fact, I do."

"You have plenty of clothes."

"Do you expect me to travel in rags? Let me remind you that when I met you, there were holes in the knees of your pants."

"There's nothing wrong with that. It gave good air circulation."

"Peter, you are being impossible."

"Me? If I let you get everything you wanted, we'd starve."

"Well, what about your new boots?"

"I needed to get them so I could walk properly. But a new outfit is just an extravagance. Peter turned and started off without Celeste. I'm not going to talk about it anymore."

"Come back here; we're not finished discussing this."

Peter kept on walking.

Celeste ran after him. "You are a miserable miser!"

"You are an irresponsible child," he said, without turning around.

"Stop!" she screamed. Then, just as Lady Sophia had warned, Celeste took out her turtle club to hit Peter. She only meant to give him a little tap to make him slow down. But she was stronger than she thought and she smacked him on the leg.

Peter whirled around. When he saw the club in her hand, he took out his to strike back. Celeste managed to block his first blow, but the second one grazed her arm.

In my dream, I feared for the worst. Fortunately, Celeste lost her grip on her club, and it dropped to the ground. At that, Peter put his club away too—but he refused to speak to Celeste for the rest of the day.

Their cords began to chafe their wrists, and the swamp became so spongy it could not support them both. Each thought it would be easier if they began to choose separate paths. Peter, with his long legs, could jump across a large tract of mud to reach a section of beach grass, while Celeste could walk on slender fallen logs that couldn't support Peter's weight. So they decided to go their own way for a while and meet up again.

Once Celeste tripped and landed in the muck. "Don't you care about me?" she shouted to Peter. "I've fallen, and it's all your fault. You're going too fast for me." Peter just kept on going and when Celeste came to a small island of firm ground, she decided to rest awhile.

Celeste watched Peter labor across the swamp until other travelers came to the island. Soon she was having so much fun talking and playing games, she didn't miss Peter at all. Late in the afternoon, she finally looked to see how far he had gotten. In the distance she saw he had become stuck in the Quagmire of Self-Pity, but she stayed on the island. Why should she do anything nice for him after he had been so mean and uncaring to her? If he was so determined to go his own way, he could figure out how to get out of the quagmire himself. Besides, he had enough of his dull rations and his guidebook to keep him happy.

Although Peter hadn't minded going off on his own through the swamp, when he got trapped in the quagmire, he felt hurt that

Celeste didn't come to help him. She had started the battle with their clubs, and now she didn't care that he was stuck. He struggled to get out, but before long he felt so neglected that he let himself sink deeper and deeper until the gooey mud was past his knees.

He discovered the mud was soothing on his sore muscles, and rather than trying to fight his way out, he leaned against the edge of the quagmire and settled in for the night. The next day he decided that he liked the quagmire's peace and quiet. He could get up as soon as the sun rose, go to bed early, and spend all the time he wanted reading the guidebook. No one ever interrupted him. He thought maybe he would just stay there.

Meanwhile, Celeste waited on the island for Peter. She didn't mind the stalemate; she enjoyed talking with the travelers who passed by, and her wound from the snapping turtle began to heal. Then one day two travelers reached the island and collapsed in exhaustion from fighting their way through the swamp.

"What are we going to do?" the woman said. "We can't go on like this."

"We don't have a choice," her partner said.

"But don't you remember?"

"Remember what?"

"Remember the gathering hut and the songs we sang and the vision of the King's City?"

"Look around. There is nothing but swamp, so get used to it."

Celeste went over to the man. "Don't you care?" she said. "Your partner is hurting. Look at all her wounds." She pointed to his wife, who was covered with leeches, dirt, and scratches. "If you really loved her, you would do whatever you could to get out of this swamp."

"But what about me?"

"Did you decide to become partners just so she could care for you? You're supposed to serve each other."

"You're one to talk," the man said. "Your partner isn't even with you. Where did he go?"

Celeste felt her cheeks turn hot. She was resting comfortably on the island while Peter was stuck in the Quagmire of Self-Pity.

She returned to her spot on the island and pondered what to do. It had been a long time since she had talked with the King or read her guidebook. She took it from the bottom of her pack and looked up a passage she had read when she began her journey. In it, the Servant said, "If any of you wants to be My follower, you must turn from your selfish ways, take up your cross daily, and follow Me. If you try to hang on to your life, you will lose it. But if you give up your life for My sake, you will save it."

She had never considered how it applied to her partnership with Peter, but now she understood she needed to sacrifice her comfort on the island and go help Peter out of the mess he was in. She hesitated a moment, then she heard the King speak to her: "Do not worry, Celeste. You have been loved. Now it is your turn."

"But how can I? It seems too hard."

"You will need the same attitude the Servant had. He did not consider being King a privilege to hold on to. Instead, He gave it up and came to the world as a humble Servant to live a life of love. He was obedient even though He was put to death for something He didn't do."

"But He was really the King, and I'm just a traveler. I'm not strong enough."

"I will be working in you as you go, helping you to want the same thing I want—and then helping you to do it," the King said. "Truly, I will be with you always."

The Breath of the King came and filled Celeste, giving her strength as she made her way through the swamp to Peter. She had to struggle mightily through the mud, and by the time she reached Peter she was completely dirty and wet, just like Peter in the quagmire.

She could hear him muttering in a pitiful voice, "Nobody loves me, everybody hates me, but who cares, who cares?"

"Peter," Celeste said from the edge of the quagmire. "I've come to help you."

But Peter paid no attention to her.

"Peter!" she shouted.

When Peter finally heard Celeste, he turned his face away from her.

She found an old branch and poked it toward him in the quagmire. "Peter, stop being so silly. Take hold of the branch."

"It's no use. You're not strong enough."

"We can do this together with the King's strength. Now grab on." Celeste dug in her heels, and once again the Breath of the King blew through her and gave her strength. She pulled and tugged, and tugged and pulled, until Peter was out of the muck. Then Celeste started to pull off all the leeches that had attached to him. It was a vile job, and several times she thought she would be sick. By the time she removed the last leech, she was worn out. Helping Peter escape his misery was the hardest thing she had ever done.

"I'm sorry I didn't come sooner," she said. "Let's stay together from now on. I promise I'll go faster."

But they were in the thickest, stickiest part of the swamp and their progress was slow. Though they cared for each other as best they could, they were always exhausted from their journey and they had no time to enjoy each other or drink from the chalice.

BENEATH THE BURDENS OF THEIR BAGS

Finally the ground grew firmer in places. They still had to make their way around quagmires, but they were able to pick up their pace. Then ahead of them, just past another quagmire, they saw a couple sitting on the ground, so weighed down by their heavy packs that they couldn't continue.

"I wonder what the trouble is," Celeste said. "The King's gifts wouldn't push them down like that."

"They must not have learned one of the most important rules of the journey: travel light."

"Can you help us get up?" the man called out.

"Why don't you take some things out of your packs?" Peter asked.

"Why would we do that?"

"Because they're weighing you down too much."

"I don't know what you're talking about," the man said. "Our bags are just fine."

"You don't see how your wife's pack is so heavy, she can't walk?"

"She's had all those things ever since we set off. But for some reason our packs seem to have gotten heavier as we've journeyed."

Celeste turned to the woman. "What exactly is in your pack?"

"Only some childhood treasures," the woman said, "and a few family heirlooms that have been passed down through the generations."

"Why do you keep carrying them if they are so heavy?"

"They're too precious to leave behind."

"But you aren't able to walk."

"If we could just get to a firmer path I think we'd be fine."

"Unless you get rid of these things that weigh you down," Peter said, "you'll never be able to go on."

"When I decided to go to the King's City, I left everything from my past behind," the man said, though his pack was bulging. "It's gone. Finished. Kaput."

Peter took one of the man's arms and Celeste took the other. Leaning back, they tried to pull the man up, but he wouldn't budge. They had no more success in moving the woman.

"Some travelers told us there is a guide who might be able to help us up," the woman said. "If you see him, can you tell him to come?"

Celeste and Peter promised they would and set off. But the couple called after them. "Wait, wait."

"What is it?"

"You're fine ones to talk about our packs," the man said, "when you're both carrying large ones yourselves."

"I don't know what you're talking about," Peter said.

The man chuckled. "That's exactly what I said."

Peter thought the man was joking. "Mine is very light. It never bothers me."

A few days later, Peter and Celeste found the guide, Truth, sitting beside a large pile of junk.

"Hello, dear ones," Truth said. "You've come to the right place with packs like yours."

"No, you don't understand," Peter said. "We're not the ones who need help. There's a couple back there whose packs weigh so much, they can't move at all."

Truth shook his head. "You have been carrying many burdens, and you haven't even known how they have weighed you down and made the hard paths even more difficult. I have seen many travelers with heavy packs like yours. Some can't stop griping about how tough the journey is. But when I tell them I want to help them lighten their load, they refuse. 'Oh no,' they say, 'the King suffered, and so I must suffer too. It is my cross to bear.' They don't understand that is not the kind of cross the King asked them to carry. He wants to give His travelers easy, light bags so they don't feel weary and burdened as they go."

He went to Celeste, opened her pack, and lifted out a few things.

Celeste was stunned at how much lighter she felt. "It's amazing, Peter."

Truth turned to Peter. "Let me take something out of your pack, too."

"You're mistaken," Peter said. "We don't have a problem. We were sent by the couple back there. They are the ones who can't even walk."

"Denying your burdens does not make them disappear. In fact, it will be too difficult for you to get through the swamp unless you lighten your load. You have spent years accumulating these burdens. Carrying them has given you bad backs and dreadful sores. The King asks sick people, 'Do you want to get well?' That is my question to you. Do you want to get better?"

Peter looked away, but Celeste said, "Truth is right. Maybe you are strong enough to walk with your pack stuffed full of unnecessary things, but I don't think I can go much farther."

"All right then, let's see what you have." Truth turned over Celeste's pack and dumped everything on the ground. A cloud of mold and dust, accompanied by a stale smell, rose from the pile. "Whew, it doesn't look like you've gone through your treasures in a long time."

Celeste winced. "I thought I left all the ugliness from my past behind."

Truth looked through the pile and shook his head. "When you took the King's path, you left much of your past, but there are still some remnants—and a fistful of chains from unconfessed sin." Then Truth picked up a large, rough stone.

When Celeste saw it in his hands, she quickly turned away and began to weep.

Truth put his arm on her shoulder. "You have been carrying many Hurting Stones that other people have tossed at you," he said gently. "In some ways these are the heaviest burdens of all because you had no choice in them."

He turned to Peter. "I'd like to look at your pack now."

"All right, go ahead." Peter was sure his would not be anywhere near as awful as Celeste's. But when Truth opened Peter's pack, a putrid puff of self-righteousness came out and Peter could see his was no better than hers.

Truth glanced at the contents. "So you grew up hearing about the King."

Peter smiled. "Yes, indeed."

"That has spared you from much harm. Do you see how your burdens are not at all like your wife's?" Indeed the stones Truth took from Peter's pack were not rough like Celeste's, but smoothly polished, some with delicate fossils imprinted in them. "A nice set of family heirlooms, but feel how heavy these are." Truth gave one to Peter. "This must be very precious to carry it with you all the way."

Peter stroked the smooth fossil. "This is one of my favorite traditions," he said. "I could never part with it."

Truth pulled out an old scroll. "And what is this?"

"My genealogy," Peter said.

"Ah, yes, I see." Truth moved his lips as he read it to himself. "Very impressive. Five generations in Upright Village, and such faithfulness and strictness in observing the law."

Peter smiled.

"It reminds me of a guide who said, 'If anyone else thinks he has reasons to put confidence in the flesh, I have more: circumcised on the eighth day, of the people of Israel, of the tribe of Benjamin, a Hebrew of Hebrews; in regard to the law, a Pharisee; as for zeal, persecuting the church; as for legalistic righteousness, faultless.' But Paul came to realize those credentials were worth nothing compared to the joy of walking on the Servant's path."

Truth looked at both of them. "Now do you understand? As

you walked, you became accustomed to the weight of these so-called treasures—even though they slowed you down and became heavier as you went. Some of these burdens you didn't even know you had in your packs when you set out. You thought others were harmless and light. In any case, you need to talk about your hurts and your treasures in the redemptive light of the King, so they will lose their heaviness. It will take a long time because you have carried them for so long. But it will make your way much easier. When I get back from dealing with the other couple, I will be happy to help you."

"How long does it take to deal with them?"

"Three weeks, maybe more."

"Three weeks? Just talking about them?" Peter asked. "Thank you all the same, but we've lost a lot of time in the swamp, and we really must be on our way."

Celeste, alarmed at the prospect of giving up her childhood treasures, didn't argue.

"I am sorry for you," Truth said, "for these burdens will not become lighter. You need to get rid of them if you want to walk more nimbly on your journey. But if you will not wait for me to deal with all of them, at least pick out a few things for the junk pile—the heaviest and ugliest burdens, I suggest."

So before Peter and Celeste went on, they sorted through their bags. As they spoke the truth in love to one another, they were each able to leave behind a few treasures. They continued making their way through the swamp. They discovered that with lighter bags they didn't sink down as much, and they had more energy to help each other. When Peter saw Celeste shivering, he took his sheepskin of humility and put it around her. And Celeste went back to singing as she walked, often choosing Peter's favorite songs.

THE LITTLE TRAVELER JOINS THE JOURNEY

Eventually they left the swamp behind them and followed a path into a deep forest of tall oaks, maples, and elms. They could no longer see the Mountains of Maturity that had towered over the swamp, and they hoped the path would lead them away from it. Some days they had time to explore the other paths that laced through the woods like they used to when they first met in the grove. They kicked pebbles and hunted for berries and often stopped to read the guidebook together. Celeste was encouraged that Peter had not turned away when Truth held up her hurting stones, and she was growing more secure in his love. Celeste thought she would be willing to give up any hope of seeing another glimpse of the King's City again if only she and Peter could walk on like this.

One night by the fire, they sang a song from the guidebook to celebrate making it through the swamp:

I called to the King for help,
and He turned to me and heard my cry.
He pulled me out of the slimy pit of despair,
out of the mud and the mire.
He set my feet on solid ground
and steadied me as I walked along.

When they finished, Celeste turned to Peter. "Will you walk on with me?"

Peter took her hand and thought how she looked more beautiful than he remembered. The look of love had returned to his eyes and covered Celeste's shortcomings. "Yes," he said, "more than ever, I want to travel with you to the King's City."

In my dream, I saw that one day a little traveler joined Peter and Celeste, bringing them great joy. It was different than the joy of the chalice, but still rich and sweet. Peter and Celeste had no Cords of Commitment for the little traveler, but they didn't need them because they loved her fiercely. They took turns holding her and rocking her and staying up all night with her without ever complaining. Without discussing it, they determined to do everything their parents had done right and nothing their parents had done wrong. They were certain their little traveler would feel so loved, she would never go through any difficulties or feel lonely or break any rules of the King.

During the day they carried the little traveler, talking and singing to her as they walked. In the evenings when the little traveler was asleep, Peter and Celeste often talked about the future.

"We have to stop and reconsider our journey now that we have a little traveler," Peter said. "It is a big responsibility to care for her, and we need to look very carefully at the map. I want to make sure we don't go through any more swamps. It wouldn't do to have her exposed to the dirt and mosquitoes and leeches."

"And I don't want to get stuck in the sand dunes. It would be too hot and too dry for her."

"I'll have to work harder to look for the best food," Peter said. "I may have to go away from time to time, if I can't find some close to the path."

"Maybe we can read the guidebook together as a family every night by the fire. I don't have as much time to spend with the King as I used to."

"Or to drink from the chalice," Peter said.

"I know, but that will change once the little traveler gets older."

YIELDING AT SUBMISSION POND

Peter always carried the map, and whenever they needed to decide which way to go he would spread it on the ground so Celeste could look too. Then they would discuss the pros and cons of each choice. But after a time, perhaps because of the little traveler or perhaps because they were still close to the great Swamp of Selfishness, Celeste became more critical of the paths Peter wanted to take. Sometimes she mocked his choice or just smirked at him. Other times she would dig in her heels and insist on her way, talking so fast and with such elaborate arguments that Peter didn't have any chance to defend his preference.

Then one day the path led them down a short incline. At the bottom it stopped at a large pond surrounded by rocks, for it had once been a quarry. Peter took out his compass and put the map on the ground in front of them. "This is interesting," he said. "The map isn't very detailed here—it doesn't show this dead end or the pond. In fact it shows the path going straight across where the pond is."

"That's impossible," Celeste said. "Let me look." Peter showed her the map, and she became quiet for a moment. "I wish you had asked for a more up-to-date map. I really don't want us to make a bad choice here. The little traveler is getting grumpy, and I want to reach the next campsite so we can all have a good rest." She peered at the map, then got up. "There must be a path somewhere."

"Wait a minute. Let me take a reading on my compass."

"You and your equipment. We don't need a compass. We just have to go around the water. I don't know whose idea it was to put a pond right in the middle of the way to the King's City."

Peter held out his compass. "Well, we want to go straight across the pond."

"Maybe we could try walking on the water?" Celeste said with sarcasm.

"Actually, that's a good idea. We could build a boat. There might be a path on the other side."

"Absolutely not."

"Celeste, we don't know how long it will take to go around the pond, and we don't even know if there's a path. You said yourself that you want to get to the next campsite as soon as possible."

"Yes, but the idea of building a boat is ridiculous."

"No, I think it's the right solution. We don't have to spend too much time on it. It will be a raft more than a boat—just sturdy enough to float us to the other side." He got out his binoculars and looked across the water. "Yes, I see an opening in the rocks. Building a boat is exactly what we need to do."

"No. We need to find a way around the pond."

Peter started looking for small tree trunks and dragged what he found to the water's edge. "Can you search over there?" He pointed to the hill they had just come down.

"I told you I don't want to do this. We have to find a path."

"It won't take long to build the raft."

"Have you ever made one?"

"Yes, I have. Soon after I left Upright Village, I made one to cross a river."

"Did it float?"

"Celeste, that's not a very kind question. But yes, it did."

"I don't believe you."

Peter sat down.

"Why are you sitting down?"

"Because we have to work this out."

"There's nothing to work out. Let's go explore."

"I told you that a raft is the best way."

"And I told you I'm not going to get on a raft."

Peter sighed.

"Stop being so stubborn," Celeste said.

"You're the one who's being stubborn."

"No, I'm not."

"Look," Peter said, "this discussion isn't going anywhere. Why don't we break for lunch?"

They sat by the pond eating their sandwiches while the little traveler splashed at the edge of the water. Then they heard a commotion at the top of the incline. "Come on. I said, come on," a woman shouted.

"No, I don't think we should go that way," a male traveler said.

"It doesn't matter what you think."

"Sounds like a teenager is giving his mother a real problem," Celeste said. Soon the travelers reached the bottom of the incline. "Your son is quite a handful," Celeste said to the woman.

"Son? What are you talking about? That's my husband. He never listens."

"Oh," Celeste said. "Don't you discuss which way to take?"

"Sure, but his ideas are always bad ones." She went over to her partner, who was chatting with Peter. "Come on" she said, "we have to get going.

The man stopped in mid-sentence and turned to follow her.

No sooner had they left when another couple came up the path on the right. The woman seemed to be sleepwalking; the man had to pull her every step of the way. When they reached the intersection, the man stopped and the woman immediately stopped too.

"Where do you think we should go?" the man asked his partner.

"Wherever you say, dear," she said as though dreaming.

"Should we swim across?"

"I don't care. Whatever you want to do."

"I want to know what you think."

"I'm sure you can figure it out," the woman said and then sat down, waiting for her husband to decide.

"We're thinking of building a raft to go across the pond," Peter told the man.

"Now that's an idea," the man said, then he shook his head. "No, that will never work with her. I have to drag her everywhere because she refuses to do anything herself. There's no way I could build a raft, pull her onto it, and then push it across. That would take two people. I guess we'll have to find a path, but if that's a dead end, I don't know what we'll do. I'd hate to have to pull her back up that hill."

Peter and Celeste finished their lunch. "Have you changed your mind?" Peter asked.

"No."

"I'm not going to be able to build the raft by myself. We have to do it together."

"It's a silly idea, and I won't do it."

"All right, then we can set up camp here for the night."

"I want to go look for a trail."

"I'm not going to argue anymore. I'm going to set up camp and we can talk about it in the morning," Peter said, remembering the lesson of the split path.

"You can do what you want; I'm going to search for a way around the pond."

"With the little traveler?"

"I'm happy to leave her with you. It's about time you took a turn taking care of her."

So Celeste took off alone. Soon she was enjoying the break from caring for the little traveler. She found a path through the woods and followed it until it came to a rushing river. A log had been placed to cross over the water. Normally she could have walked across without any trouble. But her pack was still quite heavy, and she was afraid she might lose her balance and fall into the water. As she looked to see if there was another way to cross, a guide on horseback drew up beside her.

Respect got off her horse, not looking pleased to see Celeste standing by the log. "What are you doing here?"

"I'm going to the King's City." Celeste wondered why the guide wasn't being nicer to her.

"Where's your partner?"

"I couldn't convince him to take this path."

"So you went by yourself?"

"What's wrong with that?"

Respect gave the loudest sigh Celeste had ever heard. "Did you put on the Cords of Commitment?"

"Of course."

"Then what are you doing here by yourself?"

"I told you, I couldn't—"

"I know what you told me—you couldn't convince your partner to come with you. But let me ask again. Why are you here without your partner? On what grounds did you take your leave of him?"

"The grounds of disagreement."

"Why didn't you go the way he wanted?"

"Because it seemed silly to build a raft to cross a pond. It's such a typical male approach. I prefer staying on firm ground."

"Except here you are, faced with a slippery log and no way of getting your pack across."

"I know. How are travelers supposed to get across this?"

"The same way they get across the pond."

"On a raft?"

"No, together. The only way you will get across is with your partner."

"But he's as stubborn as I am. He'll never agree to come this way."

"Then what are you going to do?"

Celeste shrugged. "I guess we'll have to spend the night here."

"And then what?"

"We'll have to decide."

"So why spend the night? Why not decide now?"

"Because it will take a night to convince Peter to come this way."

"But you said he was stubborn. What makes you think he will choose to come?"

Celeste narrowed her eyes at Respect.

"I know what men and women are like," Respect said, "and how the King designed the journey for them."

"How's that?"

"You know; you've read the guidebook. "Wives submit to and respect your husbands as to the King."

"We haven't had any problems before now," Celeste said. "We've always come to mutual agreement. We're equals, you know."

"Yes, I do know," Respect said. "You are co-heirs of the life of the King's grace. But you aren't the same. You complete each other because you are different from each other. Do you complain about being different when you drink from the chalice? Or when his strengths make up for your weaknesses and your strengths fill in his weaknesses? You are more than equal. You are one.

That's why I was so disturbed to see you here alone."

"So you're saying I should never disagree with him?"

"Of course not. How can you complete him if you say nothing and do nothing? Did you see that couple where the woman refuses to participate? That's not the way the King wants it. He asks you to yield to Peter, as you yield to Him—"

Respect held up her hand to stop Celeste from speaking. "And please don't ask the question that everyone else asks: 'But what about my husband?' Is that what you learned from the King? No. You learned to work on your own shortcomings, and let the King worry about the other person's. You are asked to defer to Peter's leadership when the two of you come to an impasse. Why is that so hard?"

"But men have abused their position. Men have done awful things to women."

"Yes, they have. People have abused a lot of the King's rules, but that doesn't mean we can ignore them. Disobedience does not justify further disobedience."

"But why should I be forced to submit?"

"You aren't forced at all. The King bought your freedom and you are free indeed. No one can make you submit. No one will force you, not even the King. The Servant laid down His life with His own free will. You have the same choice."

"But what if I don't want to?"

"It is not Peter who is asking you to do this. It is the King. Will you do it for your King?"

"It's not fair."

"Fair? Is the King's way a democracy? Look at my horse. Is it fair that the nose is not an ear or that the tail is not a leg? It's not a question of fairness but of how the world was designed to be."

"I don't want to become a nobody."

"How does yielding to Peter make you a nobody?"

"I'll have to give up all my opinions and thoughts."

"No, Peter needs you. If you always give in, it's not healthy. Iron sharpens iron, and you are meant to sharpen Peter. You are called to help him become more like the King. There are times you need to be strong, but there are also times when you should bend."

"That sounds weak."

"To bend without snapping requires great strength."

"But sometimes he is wrong. Sometimes he doesn't love me the way he should."

"And sometimes you don't love Peter the way you should. That doesn't give him an excuse to be a tyrant over you. And you're not excused from deferring to him. There will be times he will be wrong. But that does not change things. The King asks you to submit."

"I don't like that."

"Is there anything else in the guidebook you don't like?" Respect said. "Perhaps you would like to make up your own set of rules?"

Celeste thought of Pigeon Hole and shook her head. "No, I'm not the King."

"Remember, it's your decision. The King does not force you." Respect got back on her horse and took the reins. "I can take you back to your partner now if you want. It will be much easier than walking alone. Give me your hand and step up on the stirrup."

Celeste hesitated. She was very tired, and she considered how long the walk would be to return to the little traveler and Peter. She took Respect's outstretched hand, and in a flash she was sitting on the saddle behind the guide.

Respect prodded the horse and they were off. But she did not take Celeste straight back to Peter. They rode through the woods, and while they rode, Respect talked to Celeste about what it meant to treat Peter with honor. She reminded Celeste that when the King had come as the Servant, He had shown respect to His followers by washing their dirty feet. Then He had told them to follow His example. "The Servant's path is not always an easy way," Respect said, "and you need to remain attached to Him, like a branch on a vine."

When Respect dropped Celeste off at the pond, Peter and the little traveler were taking a nap in the sun. As her shadow fell across Peter, he woke up and smiled at her. "You've come back."

"Yes, I'll help you build the raft."

"Thank you," he said. "It's much harder to do it alone."

Under the Disillusioning Sun

AT THE GATHERING HUT

*O*nce they reached the other side of the pond, Peter and Celeste stopped to look at their map, and saw there was a gathering hut close by. It had been a long time since they had visited one. During their long struggle through the Swamp of Selfishness, they had lost interest in sharing with other travelers and learning more about the King. And since walking in the woods, they had gotten distracted by berry picking and exploring. Even with one close by, they debated whether they should go. As they calculated how much time the detour would take, a guide named Joyful Heart approached.

The guide spent a long moment looking them over. Peter and Celeste became self-conscious, for they were winded from climbing the slight rise from the pond. Their packs tilted with the heavy burdens they carried, and their cords were still dirty from all the swamp mud.

"What are you waiting for?" Joyful Heart said. "There's nothing to figure out. The gathering huts have been placed at regular intervals along the way to give travelers rest and encouragement. From looking at you two, it would appear you haven't been taking advantage of this benefit. It's dangerous to get out of the habit of going to the huts and receiving the support they offer. What good will it do if you set off for the King's City but give up and never arrive?"

"We've been awfully busy on our journey," Peter said. "And then we took a few wrong turns that took us off the main path."

"We have each other, too," Celeste said.

"Many traveling partners make that mistake," Joyful Heart said. "They think they do not need to go to the gathering hut as often as single travelers. But you need just as much help. The guidebook urges all travelers to meet together and encourage one another on the way. And it's not just what you can receive. You can give help to other travelers so that no one falls behind or drops out."

Peter looked at Celeste. "What do you say? I have been thinking it would be nice for the little traveler to learn the King's songs."

"And I wouldn't mind hearing from other travelers about how they take care of their children," Celeste said. "Sometimes I wonder if I'm doing what is best for the little traveler."

The path to the gathering hut followed through a gentle grove, then led them to a gate made of saplings. A sign above it

said, "Better is one day in your courts than a thousand elsewhere."
They could hear singing coming from inside the hut.

> *So here I am in the place of worship, eyes open,*
> *drinking in your strength and glory.*
> *In your generous love I am really living at last!*
> *My lips brim praises like fountains.*
> *I bless you every time I take a breath;*
> *My arms wave like banners of praise to you.*

"I had forgotten how beautiful the King's songs are," Celeste
said.

Peter sighed. "Me too."

As they entered, Encouragement, the guide of the gathering
hut, had just stood to speak. "The King designed the journey so
you could become more like Him. If you fall, remember that He
is faithful even when we are faithless, and He will teach you as you
go. Some of you have had many challenges, but these haven't
been to punish you for something you did wrong. These were
given to train you, so you could learn how to walk easily and
with a good stride. In the future as you go through hard times,
remember He is also the King of comfort who comes alongside
you."

"I need that comfort," said a traveler who walked with a
painful limp because she had broken her leg and not waited for
it to set properly.

"You are not alone," Encouragement said. "There are many
others here who are wounded. The Servant says to you, 'Are you

tired? Worn out? Burned out on religion? Come to me. Get away with me, and you'll recover your life. I'll show you how to take a real rest. Walk with me and work with me—watch how I do it. Learn the unforced rhythms of grace. I won't lay anything heavy or ill-fitting on you. Keep company with me and you'll learn to live freely and lightly.'

"When we keep company with the Servant," Encouragement said, "we will discover the help that comes from joining together. As I look out on this group, I see a lot of wounds that need to be healed." He asked people to come forward with their rags of compassion soaked in the tears of the Servant to help travelers who were hurting.

Peter and Celeste stayed at the hut for several days, singing to the King with the other travelers, enjoying the banquet feasts, and taking walks around the grove. One night Encouragement gathered all the traveling partners around the fire and instructed them from the guidebook.

"Remember that we are to bear each other's burdens. This means you can't ignore the wounds of your partner and still please the King. Some of you might be tempted to boast about how much you love the King. I've seen your looks of devotion as you sing the King's songs. I don't doubt your sincerity, but remember that loving the King is only one side of the coin. Turn it over and you will see that loving the King brings love for people. The two aren't to be separated. So if you are not loving your partner, you are not loving the King. If your partner says she needs to stop and take care of a problem, stop. Don't tell her it's not a problem just because you don't think it is. Together you make one whole traveling body and if part of the whole is hurting, the entire partnership is hurting.

"Share your struggles and your disappointments with your partner," Encouragement said. "Be honest with each other, be vulnerable. I know some of you find this difficult. If you do, don't be ashamed to ask for help. There is a guide at the Warming Hut of Revelation who can give you lessons."

Peter whispered to Celeste, "I'm sure there are other things a guide could help us with, like having a good stride." He didn't enjoy sharing his struggles with Celeste, and sometimes when she talked, he felt he would be suffocated by all her words.

"But you have a wonderful stride," Celeste said. "Other travelers always compliment you on it."

"You can always learn to have a better one," Peter replied, because like most people he preferred to strengthen his strengths and ignore his weaknesses.

Then Encouragement took out an hourglass of today. "I believe all partners are given one of these at the start. But after awhile, it is easy to forget how important it is to spend time alone together. While you are here, take the opportunity to get away by yourselves, especially if you have little travelers."

Celeste wasn't sure about that. As much as she had enjoyed the moon of honey, she didn't want to leave their little traveler behind, even for a short time. But another couple volunteered to watch the little traveler for them. The woman encouraged Celeste to go, saying she had learned it wasn't good to spend all her time with the little traveler and ignore her partner.

Peter and Celeste felt strange to be alone without the little traveler to distract them. But as they ate together by candlelight and explored the meadow paths during the day, the pleasure of being partners together returned. Celeste got up early with Peter to look at the sunrise, and Peter gathered an armful of flowers for Celeste. Peter took out their basket of remembrance so he could add a few stones. Celeste put in a bit of the raft that had taken them across Submission Pond. They drank often from the chalice, but it seemed richer and more satisfying than when they drank under the moon of honey.

"Who would have thought when we first drank from the chalice that it could be better?" Peter said.

"But what did we know of love then? Making our way through the Swamp of Selfishness, I have come to know you better than ever."

Peter laughed. "Better than you ever wanted, I expect."

One day when they were out walking, they followed a higher path that took them to an overlook. For the first time in a very long time they saw the King's City, beyond the Mountains of Maturity. As they watched, a great thunderstorm moved over the land and when it was over, a perfect rainbow curved over the mountains with a brilliant arc of purple and pink and yellow and green and blue.

"Oh look," Celeste said. "Do you see where the rainbow ends in that open area?"

She pointed to a broad alpine meadow that seemed to stretch like a long green wave all the way to the King's City.

"The Highlands," Peter said in awe.

"It looks like the most wonderful place. I do hope we get there."

"We will," Peter said. "We will."

"I am so glad we came up this path." Celeste picked up a small pine cone to put in their basket of remembrance. "I will never forget seeing the rainbow." For the rest of their time away, they took the high path every morning so they could spend the day gazing on the Highlands and the King's City beyond. On their last night they fell asleep by the fire with Celeste murmuring, "The Highlands, the Highlands."

PASSING BY THE VEHEMENT VOLCANO

The vision of the Highlands renewed Peter and Celeste as they continued their journey. Over time, two more little travelers joined them, each bringing much joy. But with three little travelers to care for, Peter had to work much harder to find food for them all. Celeste was kept busy with all the dirty clothes; no sooner had she cleaned one shirt, than two more were dirty. The little travelers seemed to take turns being fussy, which made Peter and Celeste irritable. They barely had time to linger along the meadow paths or drink from the chalice, so one of the best things about being partners became just another routine. On occasion, the forest broke open and they would glimpse the King's City or the Highlands. But when one of them pointed it out, the other was always too tired to be enthusiastic and simply said, "Yes, I see," or "Well, what do you want me to do about it?"

In my dream, I saw that the refreshment they had received at the gathering hut faded. When they managed to stop at other gathering huts along the way, they were so distracted making sure the little travelers sat still, they hardly heard anything the guide said. Soon Peter and Celeste were arguing constantly: about what paths they should take, what kind of food was best for the little travelers, what kind of clothes they should wear. Though they had often read in the guidebook that the Servant's love was not rude or easily angered, Peter and Celeste were no longer trying to imitate the Servant. They assured themselves that they were on the King's path, going to the King's City—and that would be enough. It was too hard with the little travelers to walk as the Servant had.

One day Peter decided he wanted to reach a certain cave before sundown so he would have enough time to explore it. He set off with a brisk pace, and Celeste lagged behind with the little travelers, who whined for two solid hours. Even if Celeste had wanted to stop and set up camp, she couldn't because Peter was carrying all the provisions. Then one of the little travelers developed a painful blister, and Celeste had to carry the little traveler the rest of the way.

By the time she and the little travelers finally arrived at the cave, the sun had set. Peter was glad to see them. "This is the best cave we've ever been to. I've had a grand time discovering all the nooks and crannies. I can't wait to show the little travelers everything." But the little travelers were too tired and refused to go off with him. Peter said he would go by himself then. As he did, he secretly blamed Celeste. He was sure she had been complaining all day, and that was why the little travelers had become so cranky.

While Peter was off exploring the cave a second time, Celeste made a fire and cooked supper and set up the beds. By the time Peter got back, it was quite late. When he saw Celeste asleep by the small fire she had made, he grumbled to himself. After all these years of travel, it was ridiculous that she still didn't know how to make a better fire, especially when there was plenty of wood lying around the cave that she could have collected. He went to bed angry, providing the deceiver a foothold.

In the morning he woke up as the first light came into the cave and went off, eager to investigate a few more sections in the deeper regions before it was time to leave.

Soon after, Celeste woke up, stiff from carrying the little traveler the previous day. The first thing she noticed was that Peter's bedroll was still spread out. He had not been considerate enough to fold it up. Then she saw that he also hadn't bothered to collect wood for the breakfast fire. She became very annoyed. After feeding the little travelers, she waited for Peter to help take down the camp. By mid-morning he had not returned, and she packed up as best she could. She thought how unfair it was that Peter was always urging them to go faster and farther—but when he found something he wanted to do, they had to wait for him.

Peter finally got back just before noon. Though it would have been easier to eat lunch in the cave, he said they couldn't waste any more time. They had to leave right away to get to the next campsite, so they would have to eat their sandwiches as they walked.

Along the way they passed another traveling family with six little travelers following in a neat line, not a speck of dirt to be seen on them.

"Celeste, did you see that family?" Peter said. "They're proof that it is possible to keep little travelers clean, if only you would take the time to wash them."

"I do my best," Celeste said.

"Well, obviously you could do better."

"Why do you always criticize me, and in front of the little travelers too?" she said, raising her voice.

"Why can't you take a little correction?"

When they reached the next campsite late that night, Celeste discovered she had left their best cooking pot at the cave.

"How could you have forgotten the pot?" Peter said. "There weren't any bushes for it to hide behind. It was a simple case of looking around to make sure you had everything. Are you that blind? I just don't understand why you can't be more careful about our supplies. How many times do I have to tell you that we aren't rich like other travelers?"

"There you go again!" Celeste shouted. "Why do you always blame me and say it's my fault?"

"Because it is." Peter kept his voice calm. "I'm not the one dancing up and down like a mad bee. I can control myself."

"Oh!" Celeste said, sparks coming out of her eyes. "You march on ahead, you refuse to spend any time with me, you won't discuss anything, and then at the end you say it's *my* problem?"

"As a matter of fact, yes," Peter said. "I am beginning to think that my mother was right all along. She warned me I was making a mistake because you would always be hot-tempered and emotional."

"Then why don't you go back to your mother?"

"I would like to," Peter said with his teeth clenched, "but I can't. I made a vow."

"A vow? You mean a vow to be insensitive to your wife? Or

a vow to appear righteous on the outside, but inside be full of hate?"

They were so caught up in their argument, they didn't hear the earth grinding under their feet—or the big groan as it slowly pulled apart. In the distance, a few trees crashed to the ground.

"If you would just work a little harder to keep the travelers clean," Peter yelled, "everything would be fine!"

"It's fine for you to stand there like you are some saint, but you aren't!" Celeste shrieked. "You say you love the King, but you are the most self-absorbed person I have ever met. Even my father cares more for people when he's drunk than you do when you're stone cold sober!"

"You really must control yourself," Peter said. Angry steam began to rise from the ground.

"Control myself!" Celeste shouted at the top of her lungs.

"Yes, like I do."

"I would never, ever want to be like you. You're inhuman. You can't feel *anything*!"

At that moment, a volcano erupted into the night sky ahead of them. A bright orange plume of lava shot up in front of them, spewing fiery sparks.

"This is great, just like fireworks," one of the little travelers said, jumping up and down. But Celeste and Peter went on fighting.

"Just admit you're wrong," Peter said. "Why don't you just say, 'I'm sorry I forgot the pot.' I'd love to hear you say that. Could you? Could you say that, Celeste?"

Somewhere in the forest, a clump of lava fell on a patch of dry pine needles. In an instant, a fire began to rage through the area, devouring everything in its path. Flaming lava continued to spout from the earth. Billows of smoke filled the air, and the little travelers began to break into violent coughing fits. But neither Peter or Celeste noticed.

"Not until you apologize for the way you ignored us all day yesterday and half of today."

"You deliberately went slow so you'd have something to complain about."

"How dare you say that!"

A wave of lava that had bubbled over the side of the volcano surged across the forest toward the family. Celeste suddenly realized they were in danger. She quickly put on her pack, grabbed the three little travelers by their hands, and started to run. "I will never, never, I mean *never* speak to that man again! He is a beast, a monster; he doesn't care about me, and he never has!"

"What man?" asked one of the little travelers, who looked behind to see if a monster was following.

"Never mind," Celeste said.

At first Peter was too stubborn to follow after Celeste and the little travelers. He thought she was overreacting as usual. But soon his feet became so hot that the soles of his shoes started to melt. Not wanting to ruin a perfectly good pair, he reached for his pack and began to sprint away from the lava and the fire.

All through the night, the family ran away from the flowing lava, trying to get beyond the reach of the volcano's fury. Just before dawn, they realized they were finally safe and they could stop to take care of their wounds.

The entire family suffered burns, though Peter's were the

most severe. Celeste carefully dressed the wounds of the little travelers, but she gave no sympathy to Peter. She didn't realize that the sparks from the volcano had carried venomous barbs—and that without her help and forgiveness, the poison would work its way into his heart. Peter did the best he could to put bandages on his back, then he stood up to go, grimacing as he lifted his pack. Celeste said nothing, but she was surprised he wanted to leave so soon without giving his wounds a chance to heal. Sadly, he had no kindness, not even for himself. Though the burns on his back tormented him like a thousand pricking nettles, he again started walking on the King's path.

THROUGH THE DRY WASH OF NO ARGUMENTS

Though Peter and Celeste traveled much slower than before, Celeste still managed to develop a set of nasty blisters. They preoccupied themselves with the needs of the little travelers; indeed, the little travelers were the only reason Peter and Celeste cared to keep together. They said little to each another except, "Shall we stop here?"; "All right"; "Can you light the fire?"; "Yes." Soon they stopped talking completely and walked in silence, save for their shoes scuffing across the dirt and periodic squeals from the little travelers. When they came to the Dry Wash of No Arguments, they didn't even discuss what to do. They headed down the sharp slope into the gully. At least there they would not have to worry about an angry volcano erupting.

The wide channel was quite dry, though the steep walls would fill to the top if a thunderstorm came. Everyone in the family became coated by the powdery brown dust. There was no water to clean the little travelers, who looked dirtier than ever, but Peter gave up arguing about it. And though Celeste's blisters were turning an ugly purple color, she said nothing. She was sure that if she said something, he would just tell her that her feet would toughen up.

As much as her blisters hurt, the loneliness Celeste felt as they continued walking through the dry wash troubled her more. She yearned for true companionship, not this dull, silent partnership. And in my dream, I saw how it was fortunate that no man with a smooth tongue came and talked to her, for she would have been easily led away.

After a few days, they came to a bend and saw a traveler, horribly battered and bruised, sitting on the channel wall.

"What's wrong?" Peter called to him. "Can I help you?"

"No, it's too late," the man said.

"Too late for what?"

"Too late for help. My wife has been washed away, and I don't know how I can go on without her."

"How did that happen?"

"For a long time we were fine walking in the wash, just like you are. We drifted along without saying a word to each other. With all the dust, it was easier not to open our mouths. But one day we began having a tremendous argument. It was as if all the arguments we had avoided while we were walking in the wash had combined into one giant row. Then suddenly, dark clouds covered the sky. There was a violent clap of thunder, and it started to pour. It rained so hard, the water rose to our knees within minutes. Without any warning, a tall wall of water rushed down the channel toward us, like a huge wave. By the time we saw it, we had no time to get out. It crashed into us with an awful roar. I managed to grab hold of a branch, but my wife was swept away." The man shook his head. "The wash looked so safe and dry."

Even after the disaster of the Vehement Volcano, Peter had a hard time believing that arguing could bring such a disaster. But the man's story made him worry for the little travelers. If a flash flood did come, they would be in peril. He quickly lifted the little travelers out of the wash. Celeste, not wanting to be left, scrambled after them.

INTO THE PLAINS OF DISTANCE

They brushed off the dust from themselves as best they could, then looked around. There was no sign of the Mountains of Maturity or the Highlands—and certainly no glimpse of the King's City. All they could see were the Plains of Distance that stretched all the way to the horizon. They had long since given up looking at the map to decide which path to take, and without any discussion they started walking across the flat brown expanse. There was no proper trail, just footpaths that meandered around the plains. Ahead they could make out many travelers wandering alone, even ones who wore Cords of Commitment, for in such a wasteland it was easy to drift away from one's partner.

They found a few small scrub bushes and scrawny trees by a stagnant pool, and Peter feared they would use up their food supplies before they got across the plains. He reduced their rations once and then a second time. Finally, when they had nothing left to eat, he went out to search. After a day's hunt he came back with barely enough for a single meal. In the days that followed, it became even harder for him to find enough food. He started staying away for long periods, sometimes several nights at a time. Celeste kept busy taking care of the little travelers, but she found it very tiring without anyone to help. The Cords of Commitment felt like lead weights around her wrist. How different she felt about her partnership now than when she and Peter first walked together. At the beginning, she could hardly stand to be separated from him; she had always waited eagerly for him to return so they could walk together in the woods. Now she only wanted him to return so she could fix something for the little travelers to eat and then have a bit of time to herself.

One day while Peter was gone, a family stopped by the camp. As all the little travelers played together, Celeste told the woman how lonely she was. The woman told the same tale, even though they had more food and her partner didn't have to go on long searches.

"He is with me all the time," she said to Celeste, "but he might as well not be. During the day he barely speaks to me, and at night when we sit around the fire, he plays his fiddle or repairs our bags—anything except talk with me. If we ever do get a few minutes to ourselves and take out our chalice, one of the little travelers is sure to wake up and call for me. Sometimes I think it wouldn't make any difference if I was making the journey by myself."

"But what about your cords? Would you really cut them?"

"I didn't join with my partner just so I could become invisible to him. I decided to go on the journey with him because of these." She opened her pack and took out six postcards of the most romantic spots one could imagine.

Celeste recognized the beautiful scenes. "I have my own collection too."

"Well, take a good look around. Do you see anything that comes close to one of these cards? There's nothing but dirt and more dirt. When we started off, my husband said we would be sure to visit these scenes. But we haven't been to a single one. If we don't soon, I think I will just go off on my own and try to find these places."

"What about your little travelers?"

"I'll take them with me—my husband certainly wouldn't know what to do with them."

Celeste wondered about what the woman had said. Other than her sojourns with Peter under the moon of honey and the time at the gathering hut when they had gone off alone with their hourglass, she couldn't remember much pleasure in their journey together. Why had she ever thought it would be better to walk with him? He always took the most challenging routes. He was so quiet. He liked to get such an early start. He preferred to eat the same thing over and over, and he never appreciated the elaborate meals she made.

When Peter returned with more food, Celeste told him about the scenes in her postcards. "Why don't we try to find one of those places? We could leave this plain in one long march." She thought this might appeal to him since he always liked to walk a long way without stopping.

"Impossible with the little travelers. Maybe if they were older and could fend for themselves, but I need to get food, and you need to take care of them."

"But it is so lonely and dreary here. I am tired of spending all my time with the little travelers while you go off—and when you come home you are always tired. You never ask me how my day was, and if I ask you something, you just grunt. That's not why I went on the journey with you."

As Peter listened to Celeste, he thought how Celeste used to stare into his eyes lovingly and ask how she could help him. Now she only worried about the little travelers and told him what to get for them and when to come back. Worse, she was becoming rather plump, and her skin was starting to get wrinkles.

UNDER THE DISILLUSIONING SUN

As they walked on across the plains, the sun became hotter and brighter and sharper. But this was not the King's holy light that would cause a person to shield their eyes, nor was it the healing light of salvation. Rather it was a harsh, disillusioning light that exposed things that were unlovely, things that were impure, and things that were false and undeserving of praise. Instead of looking at Celeste with an admiring gleam, Peter complained that she spent too much time looking for pebbles. And Celeste complained that he never wanted to kick them with her. She griped about the clothes he wore; he griped about the way she sighed when they began to walk. She grumbled that he never told her what he was feeling; he grumbled that she was never quiet. And because they had stopped reading the guidebook, they did not remember the passage Lord Will and Lady Sophia had underlined for them about not complaining or arguing.

The longer Celeste looked at Peter through her critical eyes, the more she doubted if she had chosen well. Peter clearly didn't resemble any of the men in her postcards. He belched after he ate, snored when he slept, and often he didn't bother to shave. She was sure that if she had known what Peter was really like before they joined together, she would not have gone with him. In truth, she had seen a vague vision of all Peter's faults when they first met in the grove. But she had expected that after walking with her, his faults would disappear. They hadn't. In fact, they seemed more entrenched than ever.

It was different for Peter. His original vision of Celeste was nothing like who she was now. At the beginning she had been so quiet and flexible, and content to stay with Peter. Now she always wanted to join up with other travelers. Somehow she had deceived him. He wondered what Faithfulness would say if he told him that Celeste was not the right one after all. She was so different from the woman she had been at the start that surely he might be excused from walking with her. Still, he remembered that Discernment had said, "It's important to choose your partner wisely, but it's even more important to choose to love her every day." Discernment would tell Peter it was his duty to walk with Celeste— no matter how much she had changed.

At a little oasis crowded with other travelers resting from the grueling journey, Peter and Celeste sat at a distance from each other. Celeste said to the woman beside her how boring the scenery was. The woman agreed. She had tried to talk her partner out of coming, but he wouldn't go any other way, so she had to follow after him.

"Why did you decide to go with him in the first place?" Celeste asked.

"That's easy. He was so cheerful all the time."

Celeste stole a glance at the woman's partner, who was napping with a scowl on his face. "And is he?"

"Well, sometimes. But the journey has been much harder than he thought, harder than I thought too. I soon discovered his cheerfulness comes out only when everything is going well. Truthfully, it's been a long time since we've been on a good solid path."

"So why do you stay with him?"

"Because of the pledge I made."

Celeste shook her head. "I know, that awful pledge."

"Why do you say that? Maybe you made different vows, but ours were for better or worse. Now we're in one of the worse parts."

"But I didn't think worse would mean this." Celeste swept her hand toward the plains.

"Neither did I."

"I feel so trapped. I thought Peter was different—or maybe I was sure the things I didn't like about him would go away once we had been walking for awhile."

"Only now they are more visible?"

"Yes, and uglier and unpleasant." Celeste rubbed the cord on her wrist. "I think I made a terrible mistake."

"Oh, I don't think you did."

"Why do you say that? You don't know me, and you don't know him."

"Because I know that you joined with him and put on the

cords. It isn't a question of making a mistake or not. You made a choice, and this is your life now."

"If you were a more caring person, you wouldn't say that. You'd understand how lonely and miserable I am."

"No." The woman leaned over to adjust the pillow under her partner's head. "I'm afraid I understand too well."

In my dream, I hoped that this would be a fairy tale—and that before long all would be well with Peter and Celeste. They pushed across the plains, and although they had moments of happiness, most of the time they plodded on, silent and dejected. Celeste was sure that Peter didn't love her anymore; he never listened to her, asked her questions, or shared what he was thinking. To comfort herself, she would take out her postcards and imagine living in one of them. The cards became blotted with tears. But she refused to give up her desire for romance, and she judged everything Peter did against the scenes in her postcards, which made his faults appear even more vivid.

From time to time, Peter would carry Celeste's pack and gather the firewood, the water, and the food. But when he did, he felt resentful. He thought back to the early days of his journey and his worry that walking to the King's City would be more difficult with a partner. His fears had now come true. Traveling with Celeste made the way much harder. Once Celeste asked him what was wrong with him, and he said nothing was wrong with him. It wasn't his problem—Celeste was the one who needed to change. Until she did, he had no choice but to keep on doing his duty.

One day while Peter was out looking for food, he came upon a traveler sitting by the path, with a grimy chalice hanging from his belt and a five-foot stack of postcards beside him.

"Would you like some pictures?" the man asked. "I have a whole collection of thrilling pictures—ones with men and women drinking from the chalice—and some real spicy ones just of stunning women. Here, do you see how this Eve tilts her head back as she drinks, and look at that drop of liquid on her lips."

"It's not good to look at those cards on the way to the King's City," Peter said. But in the bottom of his pack were a few postcards he had picked up when he was looking for a partner. He had never gotten around to throwing them away.

"I'm a traveler too," the man said. "I'll admit that before I met my partner, I had a problem looking at these cards. But now that we're together, what harm is there?"

"Doesn't it make you thirsty?"

"Sure—isn't that the whole point of looking?"

"Then what do you do?"

"Since I'm taking the Servant's path, I would never go to one of those chalice cabins to drink with a stranger. I only look at the cards by myself. That's all."

"What about your partner?"

"Well, she's nice and all, but she isn't like these women. Take a look at this beauty. Have you ever seen such a long neck? If I found a woman like this to walk with me, I'd be tempted to change partners. Imagine the drinks we'd have from the chalice." He wiped his sleeve to catch the saliva dripping from his mouth.

"But surely you drink from the chalice with your partner?"

"Yes, but it's nothing like this. It cheers me to think what it might be like."

"How can that be good?"

"Good? Good has nothing to do with it. We're men, aren't we? We get thirsty and we have to do something about it. If we don't want to drink with strangers, this is the only thing we can do."

"Wouldn't it be better to learn to enjoy drinking from the chalice with your partner?"

"No, I'm sure she doesn't want to. Besides, she spends a lot of time looking at her own postcards."

"She has those cards, the ones with romantic scenes?"

"Yes. Your partner does too?"

Peter nodded.

"Worst invention ever if you ask me. The King should ban them. All those cards do is make her mushy and want to go for a walk holding hands. Holding hands! That's not going to get the chalice filled. I say it's better to look at these pictures." The man went back to admiring the women on his postcards.

That night, for the first time since he had joined with Celeste, Peter took out his old postcards and looked at them. They stirred his thirst as much as they had before he married Celeste. He wondered if looking at them would help when he and Celeste drank together from the chalice. He would look at them for only ten minutes once a week. There wouldn't be any harm in that. After all, he didn't have a five-foot stack—just enough to fit into an envelope.

So Peter began to look at his postcards as he walked across the plains searching for food. He looked at them more often than he had promised but he justified it, thinking that since he had to be away from Celeste, he needed something to pass the time. Soon he was looking at the postcards every day, and collecting more cards that he found along the way. Then he began to look at them late at night back at the camp when Celeste and the little travelers were asleep. The cards didn't really satisfy him, and they made him even more dissatisfied with Celeste. But he couldn't seem to help it. And in my dream, I saw this was not a fairy tale, but the long, hard road of life.

Into the Orchard of Earthly Delights

INTO THE ORCHARD

After walking such a long time on the Plains of Distance, Peter and Celeste were relieved when they came to a wide river that flowed from the Mountains of Maturity. It turned the plains into a wild grassland and at a small rise, they could see that the grassland soon turned into a thick, forested wilderness that extended far into the distance. It looked like food would be plentiful, but the path was small and rugged, no more than a scar that slashed through the rough country. The thought of going through it discouraged them. Not only did they still have their heavy burdens and the three little travelers, they also had new unhealed wounds which would make hiking difficult.

South of the rise a broad path descended gently into a thriving green valley. In the middle of the valley stood a grand orchard with rows and rows of all kinds of trees that were pleasing to the eye and good for food. Beyond the orchard were squares of neatly farmed fields of vegetables and lines of fruit vines. Blessing and abundance were the staples of the land.

When Celeste saw this, she was ready to go down into the Orchard of Earthly Delights. But Peter hesitated. "Something doesn't seem quite right about it."

"What do you mean?" Celeste said. "This is the most beautiful place we've seen on our journey. And look at all those travelers down there."

"I can't put it into words," Peter said. "Maybe it looks too perfect."

Celeste became annoyed. "Of course. You don't mind walking along the ridge into the wilderness; you go off and leave me with the little travelers all day while you gather food. But if you were the one staying with the little travelers, you'd want to go down to the valley and take it easy for a bit."

"What if it takes us off the path to the King's City?"

"Look how well-watered and well-ordered and clean the orchard is. It must have been created by the King—and how can anything the King created be bad? Besides, we can always come back up and rejoin the path."

Celeste was right that the King had created everything that grew in the Orchard of Earthly Delights. Generations of travelers had come to settle there. They cultivated the fields and fruit trees and made it into a comfortable, prosperous place—without the tainted ruin of Slouching City or the stiff dryness of Upright Village.

However, as Peter suspected, something wasn't quite right.

The splendid pleasures of the orchard were meant to be only a fore-taste of what awaited the travelers in the King's City. Yet once travelers experienced all the good things the orchard had to offer, they became satisfied with the earthly bounty and often decided to give up their journey and settle down in the orchard. Over time, the path through the orchard to the King's City had become blocked by the trees and fields. The only way out of the orchard, besides the wilderness path, led directly back to Slouching City.

Peter took one more look at the wilderness that lay ahead of them and thought how hard it would be to travel on the demand-ing path with Celeste complaining every step of the way. Then he contemplated the peaceful beauty of the Orchard of Earthly Delights. "I think we deserve a rest," he said.

As they went down into the valley and entered into the orchard, they marveled at the variety and wealth around them. The best of the King's creation had been collected into one mar-velous place. There were fruit trees: apple and pear and cherry and plum and apricot and orange and lemon, and nut trees: almond and pecan and hazelnut and coconut. They saw grapevines and strawberry patches and blueberry bushes and raspberry bushes, as well as fields of wheat and corn and beans and tomatoes and cucumbers and peppers. There were cows that gave creamy milk and hens that laid rich eggs.

The little travelers could play all day, sliding down shallow waterfalls into splashing pools, and jumping into soft sand pits.

There were lakes with pleasure boats and shaded rivers to canoe through, and small woods with paths that made travelers feel like they were still walking to the King's City. In their free time, travelers could enjoy flower gardens filled with fragrant rainbows of lilies and hyacinths and irises and peonies.

There were also improvements that had been invented by the travelers themselves. Craftsmen had learned to make vibrantly dyed fabric. The furniture was carved with intricate designs, and there were colorful stained-glass windows. There were schools where little travelers could learn, and museums and concerts and plays to attend. If a traveler fell ill, doctors could cure almost any disease. But all of these advanced benefits were not cheap. Travelers who settled in the orchard eventually needed to stake out a larger claim to pay for the style of life they wanted.

The orchard covered most of the valley, and it took Peter and Celeste a long time to explore all the delights. They were happy to see that the King had not been forgotten, for many who lived in the orchard met at the gathering huts and read the guidebook. In fact, two leaders, Indulgent and Smooth Talk, were organizing people to build the biggest gathering hut in all the King's country.

But like the residents at Pigeon Hole, travelers here paid little attention to instructions in the guidebook that made them feel uncomfortable. In the lanes, one could often see a traveler in a new hat and coat greet a poor traveler who wore old, worn clothes and lacked enough food for his family. "Wear the King's garments of praise and feed on His will," the well-off traveler would say, without considering that he could give one of his extra coats and bags of food. Many travelers built large houses so they could store everything they gained, for they had forgotten that when the King called them home to His city, they would have to leave everything behind.

After Peter and Celeste had surveyed the orchard and saw how pleasant it was, they decided to stay a little while. They found a small house to settle in, and soon they began to worry about what they would eat and what they would wear. Celeste wanted to have the latest fashions like all the other travelers, and Peter thought it would be good to try all the different foods in the orchard.

The disillusionment they had experienced with each other on the Plains of Distance remained. But there was so much to occupy them—Peter working long hours at his job and Celeste fixing up the house—that they weren't bothered they saw little of each other. Celeste found plenty of friends and met with them to talk about the guidebook. Peter joined those who were making plans for the new gathering hut and started spending his free time there, proud to be involved in such significant work.

Although Peter and Celeste were still partners, there was little evidence for it except that they lived in the same house and wore their tattered cords of commitment.

"So is everything fine?" Peter would ask.

"Couldn't be better," Celeste would say.

The longer they remained in the orchard, the more their love of its pleasures grew, choking out their love for the King. They no longer thought of going back to the Servant's path. "We need to stay here for the little travelers. That's our top responsibility. They need to have the very best."

They did tell the little travelers about the King, but the little travelers preferred playing on the orchard sports teams rather than going to the gathering hut. As the months went on, Peter and

Celeste felt the strain of earning enough money to pay for all
they wanted. They were richer than they ever had been since
becoming partners, but they never seemed to have enough. They
were often short-tempered with each other, and as a result they
suffered painful attacks of the burrs. And like other travelers in the
orchard, when their unkind words were not sufficient they sometimes fought each other with their clubs. Worst of all, as their love
for the King diminished, so did their love for each other. Their
hearts became cold.

Then one day a guide in an old, long, oilskin coat and broad-
brimmed leather hat came to the orchard. He announced he was
setting up a tent, and every night he would give a talk about the
King. Many travelers paid no attention to him; others told him they
listened only to guides approved by the leaders of the gathering
hut. However, Peter was curious, since the orchard did not get
many traveling guides, and he decided to go the first night.

Heavenly Treasure stood in front of the small assembly and
cleared his throat. "My message tonight may seem strange for such
a well-fed crowd, but I believe it is what the King wants you to hear."

He took his old copy of the guidebook and began to read. "Is
anyone thirsty? Come and drink—even if you have no money!
Come, take your choice of wine or milk—it's all free! Why spend
your money on food that does not give you strength? Why pay for
food that does you no good? Listen to me, and you will eat what
is good. You will enjoy the finest food. Come to me with your ears
wide open. Listen, and you will find life."

He looked out at the crowd. "You may think you are well-fed,
living here in the Orchard of Earthly Delights. But I can see how

hungry you really are. You work so hard to feed yourselves, but you are skinny in your souls. Listen to me: call on the King. He wants to hear from you. Turn from doing things that don't please Him. Don't even think about doing something you know is wrong. Tell Him you are sorry, and He will be lavish in His forgiveness to you, for He is full of mercy."

The King's words that Heavenly Treasure had read cut through Peter like a two-edged sword. When he got home, he looked in the mirror and saw how much thinner he was than when he had first come to the orchard. Then he looked at Celeste and the little travelers. They too were undernourished. Although there was plenty of earthly food in the orchard, it didn't feed their souls or produce the King's fruit. Their hearts were starving.

The next night Peter brought the family with him to hear the guide.

"Tonight," Heavenly Treasure said, opening his guidebook, "I'd like to give you another message from the King: 'I see what you've done, your hard, hard work, your refusal to quit. I know you can't stomach evil, that you weed out apostolic pretenders. I know your persistence, your courage in my cause, that you never wear out.'"

Celeste whispered to Peter, "I don't see why people are upset about this guide's message. He is saying some nice things about us."

Heavenly Treasure went on reading. "But you walked away from your first love—why? What's going on with you, anyway? Do you have any idea how far you've fallen? A Lucifer fall! Turn back! Recover your dear, early love. No time to waste, for I'm well on my way to removing your light from the golden circle."

Celeste shifted on the bench and folded her arms. "Who does

he think he is, coming here and judging us like that? Doesn't he know we are building the biggest gathering hut?"

Heavenly Treasure wasn't finished. He turned to another part of the guidebook. "Today, if you hear His voice, do not harden your hearts as you did in the rebellion, during the time of testing in the desert, where your fathers tested and tried Me and for forty years they saw what I did . . . See to it, brothers and sisters, that none of you has a sinful, unbelieving heart that turns away from the living King. But encourage one another daily as long as it is called today, so that none of you may be hardened by sin's deceitfulness."

He raised his eyes from the guidebook and looked out on the crowd. "I do not know the condition of your hearts. But I know that your willingness to pause from your work and to focus on the King can be the beginning of a renewed faithfulness in your lives."

Peter looked over at Celeste, hoping that the King's word would cut through the hardness in her heart. But she remained sitting with her arms folded and with a scowl on her face.

"You need to be discerning of those you listen, to for the guidebook says that false teachers will come, and being greedy, they will exploit you with made-up stories," Heavenly Treasure told his audience. "However, I want you to remember: 'There's nothing to these people—they're dried-up fountains, storm-scattered clouds, headed for a black hole in hell. They are loudmouths, full of hot air, but still they're dangerous.'"

Some of the travelers began to jeer at Heavenly Treasure. Others said this was exactly what people on the other side of the orchard needed to hear, and Heavenly Treasure should take his tent over there.

"I think he may be right," Peter said to Celeste. "We have no time for the King, no time for each other. And have you noticed how much thinner we are than when we first came to the orchard, even though there is plenty of food here? The little travelers no longer remember what it was like to travel on the King's path, and you and I have forgotten all about the Highlands and how much we wanted to reach them."

As Celeste listened to Peter, she became alarmed. It was one thing to listen to the guide, and quite another to think of leaving the orchard and again taking up their journey. "That was just a fantasy." Celeste shook her head. "Maybe super travelers can make the journey, but we are just ordinary people. We have responsibilities—we just can't walk off. Think of the gathering hut and how it needs you."

"We don't have to be super travelers to make the journey to the King's City. He gives us the strength and power to walk on the path. I think we should talk to Him about what He wants us to do."

A flicker of guilt passed through Celeste. Although she spent a lot of time talking about the King, she hardly spoke to Him anymore. Then she recovered. "Go ahead, but I know what my answer is. If you want to go off and follow that crazy-looking guide, be my guest. I know I can serve the King just as well right here."

The next day, the orchard buzzed with gossip about what Heavenly Treasure had said. Some people began to question Indulgent and Smooth Talk, wondering if their guide credentials were in order. Instead of answering them, the two guides accused Heavenly Treasure of stirring up the people with unpleasant words and ordered him out of the orchard. When Peter heard that, he

realized that if he and Celeste stayed any longer, they would
wither away. But he didn't know how he could lead his family out
of the orchard. That evening, he went down to the basement and
found his old guidebook. He spent all night reading it, and stopped
when he came to these words of the Servant: "It is easier for a
camel to go through the eye of a needle than for someone who
is rich to enter the King's City . . . but all things are possible with
the King." Peter took comfort from that. Even if he didn't know
how to leave the orchard, he could trust the King to do it.

Peter was tempted to command Celeste to follow him out of
the orchard, but he remembered their argument at the split path.
To love Celeste meant he couldn't lord authority over her. He
needed to serve her just as the Servant King had come to serve
and give His life. Peter decided that from then on, instead of going
to the gathering hut to meet with Indulgent and Smooth Talk
every night, he would stay home to help Celeste with the little
travelers. He brought the garbage to the fire dump before Celeste
had to remind him, and he volunteered to wash the clothes. Every
day he asked the King to show Celeste how thin she was, and how
the little travelers were developing greedy pouts. And he often quietly sang one of the King's songs she had taught him:

> *You will go out in joy*
> *and be led forth in peace;*
> *the mountains and hills*
> *will burst into song before you,*
> *and all the trees of the field*
> *will clap their hands.*

Instead of the thornbush will grow the pine tree,
and instead of briers the myrtle will grow.
This will be for the Lord's renown,
for an everlasting sign,
which will not be destroyed.

One night as Peter sang, Celeste gave him a strange look. Then tears came to her eyes as she remembered the love she once had for the King. He had given her so many good and perfect gifts, and He had always comforted her when the way was hard. Then she thought of how the Servant had loved her so much He had sacrificed His life so she could have a full, whole life. She knew she didn't want to stop following Him. With a quiet voice, she spoke to Peter. "Soon after I left Slouching City, I met a guide who told me to keep my heart and mind set on the King's City. I had died with the Servant, and He was now my life. I think I have forgotten that. As wonderful as our life is in the orchard, it's not the same as traveling to the King's City."

"You're right," Peter said. "There is so much more than this. What we have here is only a shadow of what is to come."

"I'm sorry I lost sight of that. Can we go back and walk on the King's path together?"

"Oh, Celeste, that would make me so happy."

Celeste smiled back. "Me too."

The little travelers were sorry to leave the entertainments of the orchard behind, but Peter and Celeste promised they would have plenty of adventures on the journey to the King's City. Peter and Celeste sold all their possessions and packed their bags. Then the family said goodbye to all their friends and walked slowly up to the ridge where Heavenly Treasure was waiting. "Are you the only ones who are leaving the orchard?"

"I'm afraid so," Peter said. "We tried to talk others into joining us. Some said there were too many dangers and difficulties on the journey. Others didn't see how they could survive without the provisions of the orchard."

The guide sighed. "Many travelers want to serve both the King and money. But the Servant pointed out that this is impossible, like someone who tries to work for two bosses at the same time. You can only be devoted to one. Traveling to the King's City is not a weekend job; it's a full-time occupation."

"I'm glad to be going to the King's City," Celeste said, "but is the orchard really as bad as you say? Didn't the King create everything in it so we could enjoy it?"

"I have heard of your frankness from other guides." Heavenly Treasure smiled. "Yes, the orchard is the King's and everything in it, but people have turned it into an idol. The guidebook warns us, 'Don't love the world's ways. Don't love the world's goods. Love of the world squeezes out love for the Father. Practically everything that goes on in the world—wanting your own way, wanting everything for yourself, wanting to appear important—has nothing to do with the Father. It just isolates you from him.' The world offers us cravings we can never satisfy, but the King offers life forever. Which would you rather have?"

"So we have to give up all the pleasures of the orchard on the way to the King's City?" Celeste asked.

"Like much on the journey, it is not always a question of one thing or the other, but keeping things in their proper place. The Servant turned water into wine to keep a celebration going, and He went to parties with people who were not traveling to the King's City. Many travelers have forgotten that the King has given them gifts to enjoy on the journey. Many of them," he turned to Peter, "come from your village."

He looked back at Celeste. "But those who stay in the orchard often forget the giver. These good gifts are not just in the orchard; they are found all along the way to the King's City. The trouble comes when you make them the center of your life. That destroys your love for the King—and your love for others. Long ago, the Chosen People had the same problem. The King brought them into a good land, one with streams and springs flowing in the valleys and hills, a land with wheat and barley, vines and fig trees, pomegranates, olives, and honey. But when they had eaten and were satisfied, their hearts became proud and they said to themselves, 'Our power and the strength of our hands have produced this wealth for us.' Soon they forgot all about the King and what He had done for them.

"I want to give you some samples of the orchard's delights, so you can enjoy them as you walk," Heavenly Treasure said. "But never forget that 'people do not live by bread alone, but by every word that comes from the mouth of the King.'" With that, the guide bid them farewell.

AT THE CAMP WITH FAITHFULNESS

Peter and Celeste headed into the wilderness with the little travelers. They had to walk slowly at first, for they had gotten out of shape during their stay in the orchard. But Peter felt pleased, even proud, that he had been able to leave the comforts of the orchard behind. He was glad to be back on the trail. There was plenty of food to find, so he had time to hike up to the viewpoints along the way, and he would come back smiling, his cheeks flushed from the effort.

He didn't notice that resuming the journey to the King's City was much harder for Celeste. To her the path seemed so empty and quiet after all the activity in the orchard. She missed her friends and the conveniences she had left. The food Peter brought took longer to cook, and the little travelers complained about the taste. Without the pleasures of the orchard to distract them, Peter and Celeste had more time to pay attention to each other, but neither had enough love to cover over the faults they saw. Celeste went back to being frustrated with Peter's absences. Whenever he was around, she started hounding him to do one thing or another, and he began to stay away even longer. Soon they had their most powerful argument since the Vehement Volcano. It tore the path apart and left a dangerous crevice they had to navigate around. As they scrambled over the ragged ground, both wondered if it would have been better to stay in the orchard.

Then next day at sunset they came to a little camp and found Faithfulness, their old guide from their weaving day, sitting by the fire. He looked more frail, but also more radiant than ever.

"The King has called me ahead," he said. "I am so happy to finally be going to His city. But when Heavenly Treasure told me you would be coming by, I decided to wait so I could hear all about your journey. And look—you have little travelers now. How happy you must be. But Peter, I couldn't help noticing that you're getting a legalistic limp. I hope you are still working on walking with grace."

"Oh, that limp is nothing," Peter said. "I've just had to work a little harder after our stay in the Orchard of Earthly Delights."

"Well, come, both of you, and rest by the fire. I'm so eager for you to tell me how your partnership is going. Is your love for each other as wonderful as when you began?"

There was an awkward silence. When neither Celeste nor Peter met his gaze, he looked at the cords that had become frayed and worn on their wrists. "Oh, I see," he said gently. "That's too bad. But I still want to hear about your journey and what it has been like for you."

So Peter and Celeste told him about their detour to the Sand Dunes of Foolishness and how they crossed the Swamp of Selfishness.

"Yes, I heard that you didn't go up the Mountains of Maturity. And if I'm not mistaken, you struggled across the Plains of Distance before you were tempted by the Orchard of Earthly Delights."

"We did stay at Encouragement's gathering hut." Celeste didn't want Faithfulness to be too disappointed.

"Yes, and you're still headed for the King's City," Faithfulness said, "and that is the most important thing." As the fire flames lit up the old guide's face, Peter and Celeste saw a tear glisten in his eye.

The next morning as Peter and Faithfulness collected firewood, Faithfulness noticed something sticking out of Peter's back pocket.

"And what, dear friend, are these?" Faithfulness asked.

Peter turned red. "Nothing." He quickly stuffed his postcards down into his pocket.

"Do not hide them from me," Faithfulness said. "Do you think I don't know about the postcards men carry?"

Peter did not want to talk about the cards, especially with Faithfulness.

"Why do you keep silent?" the old guide said. "You don't want to admit you have these cards because you follow the King—and you would rather keep your illusion of godliness. Don't you remember in the guidebook where the Servant said, 'Who needs a doctor: the healthy or the sick? I'm here inviting the sin-sick, not the spiritually-fit.' You, Peter, are one of the sin-sick. No matter how long and how far you walk, you will not reach the Highlands until you admit this. Have you shown those cards to Celeste?"

"Of course not."

"To any of your friends?"

Peter shook his head.

"And why is that? Because they are so precious? Or because they are so shameful? Or both? How can it be wise to have something you cannot tell anyone about and that you hide like a schoolboy? It warps your view of your partner and gives you an unnatural thirst that can never be quenched. How often do you look at them?"

"Not often."

"Exactly how often?"

Peter looked at the ground. "Almost every day. At first it was not for very long, maybe ten minutes. But it became harder to stop, and before I knew it ten minutes turned into thirty and then an hour."

"And now they rule your life?"

"Yes," Peter said in a whisper. His longing to look at the cards had become an insatiable craving.

"Peter, these cards were not good for you when you were single—and they are not good now, when you have a partner with whom you walk as one flesh. Do you know where this will lead? Sooner or later you may not be content just to look."

"It's not fair," Peter said. "I can't help it. And Celeste is no help. She is always busy with the little travelers. When I come home she barely says hello. Why can't I have my little pleasures?"

"Because they are not so little. These cards are a corruption of the King's plan for love." Faithfulness took a card and showed it to Peter. "Did you get married for this?"

"No, but—"

"There are no buts. You have always been quick to point the finger at those who do not follow the King's path, and yet you have this secret."

"I don't know how to stop. I've tried, but I can't."

"As long as you keep these cards in your pocket, you will not be free from their power. If you do not want to look at them, you must burn them." Faithfulness took out a match and gave it to Peter. "Here, do it right now."

Peter took the cards from his pocket and looked at them.

Faithfulness watched him. "You were given a chalice to drink with Celeste. These are a dry imitation that will never satisfy you."

"Can't I keep just one? All I do is look."

"The eye is the lamp of the body. What you look at makes a difference. These cards never solve any problems; they only create problems." He put his hand on Peter's shoulder. "Perhaps it would help to think of the love the King has for you."

Peter held on to his postcards. He knew Faithfulness was right. The King had freed him from his chains and given him life. And looking at the cards would only make him more thirsty. But he found a strange comfort in how tightly the cards gripped his heart. He did not want to strike the match. "Maybe another day."

"It is best to do it now."

"I-I can't. I'm not strong enough."

"Isn't it strange? How little effort it takes to strike the match, yet how hard it is to find the will to do it."

While Faithfulness stood beside him, Peter shuffled the cards. Then he stopped, his hands trembling. "I can't," Peter said. "It's too hard."

"Ask the King to strengthen you with power through His breath in your inner being."

"O King," Peter cried, "I am powerless to do this in my own strength. Only Your grace is sufficient for me." The Breath of the King filled him, and he lit the match. The cards began to blaze and just as quickly, they fizzled into a small pile of curling gray ash.

Now it so happened that while Faithfulness and Peter had been gathering wood, Celeste had taken out her own postcards. The romantic scenes looked innocent enough, that she would often look at them as the little travelers played around her.

When Faithfulness came back to camp and saw Celeste looking at her postcards, he threw up his hands. "Not you too!" he said.

"What?" she said, for she did not feel ashamed at what she was doing. "I like to look at these scenes from time to time; they remind me of where Peter and I hope to go. I admit it has taken longer than I thought, but someday we will, I hope."

"Where exactly do you want to go with Peter?"

In lengthy detail, Celeste told Faithfulness about the dream she was looking for, and how disappointed she was that Peter did not yet share her vision. But someday he would, she was sure.

Faithfulness grew very sad, for in some ways she was more taken by her postcards than Peter.

Faithfulness pointed to Celeste's favorite postcard of a couple staring at each other. "Where is the King in this picture?"

"The King of love is the One who created the picture—surely you know that."

"No, I'm not so sure. And where is Peter in the picture?"

"He's not there yet, but someday he will be."

"But is Peter really like that? It's true there are men who also dream of this romantic love. The Peter I know is much more down to earth. He's a loyal soul, not a poetic soul. I fear you have been caught in the seductive trap of fantasy. You have taken something good—the dream of oneness—and made it into an idol. Peter resists this, as well he should. For when you dream your romantic visions, you are not really loving him at all; you are only loving your dream."

Celeste's mouth twisted into a funny shape, for she did not like what she heard.

"Now there are couples I have known," Faithfulness said, "who have shared this dream you have."

"Did they find it?"

Faithfulness shook his head. "Even those who are completely

committed to this vision find that they cannot sustain such a romance. Eventually they realize they were looking for an ideal. They wanted a perfect love that would never die, and that love does not exist in this world. Don't waste your time dreaming of things that will not be until you come to the King's City and live in His perfect love."

"But what about the Highlands?"

"To get to the Highlands, you surely have to give up the postcards, for they are a pale imitation of the joy you will have with Peter there."

Celeste pouted. "I still don't see what's wrong with my postcard dreams."

"Let me try to help you. Where are you going?"

"To the King's City."

"And what will you do when you get there?"

"Join in love and praise." She said this like she was reciting her lessons.

"And where will your postcard dreams be then?"

"Do you mean the postcards are counterfeit?"

"Remember that the King took the form of the Servant."

"So there is no romance at all?"

"There is romance," Faithfulness said. "What's in your basket of remembrance?"

Celeste showed him the pebbles and berries and pine cones.

"You have had many such times, and I hope you will have more. But romance must be kept in its proper place. Can you submit all of your dreams to the dream of the King?"

"I don't like that word," Celeste said.

"Submit?"

"It's been a problem for me."

"As it will continue to be until you learn its true meaning. Can you sacrifice your dreams of romance on the altar of love?"

"Why didn't anyone tell me the journey with Peter would be so difficult?"

"Your dream has led you astray. You are constantly critical of Peter because you focus on the fanciful—'what might be' rather than the true 'what is.'"

"But the scenes on my cards are so beautiful."

"Think of how much more beautiful it will be in the King's City. The walls are made of jasper and the city of pure gold, as pure as glass. The foundations of the walls are decorated with every kind of precious stone: pale blue chalcedony, emerald and pink beryl, yellow topaz and amethyst. And there are no tears or death or mourning or crying or pain. Everything is as it is meant to be, true and whole. But your postcard dreams with their false visions pull you away from that. The best thing for you is to bury your postcards here."

"I'll bury all of them," Celeste said, "except please let me keep my favorite one."

Faithfulness shook his head. "You will never find the Highlands as long as you are holding on to this romantic dream."

Celeste looked out into the woods for a long time. "I cannot give it up," she said, clutching the card so tightly that it bent in two.

Faithfulness took pity on Celeste. He put his hands around hers and helped her dig the hole. Celeste reluctantly dropped the cards in, one by one. Then together they pushed the dirt over the cards. As they walked back to camp, Celeste felt sad for the dreams she had left behind and wondered how she would be able to be Peter's partner without them.

THROUGH THE WAY OF WINTER

Before Faithfulness left Peter and Celeste, he told them there would be other guides ahead if they needed more help. "But even if you do not find these guides, persevere. You're on the right track. Don't give up. Forget what is behind and fix your eyes on the Servant's path. Be careful though, because you will see other travelers taking simpler paths in hope they will be able to skirt around Skull Hill and the bridges of forgiveness. But you are bound to come to these places on the way to the King's City. Though they will look unpleasant, do not turn away from them. Otherwise you might find yourself so far off the path that it will be very difficult to find your way back. And it would be better not to attempt the Mountains of Maturity during the winter cold. The climb is difficult enough in good weather."

Peter and Celeste left Faithfulness and continued through the wilderness. Celeste still pined for the comforts and dear friends she had left behind in the Orchard of Earthly Delights. She wished she could convince Peter to go back. But he was determined to march on, and she resigned herself to the hardness of the journey. Every day she felt colder than before. She was still on the path to the King's City but her love for the King, which had once been a blazing fire, now was reduced to a handful of embers. She could have fanned it into flame, but whenever she considered the idea,

she balked at the effort it would take. It seemed easier to drag
along behind Peter, who seemed in better shape. As for Peter, he
was so preoccupied with the journey, he never stopped to read the
guidebook or ask for the King's help, and his heart had also turned
cold.

They struggled to make their way over tree roots and rocks
on the narrow path. It took all their concentration not to trip and
fall. They had forgotten that when they relied on the King, He gave
them His strength, and then they could be sure-footed like deer,
leaping up to the heights. Instead they trudged on slowly and the
cold became colder. They had given up their postcard visions but
hadn't replaced them with a warm love for each other. Peter
didn't think to help Celeste over the difficult spots, and Celeste
didn't bother to say anything if she noticed a better route. And as
a result, they suffered a deep chill that shivered them to the core.

The path became steeper, but they kept on going. If they had
been talking with each other, one of them might have suggested
they stop to look at the map. They might have checked their supplies and searched for an opening in the trees where they could
see how far it was to the next camp. Then they would have seen
the path was leading them up a steep slope that ended abruptly
at the snow-covered Loveless Peak—without any way to continue. And they would have noticed a fierce winter storm was
gathering in the west.

Instead, they assumed they were heading up one of Mountains
of Maturity and they kept walking up the sharp incline. Out of
breath from the climb, they finally came to a halt. But they didn't
check their bearings. They only wanted to lighten their loads, and

they went through their packs to see what they could leave behind. Then they did the most dangerous thing of all: they took out their kingly gifts and kept their heavy burdens.

They struggled on as valiantly as they could. The trail, which had been taking them up the southern slope, curved to the east. After a brief stretch, it brought them to the north side of the peak. Clouds moved in and blocked the sun, bringing a frosty bite to the air. Even though their bags were lighter, they struggled to make the climb, and they hoped the path would soon flatten to make the journey easy again. But the trail curved around the slope and brought them to the north side of the peak. Ahead of them lay a treeless expanse covered in deep, crusty snow that led all the way up to Loveless Peak. Peter and Celeste gaped at the challenge before them.

"How did we get here?" said Celeste, irritated that Peter had not stopped to check the map. "We're getting very high up, but this doesn't look like the Highlands. I don't see how we can go on. You know how tiring it is to climb the smallest hill with the little travelers."

"Faithfulness told us to press on and keep straight ahead," Peter said. "Weren't you listening?"

"Yes, but he didn't say anything about snow."

"He said that if we came to an unpleasant stretch, we shouldn't go around it or else we would end up too far off the path."

"I think we should set up camp here and figure out another way to go. The little travelers are complaining that their fingers and toes are tingly."

Their feelings for each other had turned to ice and without

their kindling of affection or their sheepskins of humility, they spent a frigid night huddled together. The next morning they continued up the peak. A harsh wind arose, and soon the air was filled with snow. They could barely see the path. Perhaps that was just as well, because it took them across a jagged ridge with a vertical drop-off on either side. How long they walked like this, they did not know for their journey together seemed frozen in time. Peter trudged ahead to blaze a trail through the deep snow, carrying one of the little travelers on his shoulders. Celeste lagged behind with the other two. The snow turned into a blizzard, and icy flakes stung their faces. They valiantly pushed on, afraid that they would freeze if they stopped. Indeed, if Peter and Celeste had not been carrying the little travelers, who shared their own warmth, they might not have made it.

Finally the wind died and the snow lightened. In the faint winter sunlight they could see the path leading straight up to Loveless Peak. "Maybe you can climb it yourself," Celeste said, "but I'm going back down with the little travelers."

"You won't be able to find the way."

"If we go on, we'll die of hypothermia."

"All right," Peter said. He began to lead them down, retracing their steps as best he could. The little travelers didn't mind the journey. They threw snowballs at each other and jumped off the drifts, remembering the fun they used to have in the Orchard of Earthly Delights. Then one rolled into a snow-filled gully and found, buried in the snow, a sign for a warming hut of revelation. Peter and Celeste saw the sign, but they didn't stop to look for the hut. As cold as they both were, neither wanted to talk to a guide.

The sun set and the moon rose over the snowy slope. They continued descending through the night. Occasionally Peter paused to let Celeste catch up with him, but as soon as she drew near, he would start walking again.

Finally Celeste could no longer bear it. "I have to stop and rest."

"Go ahead."

"Won't you wait for me?"

"I already have." He began walking again.

"You are the most insensitive, mean, heartless person I have ever known!" Celeste yelled.

Peter turned around and yelled back. "It takes one to know one!"

Their echoes reverberated around the peak, loosening the snow. They heard an ominous rumble and in another instant, an avalanche was rushing down the slope. Celeste managed to grab two of the little travelers, and Peter reached for the third.

"Swim," he told Celeste. "We have to swim through the snow."

They flew through the cold darkness, terrified they would not survive. But when the night was again finally quiet, they found they all had landed in a clump at the bottom—except for one little traveler who was stuck upside-down in the snow and had to be dug out.

In the light of the growing dawn, they could see they were in a sorry state: their packs bent and torn, bruises everywhere. They brushed the snow off the little travelers. Celeste scowled at Peter, thinking how he had almost killed them all. Peter glared at Celeste, thinking he would have never yelled if she hadn't yelled first.

"We should stop and warm ourselves," Celeste said.

"With what? All our extra clothes are cold and damp from the snow."

Tears came to Celeste's eyes, and she closed off a little more of her heart to protect it from the hurt she felt.

They resumed their journey. There was no sun that day, and the clouds sank lower and lower until they were walking in a fog. They could barely see their cords of commitment, but they could feel them chafing their wrists in the cold. Then the path turned to a toe-numbing slush, and Peter and Celeste had to carry the little travelers to keep their feet dry. They tramped on in silence, just as they had when they crossed the Plains of Distance, and the soggy, muddy snow stayed with them for a long time.

Along Desolate Canyon to Revenge Chasm

DOWN INTO DESOLATE CANYON

*I*n my dream I saw how far Peter and Celeste had wandered from the path to the Highlands—and how much harder they had made their journey to the King's City. Yet as dark as their way appeared, there was still much hope, for the King would never stop caring for them. Indeed, He was waiting eagerly for them to turn to Him, so He could lift their burdens. Though they had given up their kingly gifts, spurned the help of His guides, and no longer read His guidebook, yet He would restore them, if only they would take His grace. His deepest desire was to give them everything they needed to continue their journey. But Peter and Celeste became so preoccupied with taking care of the little travelers that they no longer stopped to consider all the King had done for them. They forgot how He had provided food for them and how the Servant had forged the knife of grace. But the King still cared for them and helped them soldier on through the slush.

After a time they found themselves heading across a plateau of scrub desert, much like the Plains of Distance except the plateau was even hotter and drier. At first they were glad for the change from the numbing cold of Loveless Peak. But soon they regretted the new path, for there was no shade or any oasis where they could get water. So when they came to a trail that had been cut through the plateau by an ancient river, they followed it, hoping to find a stream.

Deeper and deeper they descended until they reached the bottom of Desolate Canyon. Tall rock walls blocked the sunlight, making the canyon as gloomy as a dungeon. They found no sign of water but lacked the strength to climb out of the canyon, so they started down the sandy channel. Soon the path was covered with little stones, but neither thought about how they used to kick pebbles together. Then they came to a stagnant stream dribbling out of the canyon wall. The trickle looked harmless, but Peter and Celeste didn't realize they were at the headwaters of the River of Unfaithfulness, fed by runoff from the melted snow of Loveless Peak. They didn't know that as the river went on, it broke off into many branches—making it easy for couples to become separated from each other—before it ended in the Valley of Cut Cords.

"I suppose if we follow the stream, it will take us out of here," Peter said.

"Are you so sure?" Celeste had come to detest how Peter always was convinced about his own ideas.

"Yes, I'm sure." He pulled back his shoulders. If there was

anything he hated, it was the way Celeste mocked his sense of direction.

At first the strip of water was narrow enough to step across if they wanted to. With Celeste on one side of the stream and Peter on the other, they started tracking the stream. The water quickly turned foul as it became wider and twisted through the canyon, filling the air with a rotten smell. Without the distractions of the Orchard of Earthly Delights or the comfort of their postcards, Peter and Celeste each felt a dull ache of loneliness that seemed deeper than what they had felt before they had become partners, for then they had depended on the King for comfort. Now they walked as if they were a hundred miles apart. Their steps echoed through the empty hollow canyon, punctuated only by the stones the little travelers threw at bushes clinging to the walls until Peter told them to stop, afraid they might start a rock slide.

When it was time for lunch, they sat on some boulders, Peter on his side of the stream and Celeste on hers. While they ate, they saw a woman walking toward them, right in the middle of the scummy water. She wasn't wearing cords of commitment, but they could hear her talking to herself, saying, "Where is he? Where is he? Oh my love, come back, come back." When she saw Peter and Celeste, she became distraught and rushed toward them. "Have you seen him? Have you seen my husband?"

"We've only come to the canyon this morning," Celeste said. "You are the first traveler we've seen. But tell us what he looks like, in case we find travelers ahead."

The woman sat down in the water and started to tell them her story. "What does he look like? When I first met him I thought he looked like a knight. He had an easy stride and big strong hands, and he was always so considerate—he'd lay down his coat so I wouldn't have to step in mud puddles. And he had such grand plans for the journey to the King's City. He was going to travel only on the high roads so he would always have a good view. When we agreed to become partners and travel together, it was the happiest day of my life. Then we had our weaving day and that became the happiest day of my life—until we drank from the chalice under the moon of honey. That was when I began to believe that each new day would be better than the one before, walking with my knight in shining armor.

"But I had fooled myself, for he never had any armor, shining or not—he was just an ordinary man. Soon I discovered he had a fear of heights, so we never did take the high roads he had always talked about. How disappointed I was to plod along in the valleys beside him. The only thing he talked about was himself. Day and night it was always, 'me, me, me.' I thought it would get easier when little travelers joined us, but that only made things worse. He didn't like the way I disciplined them and said I was too soft. And for all of his complaining, he never helped me with them. He just sat around the camp eating and eating until he grew pudgy. Then he turned bald and started to snore every night so I could barely sleep.

"It felt so hopeless because we didn't believe in cutting our cords. The only thing that kept us together was that he loved the little travelers as much as I did. Can you imagine how miserable I felt, trapped on the journey with such a common, uninspiring partner?

"I never meant to leave him—I swear I didn't—but how could I help it? One day a knight came by. At least he looked like a real knight, handsome and dashing and wearing shiny armor. He said he was lonely just like I was, and we started going on walks together in the meadows. Then he took me up to a high trail, and it was thrilling to finally see a view. I suppose I knew it was wrong, but I felt so alive when I was with the knight. After all those years walking with my tiresome husband, I thought the King would understand.

"Then one day the knight took out his chalice and offered me a drink. But I didn't drink just for the sweetness. No, it wasn't just for that. I loved the way he looked into my eyes as we drank, not turning away like my husband did. I felt so happy then, to finally experience what I had been missing. After that, the knight and I went walking as often as we could. It wasn't easy; we had to meet in secret. But there are so many little side canyons here that it's not as difficult as it would be someplace else. After feeling dead for so long, I finally felt alive. When I wasn't with the knight, I felt such intense anticipation at the thought of seeing him again. And then we would meet and I would see his face light up—" The woman hugged herself, as if trying to give herself comfort.

"Then one day, my husband discovered me slipping off for a rendezvous with the knight. He said I had broken my promise to him and betrayed the King—and if that was what I wanted, that was what I would get. I didn't feel too sad when he made me leave. In fact, I felt relieved because now the knight and I could go off together as we had always talked of doing. And for a while, walking with the knight was so perfect, it was like being under the

moon of honey all the time. But the excitement didn't last. I
began to notice he had his own faults, ones I hadn't seen at the
beginning when the chalice had been flashing in front of me.
That's when I realized that all I had done was exchange one set
of imperfections for another.

"We started to argue and soon he began to stay away for a
week, and then for two weeks at a time. Since we didn't have cords
of commitment, what could I say? One morning I woke up and
discovered he had left for good. He didn't even leave a note. I
looked for him for a while, but I couldn't find him. I finally gave
up and started out on my own again, but I found the way was
much harder by myself. I had always thought nothing could be
harder than living with my husband, but I was wrong. I missed
him. We had traveled so far together and had raised the little
travelers together. I realized that walking with him wasn't as bad
as I had thought. He had always been faithful to me. Maybe he
wasn't the most handsome partner, but he had never abandoned
me like the fake knight had." She started to weep. "I want to walk
with him again, but I don't know where he and the little travelers have gone. I've searched and searched, but I can't find them
anywhere. Please, please, if you see my husband, tell him I love him
and I want to come back."

Celeste promised they would. But Peter thought it was unfor-
givable that the woman had broken her vows, and her husband
should refuse to take her back. That was what he would do if
Celeste ever left him.

WITH THE HONEY WOMAN

The stream grew wider and then a long rock cut the stream in half, but neither Peter nor Celeste noticed. They had traveled so long as strangers through the Plains of Distance and Way of Winter that, whether they were together or separated it made little difference to them. When Peter finally realized he could no longer see Celeste and the little travelers, several hours had passed. The gentle flow had turned into a rushing torrent, and as the River of Unfaithfulness plunged down the canyon, dirty foam sprayed into the air. Peter suddenly felt very thirsty, but when he knelt by a side pool and cupped some of the putrid water, he could not stomach the thought of drinking it.

Night came. As the faint light disappeared from the canyon, Peter sat by the water's edge. He was happy not to have Celeste harping at him and the little travelers running around screaming. But he still felt lonely, and he wished there was someone to keep him company. Then, above the roar of the water, he heard a melodic voice saying, "Honey, honey." He thought he was all alone on his side of the river, but the voice came closer and closer. "Honey, honey."

"Who's there?" he yelled. He heard a laugh that sounded so light and carefree, he was sorry he had spoken harshly. In a quiet voice he said, "I mean, who are you? Where are you?"

"Now that's better," the voice said.

All of a sudden he felt the warmth of someone sitting beside him on the rock. He was so surprised, he almost jumped up and ran away except the woman—for it was the warmth and the voice of a woman—touched his arm and said, "Don't go, I won't hurt you."

He remained on his guard, afraid that Celeste might have sent the woman to trap him.

"I heard you say you were lonely."

"No, I didn't say that." But he wondered if he had been talking out loud to himself.

"Maybe you didn't, but anyone who comes down this path by himself has to be lonely."

"I have a wife. I just am spending the night alone."

"Then you won't mind if I just sit here with you. I promise I won't bother you. But if you want to talk, I'd be happy to listen."

It had been so long since Peter had shared his thoughts and feelings with Celeste or anyone else. His heart was so full of things to say that the idea of talking with the gentle honey woman sounded appealing. So they sat together for awhile and talked about their journeys. Then the woman stood up. "I have to go. But I'll come see you tomorrow if you want." In a flash, she was gone.

When Peter woke up the next morning, he remembered the honey woman and hoped he would see her again. When he got back to the path, she was there waiting for him. He began walking, expecting her to come, but she just stood there. He could see in the daylight that she looked perfectly harmless and beautiful too, with long honey-colored hair and honey-colored skin. "Won't you walk with me for a little?" he asked.

"All right," she said.

As they started off, Peter realized how hungry he was because he had not had any breakfast. Before he said a word, the woman brought out a jar of honey. "You must be starving," she said. She gave him a spoon of honey and as he ate it, he thought he had never tasted anything so sweet and delicious. Celeste never worried about whether he was hungry and the meals she served him were so unappetizing that he found them hard to swallow. It seemed to Peter that the honey woman wanted nothing from him except to enjoy his company.

"It's so hard to walk with my wife," Peter said. "She just doesn't understand me. She whines and harps on me all the time."

"It must be such a strain for you," the honey woman said.

"It is," Peter said, thankful he had found someone who understood how difficult his life was.

That evening she disappeared again before Peter fell asleep, and in the morning she returned once more. They walked together for another day, splashing at the edge of the water. With the honey woman's soothing words and spoonfuls of honey, Peter no longer noticed the foul smell or remembered he was playing in the River of Unfaithfulness. The river was becoming stronger and the path was filling with small boulders, but the honey woman started a game of tag to make the journey more enjoyable. As Peter scrambled over the boulders, he thought how Celeste would never have done that; she would have only complained that he had brought her on another difficult path.

Soon he could not imagine a day without seeing the honey woman. He didn't think there was anything wrong with spending time with her. After all, his chalice was packed away in his bag. What harm could there be just talking with someone? There was no traveler nearby to warn Peter of the danger, and he never thought to take out his guidebook to remind himself of the King's rules and the Servant's encouragement. All Peter could think about was the honey woman and the sweetness of her honey words, especially when the river was too loud and she had to stand on tiptoes and whisper them in his ear.

Once as he jumped over a boulder to tag the honey woman, he tripped and fell into the sand at the edge of the river, and the water splashed on him. Before he knew it, the honey woman was lying beside him. A gush of water showered down on them, and they laughed, not caring that their hair and clothes were dripping with the polluted water. That night, when it was time to sleep, the honey woman did not get up to go. She stayed beside Peter, talking and stroking his hair until he began drifting off to sleep. When he heard her get up and leave, he was too tired from playing to call her back. He fell asleep with a deep thirst.

As Peter slept, he dreamed he was drinking from the chalice with the honey woman. It was such a sweet dream, but when he woke up in the morning and remembered the dream, he was disturbed, for it had revealed his hidden desire. Then the Breath of the King reminded him what the Servant had said: wanting to drink the chalice with the honey woman was the same as doing it.

Peter sat on a rock, holding his head in despair because he knew that was true. Though he had not drunk from the chalice, he had given his heart to another woman and betrayed his vows to Celeste. Worse, the honey woman would be coming soon to spend another day with him, and he had never been so thirsty in all his life. How could he resist his desire to drink from the chalice with her? He wished there was a friend he could talk to, for that would give him strength. But he was all alone by the River of Unfaithfulness.

Peter got out the guidebook from the bottom of his pack and opened it. What he read turned him cold: "The lips of a honey woman drip honey, and her speech is smoother than oil; but in the end she is bitter as a lemon. Her way goes straight to death. She ignores the way of life. She takes crooked paths, but she doesn't know it."

What am I to do? Peter wondered. He kept reading: "Keep to a path far from her, don't spend any time with her; otherwise you'll be giving away the best part of your life to someone who is not your wife. If you do that, at the end of your life you will groan in agony. You will say, I refused to correct my way, I would not listen to the guides or the guidebook. And my error will be visible to all my fellow travelers."

And in my dream, I saw that the Servant sympathized with Peter's weakness, for the Servant Himself had been tempted in every way. But Peter condemned himself for his failure and could not forgive himself. Though it was the King's grace that had cut through his chains of debt, Peter had always taken pride in his righteousness.

"Oh, what a miserable person I am! Who will free me from this life that is dominated by sin?" he cried. Then the Breath of the King reminded Peter that he could approach the throne of grace with confidence to receive mercy and to find the grace to help him in his time of need. At that moment, Peter heard a powerful voice echo through Desolate Canyon. "Thanks be to the King! For there is now no condemnation for those who follow the King, because the law of the spirit of life set them free from the law of sin and death."

However Peter's battle was not over. Soon he heard the honey woman calling again, "Honey, honey." He put his hands over his ears and started down the trail without looking back. All day long she called after him. Peter kept his ears plugged as he walked and continued to cry out to the King. Once he caught sight of the honey woman on a boulder waving to him, and he hesitated for a moment. He could smell her honey coming on the breeze, and it was so sweet, he ached for it. What difference would it make if he just talked a little more with her? He was so thirsty, so incredibly thirsty. He started walking back to her, but again the Breath of the King spoke to him: "Flee, flee."

Peter held his nose so he would not smell the honey woman's fragrance; then he turned around and continued, not jubilant but distressed, for he was carrying a burden as heavy as a cross. When night came, he lay down exhausted. In the stillness he heard the honey woman still sweetly calling—and suddenly she was beside him again, like all the other nights.

"Why are you walking away from me? I won't hurt you. I just want to give you some honey."

Peter began to weep and again he heard the King. "Do you not know that your body is home to My Breath, which you have received from Me? You are not your own; you were bought at a price. Therefore honor Me with your body."

Peter knew he could not stay next to the honey woman. But he couldn't pull himself up. "I can't," he told the King. "I am too weak."

"Not in your strength, but by the power of My grace," the King said. "Remember the Servant. Remember I have given you My very Breath."

Peter, knowing that the Breath of the King was filling him, staggered to his feet. In the darkness he could see a vision of the way ahead of him. There were angels and demons, heights and depths, the now and the yet to come—but he saw nothing that could pull him away from the grip of the King.

"I will not leave you," the King told Peter. "I will love you. Nothing will be able to separate you from My love." Then Peter remembered something he had read in the guidebook:

> "When my heart was grieved and my spirit embittered,
> I was senseless and ignorant;
>> Yet I am always with you, you hold me by my right hand, you guide me with your counsel and afterward you will take me into glory. . . .
>> My flesh and my heart may fail, but the King is the strength of my heart and my portion forever."

Peter trudged through the night, as if crossing the Valley of the Shadow of Death, but he was no longer afraid. He held on to the King's love and faithfulness to protect himself from the urge he still felt to go back to the honey woman. By dawn he had walked some ways from the River of Unfaithfulness and found himself in a dry canyon. He still felt lonely, and he struggled again with the temptation to go back and find the honey woman. Peter had to remind himself that the Servant had died to rescue him—and that it was his duty to care for the little travelers.

Resolved to find his family, he began to shout for Celeste as he made his way back to the water. But the River of Unfaithfulness roared through the canyon and drowned out his cries. Finally he climbed a path to a small overlook and saw dozens of travelers bobbing down the river, separated from their partners with no hope of getting back together. As Peter surveyed the dismal scene, he saw a traveler wading along the shore get swept away by the current. Peter shuddered to think he too might have been taken away by the River of Unfaithfulness.

He persevered through Desolate Canyon. Eventually the channel narrowed and one day he finally spotted Celeste and the little travelers tramping along on the other side. He called to them, but the river was louder and stronger than before. He feared he would never be able to reach his family. He was not strong enough to swim to the other side, and he had seen the shattered remains of rafts that other travelers had used, trying to cross the river. He walked on, and around the next bend he found a rope of mercy that had been tied to a tree so despairing travelers could reach the other side. Peter grabbed the rope, and with one strong shove he pushed off the bank and swung over the water, landing in the soft sand.

He expected Celeste would be overjoyed to see him. When he reached her, he was ready to ask her to walk with him, as he had done at the start of their journey.

But when she saw him, she just said, "Oh, so you're back."

Irritation flared up in Peter. Although his heart was again clean, it was still empty of love for Celeste. "Yes, I am back. You have no idea how much I struggled to get here."

"You struggled? And what do you think I have been doing this whole time, left alone with the little travelers? Having a picnic?" She kept on walking as if he wasn't there.

Peter turned to the little travelers and hugged each one, pouring out his love to them, for he thought it was hopeless to care for Celeste. She would never change.

They turned away from the river, and as they walked on, the canyon became quieter. But they were not yet free of river's grasp, for one of the little travelers noticed a woman following them. "Who is that woman waving to us?"

Celeste looked behind and saw the honey woman.

"Honey, honey, how are you?" the honey woman called to Peter.

When Celeste saw Peter break into a sweat, she knew something had happened between them. She told the little travelers to sit down for a moment and marched over to Peter. "So is that what you were doing while I was taking care of the little travelers?"

Peter swore to Celeste that the chalice had remained deep in his pack the entire time and that the honey woman had never even looked at it. But Celeste did not believe him, for the honey woman was still calling after Peter, "Honey, honey, won't you have some more honey?"

"Do you mean to tell me she's following you for nothing?" Celeste asked. "That you never had any of her honey?"

Although Peter didn't want to admit what he had done, he knew he needed to confess to Celeste. He told her how he had walked with the woman and taken some of her honey, but that he had left on his own to find Celeste. He knelt before her and pledged to keep walking with her—and her alone—to the King's City.

Celeste was not impressed. "How can you expect me to trust you again? You have hurt me so much; I will never be able to forgive you for how you have betrayed me."

The honey woman finally gave up and left Peter and Celeste alone. They continued through Desolate Canyon with the little travelers. And once again in my dream I saw that if it had not been for the little travelers, Peter and Celeste might have given up and returned to the River of Unfaithfulness. For they never considered the vows they had made or the cords around their wrists.

ALONG REVENGE CHASM

The path out of the canyon led Peter and Celeste straight to Revenge Chasm. They looked across the deep black fissure that cut far into the earth. On the other side, for the first time in a long while, they could glimpse the Highlands and the King's City beyond. The view of the Highlands did not inspire them as it once had, but they still wanted to reach the King's City. However, the chasm was too wide to swing across with a rope of mercy. They followed along the edge, looking to see how they might continue their journey. After a little while they came to a bridge of forgiveness that had been built across the chasm by the Servant.

The little footbridge was the narrowest track Peter and Celeste had come to, a single plank of cedar wide enough for only one traveler at a time. And though it appeared sturdy, there was no proper railing to grasp. The only thing travelers could hold on to was a single rope of mercy that had been tied onto trees on both sides. It didn't look very taut or strong, and every traveler who contemplated the crossing wondered whether the rope would hold if he lost his footing.

Celeste was the first to reach the plank and when she did, she drew back. She knew that before she could walk across, she would have to bandage her wounds, otherwise she would fall. Most of her injuries had been caused by her partnership with Peter: the blisters from his relentless pace, the bruises and sores from his uncaring, the gashes from his anger. Whenever she felt sorry for herself, she liked to stop and catalogue her wounds. Then she would take a pick of resentment and scrape at the scabs so they never had a chance to heal. For as strange as it sounds, she had grown fond of her blisters and cuts and gashes, especially since giving up her postcards. Her wounds made her feel superior to Peter, and by keeping them fresh, he could always see the pain he had caused. And now she had received the most painful wound of all, his betrayal with the honey woman.

She had left behind her rag of compassion soaked with the Servant's tears when she had made her way up Loveless Peak. But there was another one at the bridge that travelers could apply to their wounds. Celeste didn't want to take it. To bandage her wounds and cross the bridge, she would have to forgive Peter. But then she would have no more power over him. No, she thought, she could not give that up. She wanted to punish him for what he had done to her. She had to find a way to make him pay. Until then, she would hold on to her wounds.

"We'll have to find another path," she told Peter. "My blisters make me limp so badly, I'll never make it across the bridge. If you had let me rest so they could have healed, I might have been able to cross, but I don't see how I can now."

One of the little travelers pointed to the sign at the stairs to the bridge. "Have mercy on your fellow traveler as I have had mercy on you, The King."

"This has nothing to do with having mercy," Celeste said to her family. "I simply can't walk on the bridge with my blisters."

Peter didn't argue, for he didn't want to give up his own wounds either.

As they walked away, they met a guide named Pardon. "What are you doing here?" the guide said. "Why haven't you crossed over the chasm? Didn't you see the bridge?"

"It's her fault, " Peter pointed to Celeste. "She keeps picking at her blisters."

Celeste turned red when she heard that Peter had learned her secret and then seethed inside that he had told it to the guide.

Pardon shook his head. "Loving travelers, this is not what you learned about the way of the King. You were taught to love your enemies, to do good to those who hate you, to bless those who curse you, to pray for those who mistreat you, to give without expecting anything back. Can I see your account books?"

"What are you talking about?" Peter said.

"You know what I mean. Although love keeps no record of wrongs, no one who stays on this side of the chasm does so without keeping a detailed accounting."

With great reluctance, Peter took out from his bag a small notebook in which he was keeping a ledger of Celeste's debts. Every time she wronged him, he wrote it down so he could justify not caring for Celeste. Since Celeste had failed him, he did not have to love her. Celeste was taken aback when she saw his list, though she was keeping track of his failures too, on a thick wad of paper.

Pardon talked to them a long time about the foolishness of keeping lists. "Please be merciful, like the King is merciful. Don't be unkind, stingy with your love, hard on each other, jumping on failure, criticizing faults. Love keeps no record of wrongs."

He pleaded with them to burn their accounts, reminding them the King had offered them forgiveness while they were still His enemies, before they had even wanted to surrender. "Long before you even knew you were lost, the Servant came to bring you back, though you had done nothing to deserve His selfless sacrifice. Now offer this same charity to your partner."

Celeste waited for Peter to burn his notebook. But Peter had decided he wouldn't destroy his until Celeste destroyed hers. Pardon finally left them, grieving over their stubbornness and lack of mercy.

AT THE VALLEY OF CUT CORDS

Peter and Celeste wandered along, hoping to find another way around the chasm. The path was crowded with other travelers who had balked at crossing the bridge of forgiveness. The air was dismal and dark, filled with toxic fumes and sulfur clouds of loathing that blocked the light. The travelers stumbled along, unable to see where they were going. Although they claimed to be walking in the King's light, their lack of sympathy for their partners had brought a blinding darkness.

Celeste could not bear the cloud's vile odor of old eggs. She still had knowledge of the Servant and the sweet fragrance it gave. Peter too found himself repulsed by the smell, and together they searched for fresher air. They turned onto a path that led them away from the sulfur clouds, and were surprised to see Faithfulness walking toward them.

"What are you doing here?" Peter asked. "We thought you would have gone on to the King's City by now. Did you also turn away from the bridge of forgiveness?"

"Oh no," Faithfulness said. "I've walked that bridge many times. But I wondered if you needed more help on your journey. How happy I am to see you have decided to turn away from evil."

"What evil?" Celeste said.

"The sulfur clouds are fueled by all sorts of evil things—quarreling, jealousy, outbursts of anger. The travelers who stay under those clouds may claim to love the King, but they are lying. As the guidebook says, if you love the King you must love the people you see, and that includes your partner. Come with me and I'll show you where you might have ended up if you had not turned away."

He led them to a promontory just off the path. "Do you see? The sulfur clouds go all the way down into the Valley of Cut Cords."

Celeste and Peter watched the shadowy plumes moving toward the sad place of brokenness where heaps of cords had been cut and tossed aside. Everything was coated with a dusty gray ash. There was not a drop of moisture in the valley, and the dryness was like that of death.

Dozens of couples marched down the broad way to the valley as little travelers trailed behind, sulking or weeping. Some of the couples walked together with determination, their scissors raised high. Other times, one partner dragged another who resisted violently. But in these dramas of will, the partner doing the dragging always prevailed, for what mattered was not how strong they were, but how much they desired to be rid of their cords.

"I want to remind you what you promised on that day long ago when I wove the cords around your wrists." Faithfulness took a little scroll from his pocket and read it out loud. 'Heart of my heart, flesh of my flesh, bone of my bone. What God has joined together, let no one pull apart.' The people you see heading into the Valley of Cut Cords made the same vows you did. They promised that nothing would sever their cords except death. Yet here you see them, ready to destroy the most sacred pledge one can make, other than the pledge of loving the King."

Peter and Celeste looked away from Faithfulness's steady gaze.

"Do you remember that day we talked, and you said you could not imagine why people ever cut the cords?" Faithfulness said. "You didn't even want to bring scissors with you; you wanted to throw them away. I believe you, Peter, were especially judgmental of those who would do such a thing. But the two of you have not avoided this place, though it is not on the way to the King's City. Your preoccupation with postcards, your sojourn in the Swamp of Selfishness, your splashing in the River of Unfaithfulness, and your refusal to cross the bridge of forgiveness have brought you dangerously close to this terrible place. And now you wonder if it would be better to cut your cords of commitment and go your separate ways." He started toward the promontory. "Come closer. There is something else I want you to see."

They followed him until they stood right above the entrance. Below, they could see a couple who had just arrived at the valley. A large man in a flowing red robe laughed as he took their scissors.

"Who's that awful man?" Celeste asked.

Faithfulness shuddered. "That's the cutter of the cords."

There was a screeching of metal against metal, louder than a thousand fingernails scraping a pane of glass. Celeste put her hands over her ears as she and Peter watched the cords being cut. It was much more painful than a simple snip of string, for the cords fit snugly on the partners' wrists and the cutter used the scissors like a saw, hacking away at the braid. Skin was sliced away, leaving a trail of blood that streamed down their arms. But it appeared that the partners couldn't feel this, for they took no notice as they walked away. Yet the same partners became very touchy when it came to the division of their possessions. A violent fight erupted between them over a matchbox; then they almost came to blows over an old walking stick. Even more heartbreaking was how the couple battled over their little traveler, each partner pulling one of his arms until Celeste feared the little one would be torn apart. The cutter stepped in just in time and ended the scuffle.

"Now I want you to observe the state of your own union," Faithfulness told them. It had been a long time since Peter and Celeste had looked at their cords. They saw two of the braids had completely frayed, and the gold on the third was very pale. Although it was to their credit that they had not yet cut them, they had no grounds to boast. Only their pride had kept them from doing so, each vowing it would not be on their account that the cords would be cut.

"Not a pretty sight, is it?" Faithfulness said. "These cords will have to be repaired or you will end up like those travelers in the valley."

Then a couple came walking peacefully side by side toward

the cutter. Peter and Celeste wondered what this couple was doing at the valley, for they had no marks of struggle or difficulty. In fact, their cords hung loosely around their wrists. When they came to the cutter, the husband spoke calmly.

"No, no great problem. It's just that we've grown apart. We're in perfect agreement that it would be better if we went our own ways. It doesn't make sense to stay together—it has been miles and miles since we have walked together anyway."

"It's true," his wife said. "I don't even know him anymore. He's a stranger to me."

Faithfulness faced Peter and Celeste. "Don't be fooled by what they say. Some marriages look fine on the outside, but inwardly they are rotting. Every couple here has suffered serious wounds or deep trauma—even if it is invisible to the rest of the world.

Celeste winced as the next couple came along. The woman was screaming, "Get away from me, get away from me! You have hurt me too much. I told you if you ever did that again I was going to leave. You are a brutal, hideous creature. I don't know why I agreed to walk with you in the first place."

"You're the one who has made it so horrible!" her husband yelled back. "You're a beast to live with. I never dreamed you could be so loathsome."

The wife thrust her scissors into the cutter's hands. "Quick, cut mine first, for I can't stand being joined to him another minute." The cutter took the scissors and snipped them in two, taking off a good chunk of the woman's flesh.

Faithfulness turned to Peter and Celeste. "I think you've seen enough." He took them back where the path was wider and asked what they thought.

"I wonder if those couples really tried hard enough," Peter said. "If they had worked harder, don't you think they could have avoided coming to the valley?"

"Yes, that's exactly what you'd think," Celeste said. "Just keep a stiff upper lip, and everything will be fine. Easy for you if you don't have a heart. But if you are a real human being with emotions and feelings, you can't go on day after day with such deadness."

She turned to Faithfulness. "How can it be wrong for these travelers to cut the cords?"

"Do you remember what the Servant said?" Faithfulness asked. "Anyone who divorces his wife, except for marital unfaithfulness, and marries another woman commits adultery."

"But surely the King can't expect them to keep on." Celeste's voice trembled. "If they don't cut their cords they will be doomed to years of unhappiness. Who knows what further pain they will have to endure?"

"Is that how little you know of the King? Is it for happiness that He has called you? Or for fullness of life in Him? Travelers end up here because they have slipped back into the old habit of doing whatever they want. They thought that walking together with their partner would come naturally. But you know from your own experience that isn't true. To walk as partners, your whole life has to be shaped by the King's love. That isn't a weak, dead-end love. The King's love is an energetic, blazing love that is saturated with life-giving sacrifice."

"But I have suffered much on the journey," Peter said, remembering all the times Celeste had nagged him and criticized him.

"Yes, but your suffering," said Faithfulness, "is not like the suffering of the King. You do it for show, holding it up as a virtue. Instead, you should take it as a gift. And a gift is accepted with joy—not with the grim expression you usually have."

"How can someone be happy to suffer?" Celeste asked.

"Because these trials test your faith—and the testing develops perseverance, and when perseverance finishes its work in you, you'll be mature and complete, not lacking anything. You could even welcome it as a spiritual refining process, with glory just around the corner. Don't be short-sighted; take the long view. Avoid Esau's mistake. He gave up his position as the oldest son just for a single meal. Later he regretted it, but there wasn't anything that could be done.

"Look over there to the east," Faithfulness said. "Do you see the Mountains of Maturity? That is the direction to go. The road ahead will still be hard, but the King is always ready to give you endurance and encouragement. Remember you are part of His family and He loves you. Remember what the Servant's love was like when He walked this path. It wasn't cautious; it was extravagant. He gave everything of Himself to us—not to get anything in return, but because that is what His love is."

Faithfulness looked at them. "I can see I haven't convinced either of you. Before you decide to go down to the crossroads, there is one more story I would like to share. It is about a couple who, soon after they were sent off, believed they had made a mistake. They both were young, and their parents had advised them to take more time to consider becoming partners. But they could not imagine waiting, and so they went. Immediately their journey became difficult. They were trapped in the Sand Dunes of Foolishness for so long, they almost starved. By the time they emerged, their ankles were permanently damaged, and their muscles so weak they could barely walk a mile before they had to stop. From there they went right into the Desolate Canyon, so they never got a glimpse of the Highlands. In the canyon, the wife went down the River of Unfaithfulness and drank from the chalice with another man. She stayed away from her husband for many days and nights."

"So surely," Celeste said, "the other traveler had the right to cut the cords. It's just as the Servant said, 'Except for unfaithfulness.'"

The guide looked at her with great sadness, for she had become like Peter, caring more about the letter of the law in order to justify herself.

"Yes, the husband had grounds to leave. His wife expected he would. But one night this traveler made the hard journey up Skull Hill. He realized how dark and cold the world would be if he continued alone—perhaps darker and colder than the storms he had gone through with his wife. And he thought of the little travelers they had been given. Most of all, the traveler remembered his big debt that the King had canceled. He realized he needed to do the same. He decided that even if he could not have happiness, he would stay with her and be faithful to his vow, for he had pledged faithfulness to death, not faithfulness until adultery."

"So everything worked out fine," Peter said. "That's what happens when you follow the King."

"Peter, your comment tells me you do not yet understand what it means to take up your cross daily and deny yourself," Faithfulness said. "Everything was not fine. Every day he could hear the echo of the deceiver's accusations: his wife was a whore, a harlot, an adulteress. Many times he wondered if he had made a mistake in accepting her back. No, the way he chose was much harder than going down to the Valley of Cut Cords. He had to learn to trust his partner again. And they both had to bathe in the Healing Springs and cleanse their wounds. They had to learn to walk together again. It took a very long time, and often they despaired of ever being well again. But now this couple has no regrets that they stayed together. They have learned a deeper joy; they have experienced a deeper grace. Yes, the husband was free to leave, but he remembered he was set free for freedom—freedom to love."

Celeste shook her head. "I still don't understand how they could stay partners."

"They learned it is a sacrifice to forgive like the King. When someone wrongs you, pain and loss come into your life. Someone has to right the wrong. Someone has to pay for the loss and absorb the pain. It's not enough to say, 'It doesn't matter,' because it does. A wound needs to be healed. A debt has to be paid. The King's way was to cancel our debt through the death of His Son. And that is what the King wants us to do: to absorb the pain rather than retaliate."

"But that's impossible," Celeste said.

"You're right, it is. I assure you, the only way you will be able to forgive like this is with the power of the King who has forgiven us completely. He doesn't ask us to become self-righteous martyrs. He simply wants us to forgive people by drawing on the unlimited spiritual account He's given to us—even before the other person asks to be forgiven.

"I do not tell you anything I have not had to do myself," Faithfulness said. "I know it is tempting to be here, so close to the Valley of the Cut Cords, where forgiveness has been lost. It looks so easy to walk down the hill to the cutter. You are free to do as you wish. But I beg you, don't use your freedom to go your own way. Use it to submit to each other in love. The King's rule is summed up by one very simple but very hard command: love your neighbor as yourself. Don't think that if you cut your cords, your journey to the King's City will be any easier. People think once they leave the valley all will be well. Then they round a corner and come to an endless desert—and they see they have gained nothing. So take your time before you act. Remember you can trust the King on the path of love and perseverance. He is faithful, and He will do it. Take His yoke and learn from Him—for He is gentle and humble, and you will find rest for your souls. Submit to each other and honor the Servant who died to give you life."

Faithfulness took out the scroll with the vows Peter and Celeste had pledged to each other and put it on the ground in front of them. He lifted up his hand and blessed them, saying, "As you obey the King, you will be like a well-watered garden, like a spring whose waters never fail. And now may the King bless you and keep you and make His face shine on you and be gracious to you and give you His peace."

He bowed toward Peter and then toward Celeste; then

he turned to walk up the path, leaving them to consider their decisions.

Peter stood with his arms folded. Though his stubbornness had often caused him many problems, this time it served him well. He would not cut the cords, not after his struggle to burn his postcards and his greater struggle to leave the honey woman. He would stay.

But Celeste wandered back down to the overlook and listened to the ugly grating sound of the scissors. She started to walk in a small circle, round and round, and the circle she walked was like the braid around her wrist, with no beginning and no end. She didn't know why she should go on. She thought, however, since she had buried the postcards, the journey had become much harder. And if she kept going, she had no hope it would be any easier. So why shouldn't she cut the cords, she wondered.

There was no answer, just the sound of the scissors. She kept walking in a circle, feeling the constraint of the King's love deep within her. Finally she told herself that if Peter didn't go down to the valley, she wasn't going to drag him there.

She walked back up to Peter, who was still standing with his arms folded, looking very unhappy. "Which way are you going?" she asked.

"That way." He pointed up to the path. Celeste picked up their scroll and came to Peter's side. Slowly, they walked back up to the path, leaving the Valley of Cut Cords behind them.

Through the Darkest Night

AT THE FENCING HUT

*B*ack on the path that led away from the sulfur clouds, Peter and Celeste sometimes met other couples who also were escaping the foul air. But sometimes the toxic clouds drifted all the way to Revenge Chasm, and the travelers were forced to take a narrow, rocky trail along the side of a ravine to find fresher air. None of the travelers looked happy about the difficult path, but after a little while, Peter and Celeste saw one couple holding hands and smiling. They looked so out of place, Celeste asked them why they were cheerful.

"We've just come from the fencing hut, where Gentleness taught us the kingly way of conflict," the man said.

"And you're still smiling?"

"Amazing, isn't it?" the woman said. "But you can see for yourself. The hut isn't far off the path."

Celeste could see the hut through the underbrush. "What do you think? Should we go?" she asked Peter.

"I don't know," Peter said. As usual, he was concerned what other travelers might think if they saw him going to the hut. He didn't mind meeting a guide along the way, but to look for one would make him appear weak. Then he noticed the well-traveled path leading to the hut, and he felt better knowing that he and Celeste were not the only ones who needed help. He agreed to go, but warned Celeste he wouldn't stay if he had to talk very much.

The hut was small and rustic, made of unpainted logs. When Peter and Celeste entered, they saw it was just a single room with two wooden chairs. They sat down, and soon Gentleness came in. She looked them over. "I can see from your impressive set of battle wounds that you have been engaging in some heavy guerrilla warfare."

Peter and Celeste shifted in their seats.

"Well, you've come to the right place to improve your fighting skills. You know, of course, there is nothing wrong with having a spirited discussion. The King brought you together as two different people, and I'm sure there is always plenty for you to discuss. But you have learned that conflict can be destructive if you are not working together with one mind and one purpose. Do you remember what the guide named Paul said? 'In light of all this, here's what I want you to do. While I'm locked up here, a prisoner for the Master, I want you to get out there and walk—better yet, run!—on the road God called you to travel. I don't want any of you sitting around on your hands. I don't want anyone strolling off, down some path that goes nowhere. And mark that you do this with humility and discipline—not in fits and starts, but steadily, pouring yourselves out for each other in acts of love, alert at noticing differences and quick at mending fences. You were all called to travel on the same road and in the same direction, so stay together, both outwardly and inwardly.' All right, enough talking, let's see how you fight."

Peter and Celeste stared at Gentleness.

"No, I'm serious. I can't help you if I don't know what you are doing wrong. I assume you both have weapons?"

Peter and Celeste hesitated, then took out their clubs.

"No, no. Not clubs. Where are your foils for sparring?"

Peter and Celeste didn't know what she was talking about.

"What? You didn't get them? I thought they were standard equipment for the journey. No wonder you have been having problems. Well, let's see how you use your clubs."

Peter and Celeste slowly got up and began. Peter often used his club to push Celeste along when she walked too slowly, and Celeste used hers to get Peter's attention when she thought he wasn't listening to her. And when they started to really argue, they would use them as battering rams. But it had been a long time since they had faced each other and had a proper fight.

"Come on, come on," Gentleness said. "Don't be shy."

With all the resentment Peter and Celeste had toward each other, they quickly got in the spirit of things and were coming to real blows.

"Okay, that's enough." Gentleness stepped in. "You both have quite aggressive techniques. A fencing sword would definitely help." She took out two gleaming foils for them.

Peter swished his in the air and then touched the blade.

"No, it's not sharp," Gentleness said. "These are foils, not real dueling swords. Notice the tip has a rubber cap, and the sword is thin enough to bend easily. But keep in mind that any fight can do serious damage, regardless what weapon you use: clubs, swords, rocks. Some travelers have maimed their partners for life."

Gentleness showed them how to swing the foil and let them practice until they felt comfortable with the weight in their hand. "The most important thing to keep in mind is the goal of your fighting. Can you tell me what that is?"

Peter and Celeste shook their heads.

"Understanding. Agreement," Gentleness said. "Not winning—and certainly not damage or destruction. You're on the same team, so if you disable your partner, you only hurt yourself. Think of it as a dance, not a battle."

Peter and Celeste began to fence but found themselves making wild strokes with the slender foils, which were much lighter than their clubs.

After a few minutes, Gentleness stopped them. "All right. One of your main problems is that you both lack a sense of give and take. You are either so keen on winning that you charge ahead to back your partner into a corner—or you take a defensive stance that brings you to a stalemate. I want you to practice going forward and then taking a step back, as if you are waltzing with each other. If you can master this, you will be well on your way to becoming a great fencer."

She coached them as she watched. "Back and forth. Not too defensive, Peter. Give him a chance to respond, Celeste. Respect the center line. Wait, no, no, no! Peter, it is very unsportsmanlike to get in a sneaky jab like you just did. How can Celeste trust you if she is afraid of getting ambushed? All right, that's enough for now." She handed them towels and told them to take turns drying each other off. "Remember you are partners, not opponents. Learn to cooperate with each other in everything, because love binds you together in perfect harmony."

Peter and Celeste stayed in the fencing hut a long time, practicing their moves. They were slow to learn and made many mistakes. But Gentleness trained them well and impressed on them the importance of mastering conflict. Otherwise it was unlikely they would ever reach the Highlands.

INTO THE DARKNESS

In my dream, I expected the journey would soon become easier for Peter and Celeste. They had buried their postcards, chosen to turn away from the Valley of Cut Cords, and learned to use their foils. And for a while, the way was not so hard for them. They joked and hummed as they went. One day they even kicked pebbles together. The little travelers laughed and laughed, for they could not remember when their parents had enjoyed themselves so much. Soon Peter and Celeste began to hope their muscles would grow strong enough to climb a Mountain of Maturity, and they would reach the Highlands at last.

They heeded the warning of a couple who told them to stay away from the Tar Pits of Disgust. There were dreadful reports of partners who had fallen into the sticky tar and sunk to the bottom after refusing to help each other climb out. Peter and Celeste also took a long detour to avoid the Quicksand of Abuse. They again took up the habit of reading the guidebook every night before the little travelers went to bed, and they made sure to stop at every gathering hut.

At one gathering hut, Celeste met an old friend and shared with her what had happened in the Desolate Canyon. "I've tried to forgive Peter, but how he betrayed me with the honey woman hurt me so deeply."

"Oh, Celeste," her friend said. "That must be so painful for you."

"I know the bitterness is beginning to eat at me, but I don't see how I can forgive him. What should I do?"

"Do you remember the story the Servant told about the unmerciful servant?"

"Yes, but this is different."

Her friend got the guidebook and read the story. When she finished, she again read the end: "'Then the king called in the man he had forgiven and said, "You evil servant! I forgave you that tremendous debt because you pleaded with me. Shouldn't you have mercy on your fellow servant, just as I had mercy on you?" Then the angry king sent the man to prison to be tortured until he had paid his entire debt.' I don't see how your situation is different than this. The King has been merciful to you, Celeste, and He asks you to have mercy on Peter."

"It takes time for wounds to heal," Celeste said.

"Yes, but they do not heal well if you do not use the rag of compassion or if you refuse to bandage your wounds but nurse your self-pity. I can imagine that it will be very hard to give grace to Peter. It's not something you alone have the power to do. So I will ask the King from His glorious, unlimited resources if He will empower you with inner strength through His Breath. And may you have the power to understand how wide, how long, how high, and how deep the King's love is for you."

Her friend urged Celeste to take the northern path after the gathering hut. It would lead to the bridge of forgiveness that Celeste had avoided and from there it would take her and Peter to the Mountains of Maturity.

But Celeste could not forgive Peter. When it came time for them to leave, she told Peter she wanted to take the southern route. Peter agreed, for it looked smooth and flat and headed into a flourishing hardwood forest.

They soon discovered the forest trail was not an easy stroll. The rugged path twisted like a corkscrew up and down steep ravines. For every two steps forward, they seemed to take three steps back. They became discouraged, and before long they were back to their noisy arguments and using their clubs again. When they weren't fighting, they lapsed into cold silence with quick drinks from the chalice. Meanwhile, the forest became so thick, the sun could barely shine through, making the air chilly.

But some mornings Celeste would remember that the Servant had told His followers to give without expecting anything in return. She made a radical vow to try to love Peter like that. She helped Peter with the bags and asked him how he was doing. Still, she found herself waiting for him to say a few words of appreciation or a simple thanks. But her acts of kindness seemed to make no difference to him, and he said nothing. By lunch, she was angry again and determined to tightly guard her love. Peter was not worthy of such a gift.

One day, as they struggled up a particularly hard trail, Celeste stumbled over a root and fell with a sharp cry. Peter walked on as if nothing had happened. As Celeste lay on the ground and watched him stride on, the last feeble flame of hope in her heart was extinguished. Her partnership with Peter was dead. She could call and he would not hear; she could weep and he would not comfort her. He did not love her at all.

Celeste got up and shuffled along, a dull pain filling her heart. Deeper and deeper she wandered into the dark forest. She didn't care where the path took her—or if she was on a path at all. By the time she stopped to rest, she was completely lost. She didn't care; the forest could swallow her up. She had no desire to find her way out and return to her dismal journey with Peter. Her partnership with him had only brought her sorrow.

She thought back on the trek through the Swamp of Selfishness, the Dry Wash of No Arguments, the searing Disillusioning Sun, the icy Way of Winter. All she could remember was how little he had cared for her, the arrogant way he walked, the self-righteous limp he had from carrying his pack, and his relentless pace. Her body bore scars from painful blisters, bites of the snapping turtles, and nasty burns from the Vehement Volcano.

She got up and wandered on. The darkness around her felt hollow and empty like death. She wondered if she was even still alive. But from time to time a single tear would well up, and she knew there was still some life left in her. Then she would brush away the tear, hoping it was the last.

For days and days she traveled like this, until one day a voice came out of the darkness, as soft as a shadow. "Wait."

She thought it was her imagination, and she plodded on.

"Wait," the voice said again.

But Celeste kept going.

"Wait." The voice was as patient as the first time.

Celeste finally stopped. "Who are you?"

"Don't you know Me even after I have been with you for such a long time?"

"I'm sorry. I didn't know anyone else was here."

"Where are you going?"

"Nowhere."

"That is not true. As long as you are breathing, you are on your way."

"Then I will keep on."

"And leave Peter?"

"If I disappear it would not make any difference to him."

"If you stop walking with Peter, it will be different for both him—and you."

"But we don't talk, and he doesn't care. Being partners means nothing."

"You may not be able to see it, but when you are warm, a tenderness glows within him. When you are cold, he feels a chill."

"Not anymore," Celeste said.

"It is true he does not care for you as he once did. I have seen how long and how hard you have tried to change him. Some of the changes would be good for him and help him walk with a lighter step. But some of what you want to change is part of him. You cannot fashion Peter exactly as you want."

"So I will go on in darkness and silence," Celeste said.

Suddenly Celeste could see that ahead of her the path branched into three ways. To the left, it led into the Desolate Canyon and the River of Unfaithfulness. To the right, it headed down toward the Valley of Cut Cords. In the middle, it continued into the Plains of Distance.

"I know those ways," Celeste said. "It doesn't matter which path I take. I will suffer no matter which one I follow."

"Oh, but you are wrong—as you are in many things. If you were wiser, you would understand the difference each path would make to you, to Peter, to your little travelers, and to all the other people in your life."

"So tell me which one to take," Celeste said. "Tell me which is the best."

He sighed. "Do you know so little of Me? These paths have been chiseled out by sinful feet and devilish desires. They were never in My original design or on the Servant's path."

Celeste stood waiting.

"You know the Servant's path—or at least you once did. But perhaps you have forgotten it. Look behind you and see what you just passed."

Celeste turned around and saw a fork in the path that went up a short slope and into a walled garden. She had thought she was past caring. Yet when she looked at the three branches that would take her to what she had already suffered, she decided to go back to the fork and follow the path into the garden.

As she entered the garden doorway, she found it was not as dark as the forest. But what she saw in the faint light made her recoil; the stone walls were covered with snakes slithering among the vines. In their hissing, she thought she could hear them speak. "He doesssn't love you, he'sss an awful man, what doesss he expect you to do? Sssuffer forever? Yesss, that isss what he wantsss. You to sssuffer."

"Do not listen to the snakes," the King said. "For they only seek to do you harm."

"Sss," hissed the snakes. "What harm to sssave yoursssself? No one elssse will do it for you. Go back, choossse your own path. Three to choossse from. Yoursss to decide. Follow what you desssire. Ssso much better than thisss garden. Ugly plantsss."

But Celeste could see the snakes were wrong. The vines on the wall were covered with the most exquisite blossoms she had ever seen along the trail or in the Orchard of Earthly Delights—even in her postcards. The multi-layered passion flowers had white petals and blue fringe, green and yellow stamens, topped with purple stigma. The fruity fragrance they gave off was so rich, Celeste felt a tremendous ache in her heart. She thought she might cry.

"If you want to follow Me," the King said, "take the path that leads up Skull Hill."

Through the doorway on the other side of the garden, Celeste could see the beginning of a steep rise.

"If you want to save your life, you will lose it," the King said. "But if you lose your life for Me, you will find it. What good will it do if you lose your very soul?"

"Follow what you desssire," the snakes hissed.

"To go up Skull Hill, you will have to leave behind your dream of being loved by Peter. More than that, you will have to leave your selfish desires behind and love him without any conditions."

"Choossse your own path. Yoursss to decide."

"The snakes are right. You must choose your way. I will never force you."

Celeste thought of the scenes in the postcards she had buried with Faithfulness. When she had given up her dream of romantic love, she had expected to get something better in return—a whole, true love with Peter. She wanted the give-and-take of two equals. But if that was denied as well, how could she go on? How could she give up her desire for completeness? How could she walk without that? Surely she would die. "Please, oh please, give me another way." Sweat began to fall from her forehead to the ground like drops of blood.

The snakes on the walls continued hissing. She stood there a long while, for she could not bear to go back. Again she asked for another way. She waited for His reply, but received only silence.

She began to weep with deep sobs of agony. She didn't want to give up her hope of love—she didn't see how she could. But if she went back and took one of the three branches, she would find only more sorrow. Never had her heart felt such pain. How could she let go of all expectation that Peter would love her? Or give up the right to be cared for? Or to be cherished? She would do anything for the King—if only she could keep her desire to be loved in return. "Please. Please give me another way."

"When you pass through the waters, I will be with you, and

when you pass through the rivers, they will not sweep over you. When you walk through the fire, you will not be burned; the flames will not set you ablaze."

She knew the King was right and loving and wise. She knew the three other paths would only lead her to deeper misery. She thought of the Servant dying, nailed to the cross, suffering in anguish—and she knew that if she wanted to follow the Servant's way, she needed to go up Skull Hill. There was no other way.

For a long time she stayed there though, crying in agony. She had once grieved the death of her old life when she first joined the King's family. But then she had been given freedom from her chains and the promise of new life. The death that lay before her now was different. It meant destroying what she held most precious. She would be giving up her right to expect that Peter love her.

"Peace be with you," the King said.

And a little while later she heard, "My peace I give you."

Soon Celeste was no longer crying. She bowed her head. If going up Skull Hill was the only way to save her life—and perhaps her partnership with Peter—it was worth trying. "Not my will, but Your will be done," she said, sobbing.

The snakes on the walls hissed and writhed in torment.

She started walking slowly across the garden. As she stepped through the doorway that led up the hill, the snakes slid off the walls and fled the garden in silence.

There was darkness all around, but the path was lit by a beacon of fire burning on Skull Hill. She made her way across a small field, then came to the base of the hill where a narrow trail led the way up the steep slope. She saw the path was blocked by two objects, and fresh anguish flooded her heart. She understood she was meant to carry them to the top of the hill and destroy them there.

The first object was a glass case about the size of an aquarium. When Celeste looked at it closer, she gasped, for the case contained gruesome specimens of every wound she had suffered from walking with Peter. There were vials of blood, bruised flesh, scabs, and bits of broken bones. Each specimen was clearly labeled with a date and a brief description. "12/3 Flesh wound from uncaring," "4/21 Bone chip from long fall," "6/15 Bite from snapping turtle."

"I have suffered so much," Celeste's voice quivered. "Please do not ask me to sacrifice this."

"I have also cried over all these wounds," the King said. "And by My wounds, you have been healed."

"But if I destroy the evidence, what justice will there be? Who will pay the price? Who will bear the suffering? You ask too much."

"No more than I gave Myself."

"But who will love me? Who will love me?"

"You are My beloved. Remain in My love."

Celeste remembered a song from the guidebook: "How great is the love the King has lavished on us, that we should be called children of the King—and that is what we are!" She felt the love of the King warm her heart, and she reached to pick up the case. But it was so heavy, she did not have the strength to lift it. "I am sorry," she said. "But I am powerless."

"Not by might, nor by power, but by My Breath," the King said. "Surrender, and I will do it. Everything is possible for the one who believes."

"I do believe; help me overcome my unbelief."

The Breath of the King came and filled her, and she picked up the case—though even with His power, it was the hardest thing she had ever done.

Now that she held the case, she could identify the second object on her path: her club. Although she had used it often, she had never really seen it when it wasn't in her hands. It looked dreadful, with bits of dead skin and blood from the wounds she had given Peter. Even when she had received a foil from Gentleness, she had held onto her club, for it was her shield as well as her weapon. Without it she would be truly vulnerable. She could not attack, and neither could she defend herself. She would be nothing more than a humble servant, loving Peter regardless of how he treated her. She would sign away her rights, give up her demand for love. Only the love she offered Peter would remain.

"You are My beloved," the King said. "Rest secure in Me, for I shield you all day long. Remain in Me."

Trusting in the King's unfailing love, she picked up the club and started up Skull Hill.

UP SKULL HILL

As Celeste trudged up the slope, one slow step after the other, she still hoped she would be spared from going to the top. She hoped that Peter would come running after her and say he was sorry. She hoped that the King would come and carry her away.

She hoped that Skull Hill would melt away in front of her. But nothing happened, and she continued her long, painful climb.

Sometimes she had to stop because the path was almost vertical and gravity pulled her backward.

Humility joined her as she struggled on. "Fix your eyes on the Servant. For the joy set before Him, He endured the cross, scorning its shame, and sat down at the right hand of the throne of the King."

Her pack weighed her down so she couldn't look up to the top. But as she looked at the ground, she thought of the Servant who had been shamed and broken. She thought of the scars from His wounds, the stripes from lashes, the cross He had carried through the streets of the Chosen City. Drawing strength from His example and fueled by the Breath of the King, she was able to reach the top of Skull Hill.

The summit was bare except for a fire burning in a pit. The flames blazed strong as a wind howled in the trees below, and Celeste shivered. Weak from carrying the case and the club up the hill, she stumbled as she made her way forward. When she reached the pit, for once she did not hesitate. She wanted to be free of the burden of resentment and anger. Gathering all her strength, she thrust the club and the case into the fire.

The flames roared up. As she watched them, she thought of one more thing she must do. She took out the paper on which she had kept account of the debts Peter owed her. Then she crumpled the list and threw it into the fire. It was saturated with hostility and resentment, and the flames blazed so hot that Celeste had to take a step back. The ground began to throb with a deep harmonic resonance, and Celeste heard a large choir singing: "And hope does not disappoint us, because the King has poured out His love into our hearts through His Breath." A great cloud of witnesses had been watching as she had made her sacrifice. Now their song turned into cheering. Humility came alongside Celeste, and together they started down the other side of Skull Hill.

As they walked, Humility counseled Celeste. "Do not assume Peter will be different because of what you have just done. Most likely, you will find him just the same. But you are free now to love him without expectation and to give without hope of return. Care for him as you would want him to care for you. Desire what is best for him, loving him as you have been loved."

At the bottom of Skull Hill, they came to the path that led to a bridge of forgiveness. Celeste was filled with dread; she did not know if she could love as the King had loved her. "It's too soon to cross the bridge," she told Humility, thinking of the narrow plank and slender rope stretched across the chasm. "I'm not ready."

"If not now, when?" Humility said.

So with Humility beside her, Celeste headed down the path. When they reached the bridge, Humility took the rag of compassion and tended to Celeste's wounds. As she did this, she told Celeste about an old couple she had once met. In their younger days, they had done much for the King. The husband had been very gifted at blazing new trails for the King, and the wife was bright and quick, always eager to help. As they traveled together, she enabled him to do great things for the King. But then she grew old faster than she should have. She lost her ability to remember and speak, and even to think and dream and plan.

Sometimes she would wander away by herself, drooling and muttering. The husband could not take care of her and continue his work for the King. So he gave it up."

Celeste wondered about the husband's decision. "But think of all the good things he could have done without her."

"Do you remember the friend of the Servant who complained about perfume being wasted on the Servant's feet? He said the money could have been given to the poor, and that was true. But the King's economy is not like ours. Many travelers think that serving the King dutifully is the most important thing on the way to the King's City, but they often look no different than the people in the Orchard of Earthly Delights or Slouching City or Upright Village. If you are going to stay on the King's path, you cannot put serving the King ahead of loving the King."

"But this man wasted his life caring for his partner."

"It is never a waste to love or to take the Servant's path to Skull Hill. This husband had vowed to care for his partner no matter what happened, and he did as he promised."

ACROSS THE BRIDGE OF FORGIVENESS

Celeste knew it was time for her to cross the bridge. Although the list of Peter's debts lay in ashes on Skull Hill, she still could recite all the ways Peter had failed her. He had closed himself off from her, he had not listened to her, he had gone off with the honey woman, he had been cold and callous, he had refused to stop for her. . . .

"Release, let go," Humility whispered. "Cancel the debt. Remember you too have been forgiven. Follow the Servant's footsteps."

"All right, I'll go," she said. She threw back her shoulders and walked quickly onto the bridge, her eyes fixed on the other side. She had gone a quarter of the way when she made the mistake of looking down into the black, endless chasm. A wave of dizziness came over her. But she forced herself to press on.

Pardon was waiting on the other side, and when Celeste reached the end, the guide held out his hand to help Celeste off the bridge. Celeste looked at him expectantly, thinking he would congratulate her. But all Pardon said was, "Do not be fooled into thinking that you will not have to do that again."

"But I crossed the bridge. I've forgiven Peter."

Pardon shook his head. "There will be other chasms ahead of you, and each time you will need to walk over a bridge."

"How many more times will I have to walk over it?" She was about to add, "And what about Peter; when will it be his turn to walk across it?"

"That is what everyone always wants to know," Pardon said. "But there is no magic formula. And there will never come a time when you will be able to say to Peter, 'I won't forgive you again because you've used up all of your chances.'" Pardon looked at Celeste with understanding. "Think of some small sin you do every day. Multiply it by the number of days you have walked. How many times in all is that?"

Celeste shook her head.

"It's a lot to forgive, isn't it? Yet the King has forgiven you that many times, and will still forgive you even if you commit this one sin a hundred times a day, every day, until you reach His city. That's how many times you should be prepared to cross a bridge of forgiveness. We have been given grace without measure, yet we would parcel it out in drops to someone else." Pardon sighed. "The King is very patient. You must be patient too. We hope Peter will respond to the grace you give him, as you have responded to the King's. But there is no guarantee. You must continue to love, without rules, without conditions, without expecting anything in return."

Celeste continued on the path and soon found Peter and the little travelers napping in a grove near the chasm. Peter woke up and looked at her without smiling.

"I'm sorry to keep you waiting," she said.

"What do you mean? We just got here an hour ago. It took me days to find a way around the chasm."

"So you didn't walk over the bridge?"

"How could I do that after you walked off and left me with the little travelers? Anyway, it's time to go. Let's not waste the rest of the day."

Celeste quickly woke up the little travelers and got their bags ready. Before they all started off again, she went to Peter. "Will you walk with me?" she asked.

A faint smile came to his face.

The path took them into woodlands interspersed with pastures, all showing the first signs of spring. The bare branches were tipped with green buds, and the first tiny wildflowers blossomed in the hollows. Celeste felt a sweetness carry her along as she walked. In spite of Humility's warning, she was confident that after her sacrifice at Skull Hill and crossing the bridge of forgiveness, their path would take them on to the Highlands. She worked hard to keep up with Peter without a single grumble, and often she hummed one of the King's songs to herself.

But Peter was so used to her complaints, he still heard them in his head. Once he turned around and said, "Oh stop complaining, will you?"

Celeste looked at him bewildered, and then replied calmly. "I wasn't saying anything." She was determined to keep answering him with tenderness, hoping that soon he would start to show signs of change.

Peter kept to his pace even when the track became rocky and then turned slippery after a gentle mist. He still wanted the campsite neat and orderly, even if they stayed for only a night. Food was still scarce, and he had to leave Celeste alone with the little travelers for long periods while he searched for something to eat. Soon her old bitterness and resentment returned. Didn't she deserve an easier journey after what she had sacrificed?

One day when he snapped at her, she snapped back. "I've been so patient with you, why can't you be nice for once?"

But he only scowled and said he didn't know what she was talking about.

Just then a strong wind came up. Turning around, she saw Skull Hill behind her with a fire blazing on top. She remembered the death she had died, and she gave a little sob.

There was no way around it; she really had to love Peter without expecting anything in return.

She started to spend time alone with the King every morning before setting off. During the day when she felt too weak to give, she asked the King for what she needed—again and again.

"I do this to please the King and no one else," she told herself. "As I die the Servant's death, I will reveal the Servant's life. And I trust the King to love me."

She worked hard to keep up with Peter. And as she yielded to Peter, her muscles became stronger and she found the walking easier. Although the path was still very rugged, she was able to scramble up the direct, rocky paths Peter loved to take. She let Peter have the biggest log to sit on when they stopped to rest; she gave up asking him to help her with the little travelers when he was tired. Instead of cutting Peter down with unkind words, she complimented him on his stride and thanked him for the warm fire he made every night. She told him how much she appreciated the way he repaired their packs and gathered food for them.

Peter was still judgmental and rigid, but as she looked on him with the King's eyes, her love covered over his sins.

One day she fell and sprained her ankle. She limped on as best she could, not wanting to slow Peter down.

Peter noticed her grimacing. "What's wrong?"

"I twisted my ankle."

He carefully bound it up and carried her bags. Celeste was amazed at his kindness. She walked on behind him—and remembered other times he had cared for her. He had helped her out of the Sand Dunes of Foolishness and gone down the path of co-heirs and waited for her at Submission Pond. She thought of how he played with the little travelers. Though he had gone astray with the honey woman, he had not shared the chalice with her, and he had come back to Celeste with remorse. Celeste thanked the King for Peter.

The days were getting warmer and food easier to find, but Peter still liked to take his time when he looked for provisions. Often he would leave first thing in the morning and not return to Celeste and the little travelers until sunset. But he did not spend the whole day searching for food. Instead he would go off and hike to overlooks, as he had before he became partners with Celeste. Then one day he walked quite far to climb a steep peak that overlooked one of the chasms. When he got to the top, the sun was already low and he decided to take a shorter route down the other side. As he descended, the air turned colder with a sharp wind, and he thought how nice it would be to get back to a warm fire. Much to his surprise, Celeste had become an expert fire builder, and he was certain she had already started one back at their campsite.

But when he reached the bottom, he discovered a rock slide blocked the way back to the main path. The sun had almost set. He didn't think it would be safe to retrace his steps or find a way through the wilderness that lay behind it, and he didn't like the idea of spending a cold night alone. The only other option was to cross a bridge of forgiveness he could see just a little ways down the chasm. When he got to the bridge and looked at the single narrow plank, he shook his head. How could the King expect him to cross such a dangerous bridge? He stood in the growing dark, feeling colder and colder while he wondered what to do.

Before long, he saw Pardon coming toward him.

"It's getting dark and cold," Pardon said. "I can see the campfire Celeste has made for you, up ahead on the other side of the bridge."

Peter nodded, rubbing his arms to stay warm.

"Have you noticed how she has changed lately? She's become more considerate and caring, hasn't she?"

"Yes, but—"

"Why is it so hard for you to appreciate what she has sacrificed for you?"

"Because she doesn't appreciate what I've done for her!" Peter took out his account book and showed the guide. "Do you see all the ways she has failed me? Arguing, yelling, how she always needs to be right, not understanding how hard I work to find food, not giving me love or even sympathy, criticizing my choices—in front of the little travelers too. And she holds it over my head that I went off with the honey woman instead of thanking me that I came back to her."

"Peter, the King calls you to love, not measuring it out drop by drop, but turning on the faucet and letting it flow freely. Do not react to anger with anger, or fault-finding with blame. Give even more than is asked of you, not in your own strength, but filled with the King's Breath and power."

"But my complaints are just. It's not fair that I have to cross the bridge."

"Do you remember what I said the first time we met? You need to burn that account book. Extend to Celeste the same grace the King gave you. Or have you forgotten His mercy?"

Peter remembered the moment long ago when he had first set out on the King's path and Freedom had cut through Peter's chains of debt.

"Act on your love for the King," Pardon said. "Throw your

account into the chasm and walk across the bridge. It may be difficult this time, but it will get easier as you practice."

Peter took a deep breath. "If there is no other way . . ." He grabbed onto the rope of mercy. But the rope was slack, and he could feel himself begin to sway.

"Hold it lightly," Pardon said. "Move on and you will be fine, for the Servant has gone before you and the way is firm."

Peter relaxed his grip on the rope and felt his balance return. Keeping his eyes fixed on the campfire Celeste had made, he walked safely across to the other side.

AT THE QUIET POOL

One afternoon Peter and Celeste came to a series of waterfalls like the one they had enjoyed in the Orchard of Earthly Delights. They stopped to let the little travelers play in the shallow pools while they rested. Spring had come in all its glory, and they took in deep breaths of fragrant air while they listened to the birds' cheering songs. In the warmth of the sun, they dozed off. When they woke, they discovered one of the little travelers had wandered off. They began calling out for him and searching all the paths that led away from the waterfalls, but they couldn't find him. Then they saw a guide leading a flock of sheep down a path, and on his shoulders rode their little traveler. Abundant Provision told them one of his sheep had gone astray the day before, just like the little traveler, and he too had searched until it was found.

Then Abundant Provision noticed the frayed cords of commitment on their wrists. "Travelers are often like sheep who wander far from their good shepherd," he said. "But the King is always looking for them, so He can bring them back to the resting place He made for them. It looks like you have strayed far from the straight path to the Highlands and the King's City, and you have suffered much: hunger and thirst and great loneliness. But the King longs to be gracious to you. When you call to the King, He will deliver you from your distress. He will lead on a good way; He will satisfy you when you are thirsty and fill your hunger with fine food. He will heal your brokenness and let you feast on His unfailing love to you."

Then Abundant Provision led them into a soft green meadow with a quiet pool. The guide took out some bread of life and living water and gave it to them. As they ate and drank, he advised them. "Because the King is your Shepherd, you won't lack anything on the journey ahead. He will bring you again to green meadows, and He will lead you again to quiet waters where He will restore your soul. You may walk through dark valleys, but you need not fear. No evil will come to you, for He will be with you and will give you His strength."

They remained in the meadow for some time, refreshed by the King's goodness. Abundant Provision gave them new kingly gifts to replace the ones they had lost: a new basket of remembrance and new sheepskins of humility, garments of praise, and rags of compassion. Then he sang to them:

> *May the King strengthen you with His Breath,*
> *May you always walk on the path of His love.*
> *And as you walk, may you see—really see—the range of*
>   *His love.*

*May He help you to grasp how far it goes, how long, how
    high, how deep.*
*May you experience this vast, unmeasured love,
and it will fill you up and make you complete.*

When it was time to leave, Peter and Celeste studied the map
carefully so they would follow the best path. But they were dis-
mayed to see that many dangers still lay ahead. There were more
dry washes and vehement volcanoes and desolate canyons to
avoid. Abundant Provision pointed out that several revenge chasms
snaked through the land, and they would have to be prepared to
cross bridges of forgiveness many times, for there was no other way
to reach the Highlands.

"Do not be terrified, do not be discouraged, for the King will
be with you," he said. "Make every effort to stay on the path. If
you do find yourselves off of it, stop immediately and make your
way back."

And in my dream, Peter and Celeste resumed their journey.

Up to the Highlands

AT THE WARMING HUT OF REVELATION

With Abundant Provision's cautions in mind, Peter and Celeste carefully kept to the path. The trail rose through a thick forest, occasionally going through a meadow before continuing up. Soon it became so narrow that Peter and Celeste had to walk in single file. They had little chance to talk, but it was a comfortable, peaceful silence. Peter was glad to be climbing after their long sojourn in the plains and valleys. Even if there were no scenic overlooks, he made sure he didn't get ahead of Celeste and the little travelers. And Celeste was pleased that Peter kept pace with them, for there were fewer travelers in the region. Even though they didn't speak, his presence comforted her.

Then one morning, after spending the night in a meadow, they awoke to find a bank of thick clouds moving toward them, driven by a stiff, biting wind. By the time they packed up, the clouds had surrounded them and they couldn't find the path. They heard something clinking, and when they headed toward it, they almost bumped into a couple. The husband was wearing a complete set of armor; other than a small slit for his eyes, he was covered in metal.

"Where did he get that?" Celeste asked the wife.

"It's hard to say. He had a few of the pieces when we first met. But he's picked up more along the way."

"Where does he find them?"

"I don't know. I think they just appear on him."

"Can he speak?" Peter asked.

The husband raised an armored flap that covered his ears, then lifted his mouthpiece.

"What?"

"I asked if you could speak."

"Yes," the husband said.

"But he prefers to keep to himself," the wife said.

"Aren't you lonely, never talking together?" Celeste noticed his chainmail gloves. "You can't even hold hands properly." She wondered how they drank from the chalice together.

"What are you protecting yourself from?" Peter said. "She's not going to hurt you."

"It's no use," the wife said. "We've just come from the Warming Hut of Revelation and the guide said he could help us, but my partner refused to take off his armor. So we're going back down where the walking is easier."

The husband tugged at his wife's hand, and they shuffled on.

Peter and Celeste and the little travelers pressed up the path to the hut. Because they could barely see the path, Peter made sure they held onto each other, so no one would get lost. Sometimes the fog was so thick, even the trees disappeared. They had no idea where they were going. But they knew the path was still rising steeply, for the air became cooler and they could feel their muscles aching as they climbed. Each day they were less winded, and their legs became stronger. But Celeste suffered from the cold; her lips turned blue, and she could barely feel her fingers and toes.

They finally reached the warming hut and huddled together inside. "What a strange place," Peter said. "It's not even heated. You'd think the owners would have installed central heating or at least kept the firebox full. There are just a few pieces of kindling of affection, and I don't see how they can keep us warm."

"And where's the guide to welcome us or the books that will teach us how to restore the warmth between us again?"

"You are always relying on guides and reading books about how to be partners," Peter said.

"Because I don't know what to do. When I want to get closer to you, you always pull away from me."

"Aren't things better between us?"

"It's true we spend more time together. But I wished we shared more. When we talk, it's just about practical matters—what to feed the little travelers, which path we'll take. Don't you remember how we used to talk and talk all night in the woods before we became partners?"

Peter didn't answer. He was thinking there was nothing to talk about. He knew everything about Celeste; he could even predict her questions and her responses. Then he heard the King say to him: "Do you? Do you really know what Celeste is feeling right now? Do you really know how she suffered in the Desolate Canyon? If you knew more about her, you would be able to love her better."

Peter thought maybe he should try the kindling after all. He rubbed two sticks together, and instantly the kindling started to blaze with a powerful heat. "Come sit by the fire, Celeste." He lay his coat on the floor in front of the fireplace.

"What a wonderful fire," Celeste said.

"So what is wrong?" Peter said. He feared that simple question would open up a torrent of conversation from Celeste.

Celeste stared silently at the fire, wiggling her fingers and toes. She didn't know if she could bear it if she started to talk and Peter didn't listen.

Peter was glad Celeste didn't want to talk. But the King spoke to him again. "Of course she doesn't want to talk with you when you look so impatient."

So Peter tried once more. "Tell me, what has been hard for you?"

"Do you really care?"

Peter nodded. "Of course I do. I'm your partner."

"But you get so caught up in walking and gathering food," she said. "Sometimes I really wonder if you still love me."

"How was it for you in the Desolate Canyon?" he said gently. "I really want to hear."

Celeste took a deep breath. Warmed by the kindling's fire, she gathered her courage to share again with Peter. Slowly she began to tell him how lonely she had been, and how hurt she had felt when she learned of the honey woman. She didn't think it was time yet to tell him about Skull Hill, but she did tell him that she was learning to rely on the King to meet her needs and not Peter.

When Peter heard this, he was relieved, for he had felt so overwhelmed trying to care for Celeste.

"You know sometimes," Celeste said, "I think you'd rather not be married."

"Being partners has turned out so much harder than I expected," Peter admitted. "I used to have such warm deep feelings for you, and now I often don't feel anything."

Celeste wasn't offended. "It's that way for me too sometimes. But I want to remain faithful to the vows I made with you, regardless of how I feel. It's hard though, and sometimes I sense myself pulling away from you and becoming distant."

Peter put more wood on the fire. "You know, when we were at the Valley of the Cut Cords, I realized how much duller my journey would have been without you."

"Really?" Celeste brightened. "You really thought that?"

"I've wondered if you love the little travelers more than you love me," Peter said. "You spend so much time with them, and it takes you so long to put them to bed at night and then you are too tired to drink from the chalice. When you wake up, the first thing you say is, 'I wonder how the little travelers are doing.' I think if I disappeared, it wouldn't really bother you—you'd be happy enough with the little travelers."

Celeste had never imagined that Peter felt that way. She took his hand. "Oh Peter, what would I have done without you? You were brave enough to ignore Mr. One Verse and leave Pigeon Hole, and you rescued all of us from the Orchard of Earthly Delights."

The fire burned on, warming them as they talked into the night. Although Peter didn't tell Celeste about his postcards, he talked about the chalice and how important it was to him. And Celeste told him how much she needed time alone with him before they drank from it. They listened with kindness and gentleness to each other, and as they shared their joys and sorrows, the numbness left Celeste's heart, and Peter's cold fear thawed.

IN THE HIGHLANDS

In my dream, I saw that when morning came, the sky had cleared to a brilliant blue. Outside the warming hut, Peter and Celeste looked around in astonishment. They hadn't realized that as they hiked in the fog, they had been climbing a Mountain of Maturity. Now they found themselves in a velvet green meadow that seemed to float high above the rest of the world. Ahead of them on the horizon, the King's City rose even higher.

"I can't believe it!" Celeste said. "We've reached the Highlands."

Just then, a mountain guide was walking by. When Patience heard what Celeste said, he laughed. "Most people who reach the Highlands have the same reaction. You have taken a slow and gradual ascent up the Mountains of Maturity, and Skull Hill blocked the last view of the Highlands for you. You were walking in faith for quite some time."

"We almost lost all hope," Peter said.

"But no matter how hard the path was, you remained committed to each other, and now you see the reward for your faithfulness."

Peter and Celeste smiled, thankful they had not given up.

"You must be hungry from the climb. Here, take some of this." Patience offered them some milk, and it was like nothing they had ever tasted, so rich and creamy. Then he gave them honey made from the highland flowers.

Peter and Celeste spent the rest of the morning exploring the Highlands. Flocks of sheep and herds of cattle grazed in the fields with bells around their necks ringing out between the Peaks of Maturity. In some places, purple and yellow and pink flowers flowed like bands of the rainbow through the mountain crevices.

They saw many travelers they had met on their journey, though at first Peter and Celeste barely recognized their old friends. For people who reached the pastures moved with the joy and freedom of well-loved children, appearing younger, not older.

On the way back to the hut, Peter wanted to take a path that followed beside a roaring cascade. The water's mist drenched them, but Celeste did not grumble about getting wet. In fact, she was thankful because it was getting hot in the sun and the mist kept them cool.

"Thank you for not complaining about this way," Peter said.

"Oh Peter, I am so sorry for the way I used to gripe all the time. How frustrating that must have been for you. Sometimes I wonder why you put up with me."

"Because I love you," he said. Then a shadow came to his face. "I am sorry for going off with the honey woman. You were patient with me then. What I did was so wrong."

"But it would have never happened if we had avoided Desolate Canyon, and that was as much my fault as yours. And I am to blame that you found her words so sweet, for I wasn't a pleasant companion. But you left her and came back, and I know that couldn't have been easy." Celeste saw Peter tremble. She touched his arm and said, "It's all right."

Peter looked across the mountain peaks. "I have never done anything so difficult. I felt like I was going to my death, and a dream did die. Then when I came back and you were hurt and angry, I wondered if I had made the right choice. But I know now that I did—and I am so grateful that the King saved me."

Celeste thought of her own dying. "How could we ever do this without the Servant?"

Soon after they returned to the warming hut, a guide came by. "I wanted to check that you have everything that you need," Understanding said. "I see you used the kindling of affection. Very good."

"But why didn't you come to see us last night?"

"You didn't need me, did you?"

"No, we had a very nice time talking."

"We generally think it's best for partners to spend time alone listening and sharing with each other. A guide only comes to help if they need a referee or a little instruction."

The guide filled up the firebox with more kindling and before he left them, he said, "Don't forget that you were made for giving as much as you were made for receiving. That's how to discover all of who you are."

Peter and Celeste stayed at the warming hut for several days. When they continued their journey again, the paths in the Highlands were steeper and more challenging than anything they had encountered before. They were glad to discover that they had developed new strength, for the views were clearer and more spectacular, and the King's City was always in sight. Often Celeste would sing one of the King's song to lighten their hearts as they climbed:

> *I lift up my eyes to the mountains—*
> *where does my help come from?*
> *My help comes from the Lord,*
> *the Maker of heaven and earth.*
> *He will not let your foot slip—*
> *He who watches over you will not slumber . . .*
> *The Lord watches over you—*
> *the Lord is your shade at your right hand;*
> *the sun will not harm you by day,*
> *nor the moon by night.*
> *The Lord will keep you from all harm—*
> *He will watch over your life;*
> *the Lord will watch over your coming and going*
> *both now and forevermore.*

IN THE HEALING SPRINGS OF RESTORATION

However, Peter and Celeste were still hampered by their wounds, and they could not take the highest paths. They used the rag of compassion often, but some of their wounds were too deep.

As they struggled along, they came to a guide sitting by the path.

"Dear travelers, I can see your journey has been rough," Peace said. "Ahead you will find the Healing Springs of Restoration where you can recover from your most serious wounds." He showed them on the map how to get to the springs and told them to pay attention, for the turn was easy to miss.

They followed his directions until they came to a huge boulder that blocked the path. "I don't think this is right," Peter said. "There doesn't seem to be a way around the boulder. We must have passed a turn back there."

"No, we were very careful to follow the directions Peace gave us."

Then Peter noticed a small sign in front of an area of thick brush. "Healing Springs of Restoration," the sign said, with an arrow pointing through the brush.

"No wonder people miss the turn," Peter said. "We're going to have to crawl on our hands and knees to follow the path, and that will be difficult with our blisters and sore muscles."

"I wouldn't have been so eager to go this way earlier in our journey," Celeste said. Kneeling, they pushed their bags in front of them and crawled a short way into a broad, sunlit spot. Before them a chain of hot springs from the King's City bubbled out of the rocks. In the center was a deep, broad pool, as blue as the sky.

Peter put his toe in. "Oh Celeste, this is the most delightful water I have ever touched—warm but fresh, flowing strong but soothing." The water, filled with the power of grace, tingled his skin.

But Celeste hesitated. The reflection she saw revealed all the dirt of her sin. She realized that when she entered the pool she would muddy the water, and she wished she could get clean first. Then she became afraid. Dirty and disgraceful as she was now, she was sure the King would disown her. A condemning buzz in her head told her she did not deserve to be healed.

Then she heard the King say, "Can you love yourself like you love others? Be bold; you are free."

Celeste remembered one of the King's songs: "You are a compassionate and gracious King, slow to anger, and overflowing with love and faithfulness. Have mercy on me." She stepped into the pool and as soon as her feet touched the water, the dirt on them vanished, leaving a sharp line between her ankles and her now spotless feet. And the graceful water remained as clear as before.

Peter and Celeste sank into the pool. Sitting in the transparent water, they began to see more clearly their own weaknesses and sins. Yet as soon as a cold wave of shame came over them, a warm surge of water welled up and pushed it away. And a chorus rose up from the springs singing:

Let all that I am praise the King;
with my whole heart, I will praise His holy name.
Let all that I am praise the King;
may I never forget the good things He does for me.
He forgives all my sins
and heals all my diseases.
He redeems me from death
and crowns me with love and tender mercies.
He fills my life with good things. My youth is renewed like
*   the eagle's!*

Then the water bubbled with greater strength, massaging their wounds: every injury they had received, every anguish they had felt. In the warm healing water, they soaked in the forgiveness of the King, and the painful memories dissolved away. When Celeste looked at Peter's wounds, she was filled with compassion for what he had suffered. She dipped the rag of compassion in the water and began to caress his hurts. There were the bruises where she had hit him with her club, a gash from when he had fallen on the rocks with the honey woman, and the lava burns from the Vehement Volcano.

Some of his wounds had become infected. "I'm afraid to scrape away the scabs," she told Peter. "I don't want to hurt you."

"Don't stop. That is the most loving touch I have ever felt," he said.

As she continued to wash his hurts, she started to cry, and her tears softened his skin.

"Don't you feel any pain?" she asked, for at that moment she was cleaning the biggest, ugliest wound on his back.

"I feel love and grace—and such an amazing kindness."

When Celeste finished treating Peter's injuries, she leaned back against the side of the pool and thought back to when she had desperately wanted Peter to make her complete. Now all she wanted to do was to help him become more whole, and she rejoiced that the King had led them to the healing springs.

"But what about your wounds?" Peter said.

"Mine?" Celeste had completely forgotten the ways Peter had wronged her. All she could remember were her own failures and weaknesses, how she had not fulfilled her vows, the times she had given Peter a cold shoulder or spoken a cruel word. "They don't bother me anymore."

"You have a nasty one on your side—it's all scarred over and maybe that's why you can't feel it," Peter said. He began to wipe her wounds, and Celeste had never felt such tenderness from him. "And these blisters on your feet—why didn't you tell me they were so bad?"

"I tried once, but you were busy."

"I am so sorry for the pain I caused you."

"It was I who failed you," Celeste said.

They almost began to argue about which of them had acted worse, but they quickly realized what a silly argument that was.

Peter and Celeste stayed in the pool all day, experiencing the glorious freedom of being fully known and yet accepted and loved without shame. As they gave each other compassion and kindness, they were renewed in the knowledge of the King and their brokenness turning to wholeness. Their scars didn't disappear, but by the time Peter and Celeste were finished, their old wounds almost looked beautiful, infused with love and understanding.

"Think how close we came to cutting our cords," Celeste said. "If we had, we would have never experienced this miraculous healing together."

Their cords, now cleaned and rewoven, began to shine brightly again on their wrists. Peter and Celeste repeated the pledge they had made to each other on their weaving day:

> "I will love you, I will honor you,
> I will give you my affections.

I will walk with no other partner,
and no matter how dark or how cold the way,
no matter how weak you become,
I will love you always and walk together with you
until we reach the King's City."

But for all the joy and blessings Peter and Celeste found at the healing springs, they did not want to stay there. As their love again grew strong, so did their desire to reach the King's City. Gathering the little travelers, they set off once more.

AMONG NEW MEADOWS

Back on the path they came to a crossroads with a sign that pointed to the left branch. Celeste started toward it. But because the branch headed down into a valley, Peter wanted to double check the map. An old impatience rose in Celeste, but she told herself there was no harm in stopping for a little rest. While she sat with the little travelers, she discovered a patch of the tiniest wildflowers growing alongside the path. She was thankful she had kept her temper because she would have never seen them if Peter hadn't wanted to stop.

"Some spiteful person must have turned the sign around," Peter said. "Both the compass and the map are clear that we should take the right branch." Peter pointed to a rocky way.

"Oh no, Peter, look at how bad that path is—" Then Celeste remembered the wildflowers. "Okay, let's go the way you think we should."

They journeyed on, attentive to keep on the path. The way

became straight, and the rough ground grew smooth. They followed a small brook, with sprays of ferns bordering the path. It lead them into another meadow—like the first chalice meadow they had gone to, only more lovely and fragrant.

Celeste began to understand how poor the scenes on her postcards had been. If she had followed those visions, she would have never gone up to Skull Hill; she would have held onto her postcards until they dissolved into scraps. But when she buried the dreams, she was able to experience a deep oneness with Peter—something so extraordinary she had never imagined anything like it in all her dreaming. Peter also realized what a pale imitation his postcards had been; drinking from the chalice with Celeste satisfied him like no postcard could.

They took turns setting the pace and choosing the route, sometimes going fast and sometimes slow, sometimes taking the upper paths and sometimes the lower paths.

Celeste would go through the small tight spots for them, and Peter would reach up to the high places for the handholds. Peter began to search out the most flower-filled meadows for Celeste to enjoy, and Celeste began to urge Peter to climb up to the best overlooks. At night when the air grew chilly, Peter would get the sheepskin of humility from the pack and put it around Celeste. When he grew tired from chopping wood, she would rub his shoulders as she did long ago in the grove. And when they drank from the chalice, it was the sweetest drinking they could ever remember.

It was as if they were dancing together, giving and receiving without thinking, for they were walking together as one.

But in time, a deep drought came over the King's country, even in the Highlands. Green gave way to brown. The birds flew away in search of water, and the weather turned from hot to cold and back to hot. The journey through the dry, weary land was as difficult as anything Peter and Celeste had experienced as partners.

The days turned into months and still there was no relief. They began to disagree about whether they should stay together or have Peter go off in search of food. They had no energy to kick pebbles. Though they still made sure to sing to the King and read the guidebook every day, they suffered a terrible thirst. Celeste remembered the Healing Springs and the grassy meadows, and it seemed like the King was playing a cruel joke on them. But Peter reminded her that not every difficulty came from their stubbornness. No matter what hardships they went through, nothing could separate them from the King's love. That night by the fire, they read from the guidebook:

> "I've learned by now to be quite content whatever my
> circumstances.
> I'm just as happy with little as with much, with much as
> with little.
> I've found the recipe for being happy
> whether full or hungry,
> hands full or hands empty.
> Whatever I have, wherever I am,
> I can make it through anything in the One who makes
> me who I am."

They decided to climb higher, hoping to find a stream from a mountain's melting snow. After an exhausting ascent they came to a green plateau fed by a small spring. Suddenly Peter stopped.

"I don't need to rest," Celeste said.

"Look," he said quietly.

She gasped. The plateau was rapidly becoming a wasteland. The plants curled up and the trees shriveled. Then suddenly, the ground sprouted thorns as sharp as daggers.

As they walked on, the thorns ripped their clothes and cut their arms and legs.

"What's happening? Did we take a wrong turn or disobey a sign?" Celeste said.

Peter shook his head. "We are still the children of the King, but the world remains under the control of the evil one."

"Maybe we can just set up camp here," Celeste said. "We could clear a little space. I'm sure we can find something to eat."

"If we camp here, we'll never get out," Peter said. He had them all hold hands, and they continued slowly, but they could not avoid being cut by the thorns. "We need to protect ourselves," Peter said. "Wrap your robe of righteousness and your sheepskin of humility tightly around you."

Doing this they were able to make their way back to a clear path just before the sun set. They spent an uneasy night close to the thorn land and to encourage them, Peter read from the guidebook:

"Therefore we do not lose heart. Though outwardly we are wasting away, yet inwardly we are being renewed day by day. For our light and momentary troubles are achieving for us an eternal glory that far outweighs them all. So we fix our eyes not on what is seen, but on what is unseen. For what is seen is temporary, but what is unseen is eternal."

They got up as soon as the sun rose and started off again. By mid-morning, they reached a small hut where a guide named Courage lived. He invited them in and spoke to them about the journey ahead. "You have learned that the highland meadows are not the end of your journey. There is still a long way to go before you reach the King's City and until then you will never be finished with burdens and struggles. There will always be new challenges to face: the little travelers will leave you, and you will grow old. Another drought may come, and the roaring lion continues to prowl. But all these trials come so your faith may be proved genuine—and will result in praise and glory and honor for the King. So do not be ashamed. You can boast of your weaknesses, because His power is made perfect in weakness."

Courage suggested that they stay with him for a few days so he could help them go through their bags, for they had picked up new burdens along the way. This time Peter and Celeste didn't mind getting rid of their unconfessed sins and rusty treasures.

When Celeste looked at the pile, she sighed. "Look at all these unnecessary burdens. Is there any way we could have avoided getting them?"

"It would have been possible to come directly to the Highlands over the Mountains of Maturity, except you wanted to find an easier way because your legs were weak and your hearts were faint. I think you've learned now that it does no good to take a detour when you come to a challenging section."

"Yes, but only through painful experience," Peter said.

"Don't be discouraged. There are some travelers who choose harder routes and are able to bypass many of the dangers in the Low Country. But I have never heard of any traveler who was able to completely avoid the Swamp of Selfishness."

That night by the fire, Courage reminded them again that life would not always be sweet, even in the Highlands.

"Your postcard dreams led you astray. Those scenes seemed ideal, but you learned they were a weak and incomplete picture of true love. Even after you burned and buried them, you expected the Highlands would be like a fairy tale. Now be careful not to fall back into the trap of thinking that romantic love will solve your problems."

Peter and Celeste nodded.

"It's not easy. Remember that you did not start on the journey to the King's City for pleasure's sake, but because you loved the King and you longed for a better country. Those who belong to the Servant have nailed the passions and desires of their old selves to the Servant's cross and killed them there.

"But what glories are waiting for us in the beautiful city the King has prepared for us. Just think—when we get there we shall be like Him, for we will see Him as He truly is. Hallelujah!" The guide jumped to his feet and danced a little jig; he was so full of joy. Together they sang and praised the King as long as the fire's coals still glowed.

The next morning, Peter and Celeste gathered their little travelers and prepared to leave. Before he said goodbye, Courage sang one more song:

Be blessed as you journey, following the path of the King.
Be blessed as you listen to His instructions and obey His directions.
Walk in His way only and pay attention carefully. Praise the King!

TOWARD THE KING'S CITY

In the summer, Peter and Celeste decided to climb the highest peak by themselves. When they reached the summit, they saw the clearest and closest view yet of the King's City. The city appeared as an unshakable mountain filled with thousands upon thousands of angels in joyful assembly. Surrounded by a wall of dark green jasper, it shone like a brilliant diamond, made of gold so pure it was like glass. It did not need the sun or the moon, for the glory of the King gave it light. The River of the Water of Life, clear as crystal, flowed from the King's Throne through the middle of the city, and there was no mourning or crying or pain anywhere.

Peter and Celeste could see a crowd of redeemed travelers streaming into the city, with joy crowning their heads like halos, and singing:

How beautiful is the place where You live, O King,
How eager I am to enter into Your city, to come into Your courtyard.

All of me, body and soul, shouts with joy to You.
How wonderful to live in Your house and sing Your praise.

"That's where we're headed!" Peter said. "Someday we'll join them loving the King and glorifying Him forever."

"I've never heard anything so beautiful," Celeste said. "It will be wonderful to sing in that choir."

"Look—over there," Peter said. At the gates to the city, a traveler was getting ready to enter. They saw him turn to kiss his partner goodbye, then he went through the gate. "Well done, good and faithful Servant," they heard the doorkeeper say to the traveler.

For a long while, neither Celeste nor Peter spoke. Each was thinking what a painful separation it would be if the King didn't call them together and one of them had to stay behind.

They stood there silently, with the light of the King's glory shining on them. Then they turned to each other—and for a brief moment saw each other whole and complete in the King's love, as He had created them to be.

"This was always my favorite postcard," Celeste said quietly.

"You and I were in the postcard?"

"It was another couple, though I dreamed that someday it would be me." She took Peter's hands. "But what a dim reflection my postcards were of what could be. We've gone through so many difficulties—some of our own choosing, some we had no control over—and so many times I lost all hope for our partnership. But the King gave us strength to save it. By His grace we are still partners, and by His grace I have experienced a love with you that is so much richer and fuller than I ever imagined when we first set out."

"Truly you have become heart of my heart and flesh of my flesh," Peter said.

Holding hands, they turned again toward the far horizon, looking to that day when they would stand before the King and all their incompleteness would be made whole in the great Complete.

Then they looked around the Highlands and saw how the love of the King and His faithfulness reached all the way to the sky. Together they pledged to keep walking on the path of love, as the Servant had done. They would continue to teach the little travelers the way until it was time for them to set off on their own. They would keep praising the King and doing good, sharing with other travelers along the way.

They knew they would still face trials, but whatever happened, they would always find refuge in the shadow of the King. Through storms and droughts and floods, mudslides and swamps and canyons, He would never give up on them. He would always go with them, giving them everything they needed to follow His path home.

The last light of the sun was disappearing behind them. It was time for them to go back down to the Highlands.

Peter faced Celeste. Taking her hands, he asked her, "Will you walk with me?"

And Celeste said, "Yes."

Scripture References and Sources

....

1: ON THE KING'S WAY

"had sent the Servant, not to condemn them": See John 3:17

"by giving them His very Breath": See John 20:22

"my Robe of Righteousness": See Isaiah 61:10

"the stains of your guilt": See Jeremiah 2:22

"But she pressed on, working to strengthen her flabby muscles":
    See Hebrews 12:12

"ask other travelers which direction to go": See Proverbs 2:6–13

"travelers who no longer cared": See 2 Peter 2:15–18 THE MESSAGE

"not meant to be taken alone": See 1 Corinthians 2:25–26

"how great was the love of the King": See Ephesians 3:18

"She knew she would never go back": See Hebrews 11:15–16

"to give those who followed Him life to the full": See John 10:10

"streams of living water would flow from within": See John 7:37

"his real life was on the Servant's path": See Colossians 2:20–3:4

"The Roaring Lion prowls around": See 1 Peter 5:8

"the Weights of Decrees and Regulations": See Matthew 23:4

"the Servant died to free the prisoners from their chains": See
    Luke 4:18

"the Knife of Grace can cut through your chains": See Romans
    3:21–26

"tell the King he was sorry": See 1 John 1:9

"Anyone who cuts the cords, except for unfaithfulness": See
   Matthew 19:8–9

"there is no partnership in the King's City": See Matthew 22:30

"He created the first partners in the Great Garden": See Genesis
   2:21–24

"You could put every mountain into the ocean": See 1 Corinthians
   13:2b

"your songs will sound like rusty hinges": See 1 Corinthians 13:1

"Make allowance for each other's faults": Colossians 3:13 NLT

"the King's love never gives up and never loses faith": See
   1 Corinthians 13:7 NLT

"Place me like a seal over your heart": Song of Solomon 8:6–7

2: IN THE LOW COUNTRY

"Printed in large letters": See Genesis 2:15–17

"they hid behind some trees": See Genesis 3:8–11

" use your freedom to serve one another in love": See Galatians
   5:13–14

"If you have never disobeyed a sign, go ahead and judge her": See
   John 8:7

"Garments of Praise": See Isaiah 61:3

"remember what the King has done for us": See Psalm 77:11–12

"to encourage each other daily": See Hebrews 3:13

"do not let the sun set on your anger": See Ephesians 4:26

"be careful not to turn away": 1 Peter 1:14–18 THE MESSAGE

"Do everything without complaining or arguing": Philippians
   2:14

"Do not let any unwholesome talk": Ephesians 4:29

"pay attention to each other's weaknesses and troubles": See
   Philippians 2:4

"If you feel a little twinge": See James 1:14–15

"Serve Him with all your heart and with all your soul": See
    Deuteronomy 10:12–13
"be careful not to turn away": See 1 Peter 1:14–18 THE MESSAGE
"some travelers have been tortured and stoned": See Hebrews
    11:35–38
"courage to walk on water": See Matthew 14:29
"not brave enough": See Luke 22:56–60
"For this reason a man will leave": Matthew 19:4–6
"store up my treasures in the King's City": See Matthew 6:19
"I gave up my citizenship": See 1 Peter 2:11
"The logs, dear mother": See Matthew 7:3–5 ESV
"Get rid of all bitterness": Ephesians 4:31–32

3. AROUND THE MOUNTAINS OF MATURITY

"the Course of Testing": See James 1:2–4
"guides disguised as harmless sheep": See Matthew 7:15 NLT
"thinking only about their own comfort": See Philippians 2:3–4
"All day, the rain poured down": See Matthew 7:24–27
"not give up until we get to the King's City": See Philippians
    3:12–14
"he sang to the King": See Colossians 3:16
"Turn your ear to listen to me": Psalm 31:2–3 NLT
"Oh, that my steps might be steady": Psalm 119:5–6
    THE MESSAGE
"My sad life's dilapidated": Psalm 119:28–30 THE MESSAGE
"The King knows your weakness": See Isaiah 40:27–31
"Self-Control in front, followed by Patient Endurance": See
    2 Peter 1:5–7
"For a moment Celeste thought he looked like a wolf": See
    Matthew 7:15
"there should be a stream of living water": See John 7:37–39

"These people come near to me with their mouth": Isaiah 29:13
"strain out a gnat from their cup": See Matthew 23:24
"cares more about the regulations": See John 5:39–40
"The inside was as dirty as the outside was clean": See Matthew
    23:25–26
"listen to the rules but don't put them into practice": See James
    1:22–25
"like clanging gongs, screeching hinges": See 1 Corinthians 13:1
"I don't see any fruit here": See Galatians 5:22–23
"a rule that says you should sing": See Psalm 47:6–7
"The King's truth will set me free": See John 8:32
"I have my Guidebook to light my way:" See Psalm 119:105
"Wives, submit to your husbands": paraphrase of Ephesians
    5:22–24
"Yes, just like the one hundredth sheep": See Luke 15:3–7
"Husbands, love your wives": paraphrase of Ephesians 5:25–30
"You know that the rulers": paraphrase of Mark 10:42–45 NLT
"to love your neighbor as yourself": Matthew 22:39
"a story of mercy and compassion": See Luke 10:25–37

4. ACROSS THE SWAMP OF SELFISHNESS

"Tree of the Knowledge of Good and Evil": See Genesis 3:16–19
"filled with all kinds of evil": See 2 Timothy 3:2–5; Galatians
    5:19–21
"don't think the King's path is supposed to be like this": See Psalm
    37:23
"show us a way out": See 1 Corinthians 10:12–13
"each of us being quick to speak": See James 1:19
"We are trying to be patient with each other": See Ephesians 4:1–2
"If any of you wants to be my follower": Luke 9:23–24 NLT
"You will need the same attitude": paraphrase of Philippians 2:5–8

"I will be working in you as you go": See Philippians 2:13

"important rules of the journey: travel light": See Hebrews 12:1b

"He wants to give His travelers easy, light bags": See Matthew 11:28–30

"The King asks sick people": See John 5:6

"If anyone else thinks he has reasons": See Philippians 3:4–6

"realize those credentials": paraphrase of Philippians 3:7

"As they spoke the truth in love to one another": See Ephesians 4:15

"I called to the King for help": paraphrase of Psalm 40:1–2

The look of love had returned": See 1 Peter 4:8

"You are co-heirs": See 1 Peter 3:7

"The Servant laid down his life": See John 10:17–18

"Iron sharpens iron": See Proverbs 27:17

"washing their dirty feet": See John 13: 4–5

"told them to follow His example": See John 13:15

"remain attached to Him": See John 15:4

5. UNDER THE DISILLUSIONING SUN

"to meet together and encourage one another": Hebrews 10:25

"Better is one day in your courts": Psalm 84:10

"So here I am in the place of worship": Psalm 63:2–4
    THE MESSAGE

"If you fall, remember that He is faithful": See 2 Timothy 2:13

"These were given to train you": See Hebrews 12:5–13

"He is also the King of comfort": See 2 Corinthians 1:3–4

"Are you tired? Worn out? Burned out on religion?": Matthew 11:28–30 THE MESSAGE

"if you are not loving your partner": See 1 John 4:19–21

"Together you are one whole traveling body": See 1 Corinthians 12:25–27 "love was not rude or easily angered": See 1 Corinthians 13:5

"He went to bed angry": See Ephesians 4:26–27

"spewing fiery sparks": See James 3:5–6

"man with a smooth tongue came": See Proverbs 6:24

"the King's holy light that would cause a person to shield their eyes": See Exodus 33:18–20

"things that were unlovely": See Philippians 4:8

"not complaining or arguing": See Philippians 2:14–15

6. INTO THE ORCHARD OF EARTHLY DELIGHTS

"one could often see a well-off traveler": See James 2:14–17

"Rich travelers built large houses": See Luke 12:13–21

"to worry about what they would eat": See Luke 12:22–31

"their love of its pleasures grew": See Mark 4:19

"felt the strain of earning enough": See James 4:1–3

"Is anyone thirsty? Come and drink": Isaiah 55:1–3 NLT

"Call on the King": paraphrase of Isaiah 55:6–7 NLT

"lavish in his forgiveness": paraphrase of Isaiah 55:7b THE MESSAGE

"the King's words cut through him like a two-edged sword": See Hebrews 4:12

"They were dying for heart food": See John 4:34; 6:35

"But you walked away from your first love": Revelation 2:4–5 THE MESSAGE

"I see what you've done": Revelation 2:3 THE MESSAGE

"Today, if you hear His voice": Hebrews 3:7b–9

"See to it, brothers and sisters": paraphrase of Hebrews 3:12–13

"false teachers may come among you": 2 Peter 2:1, 3, 14, 15

"it is easier for a camel": paraphrase of Matthew 19:23–24, 26

"responsible to love Celeste": See Ephesians 5:25

"not by lording it over her": See Matthew 20:25–28

"You will go out in joy": Isaiah 55:12–13

"There's nothing to these people": 2 Peter 2:17–18a
THE MESSAGE
"all the good and perfect gifts": See James 1:17
"keep my heart and mind set": See Colossians 3:1–3
"Many travelers want to serve both the King and Money": See
Matthew 6:24
"Yes, the orchard is the King's": See Psalm 24:1
"Don't love the world's ways": 1 John 2:17–18 THE MESSAGE
"The Servant turned water to wine": See John 2:7–9
"went to parties with people who were not traveling to the King's
City": See Matthew 9:9–12
"the Chosen People had the same problem": See Deuteronomy
8:7–17
"People do not live by bread alone": Paraphrase of Matthew
4:4 NLT
"enough love to cover over the faults": See 1 Peter 4:8
"Who needs a doctor": Mark 2:17 THE MESSAGE
"The eye is the lamp of your body": Matthew 6:22
"Ask the King to strengthen you": See Ephesians 3:16–17
"Only Your grace is sufficient for me": See 2 Corinthians 12:9
"The Breath of the King filled him, and he lit the match": See
Philippians 4:13
"The walls there are made of jasper": See Revelation 21:18–21;
21:4
"Forget what is behind": See Hebrews 12:2
"surefooted like deer": See Habakkuk 3:19

7. ALONG DESOLATE CANYON TO REVENGE CHASM

"the King still cared for them": See Isaiah 44:21–22
"the Breath of the King reminded him": See John 14:26
"wanting to drink the chalice": See Matthew 5:27–28
"The lips of a Honey Woman": See Proverbs 5:3–6

"Keep to a path far from her": See Proverbs 5:8–14

"the Servant sympathized with Peter's weakness": See Hebrews
    4:14–15

"Oh, what a miserable person I am!": See Romans 7:24

"could approach the throne of grace with confidence": See
    Hebrews 4:16

"For there is now no condemnation": See Romans 8:1–2

"the Breath of the King spoke to him: 'Flee, flee'": See 1 Corinthi-
    ans 6:18

"Do you not know that your body": paraphrase of 1 Corinthians
    6:19–20

"angels and demons, heights and depths": See Romans 8:38–39

"When my heart was grieved": paraphrase of Psalm 73:21, 23, 24,
    26

"Have mercy on your fellow traveler": See Matthew 18:17–25

"You were taught to love your enemies": See Luke 6:27–30

"love keeps no record of wrongs": See 1 Corinthians 13:5

"Long before you even knew you were lost": See Romans 5:8

"they claimed to be walking in the King's light": See 1 John
    2:9–11

"knowledge of the Servant and the sweet fragrance": See
    2 Corinthians 2:14

"all sorts of evil things—quarreling, jealousy, outbursts of anger":
    See Galatians 5:19–21

"if you love the King you must love": See 1 John 4:20–21

"Anyone who divorces his wife, except for marital unfaithfulness":
    See Matthew 19:9

"your whole life has to be shaped": 1 Peter 1:13–16 paraphrase of
    THE MESSAGE

"Because these trials test your faith": See James 1:2–4

"a spiritual refining process, with glory just around the corner":
    1 Peter 4:13 THE MESSAGE

"Don't be short-sighted": See Hebrews 12:16–17

"and He loves you": Ephesians 5:1–3 paraphrase of
THE MESSAGE

"remembered he was set free for freedom": Galatians 5:1

"the King has forgiven us completely": I am indebted to Tim
Keller's sermon, "And Kissed Him" for this explanation of forgiveness. http://sermons2.redeemer.com/sermons/and-kissed-
him

"don't use your freedom to go your own way": See Galatians
5:13–14

"Take his yoke and learn from him": See Matthew 11:29

"submit to each other": See Ephesians 5:21

"He is faithful and he will do it": See 1 Thessalonians 5:24

"As you obey the King": See Isaiah 58:11

"may the King bless you": See Numbers 6:24–26

8. THROUGH THE DARKEST NIGHT

"working together with one mind": See Philippians 2:2 NLT

"In light of all this": Ephesians 4:1–4 THE MESSAGE

"love binds you together": See Colossians 3:14 NLT

"Then the king called in the man he had forgiven": See Matthew
18:32–34

"So I will ask the King": Ephesians 3:16–18 paraphrase of NLT

"to give without expecting anything in return": See Luke 6:35

"Don't you know Me after": See John 14:9

"If you want to save your life": See Matthew 16:25–26

"Please give me another way": See Luke 22:42, 44

"When you pass through the waters": Isaiah 43:2

"Peace be with you": See John 20:19

"My peace I give you": John 14:27

"Not my will, but Your will be done": See Luke 22:42

"by My wounds, you have been healed": See Isaiah 53:5

"Remain in my love": See John 15:9–10
"How great is the love": 1 John 3:1 paraphrase
"Not by might, nor by power": Zechariah 4:6 paraphrase
"Everything is possible": See Mark 9:23
"I do believe; help me overcome my unbelief": Mark 9:24
"You are My beloved": See Deuteronomy 33:12
"trusting in the King's unfailing love": See Psalm 13:5
"Fix your eyes on the Servant": Hebrews 12:2 paraphrase
"And hope does not disappoint us": See Romans 5:5
"a great cloud of witnesses": Hebrews 12:1
"The husband could not take care of her": The story of Robertson McQuilkin is told in his book, *A Promise Kept*, Tyndale House Publishers, 1998.
"money could have been given to the poor": See John 12:4–5
"Cancel the debt": See Romans 13:8
"How many more times will I have to": See Matthew 18:21–22
"she asked the King for what she needed—again and again": See Luke 11:8–13; 18:1–8
"She worked hard to keep up with Peter": See Ephesians 4:2–3
"have the biggest log to sit on": See Philippians 2:3–7
"how much she appreciated": See 1 Peter 3:9
"her love covered over his sins": See 1 Peter 4:8
"amazed at his kindness": 1 Peter 3:7
"the King calls you to love": Matthew 5:38–42 paraphrase
"one of his sheep had gone astray": See Matthew 18:12–14
"the King longs to be gracious to you": Psalm 107:4–9 paraphrase
"the King is your shepherd": Psalm 23 paraphrase
"May the King strengthen you with His Breath": Ephesians 3:16–19 paraphrase.
"Do not be terrified, do not be discouraged": See Joshua 1:9

9. Up to the Highlands

"listened with kindness and gentleness": See Galatians 5:22–23
"moved with the joy and freedom of a well-loved child": See
    Romans 8:5–17 THE MESSAGE
"I lift up my eyes to the mountains": See Psalm 121:1–3, 5–8
"Be bold; you are free": 1 John 3:21 paraphrase of THE MESSAGE
"You are a compassionate and gracious King": Psalm 86:15–16
    paraphrase
"Let all that I am praise the King": Psalm 103:1–5 paraphrase of
    NLT
"freedom of being fully known": See 1 John 3:19–22
"renewed in the knowledge of the King": See Colossians 3:10, 12
"The way became straight": See Isaiah 40:1–5
"It was always dry": See Psalm 63:1
"they were still thirsty": See Psalm 42:1–2
"they were bound to have hardships": See Romans 8:35
"I've learned by now to be quite content": See Philippians 4:10b–
    13 THE MESSAGE
"We are still the children of the King": 1 John 5:19 paraphrase
"Therefore we do not lose heart": 2 Corinthians 4:16–18
"all these trials come": See 1 Peter 1:7
"you can boast of your weaknesses": See 2 Corinthians 12:8–9
"you will always have difficulties": See John 16:33
"you longed for a better country": See Hebrews 11:13–16
"Those who belong to the Servant": See Galatians 5:24
"we shall be like Him": See 1 John 3:2
"Be blessed as you journey": See Psalm 119:1–7 paraphrase
"The city appeared as an unshakable mountain": See Hebrews
    12:22
"shone like a brilliant diamond": See Revelation 21:11
"made of gold so pure": See Revelation 21:18

"it did not need the sun or the moon": See Revelation 21:23

"the River of the Water of Life": See Revelation 22:1

"no mourning or crying or pain": See Revelation 21:4

"a crowd of ransomed and redeemed travelers": See Isaiah 35:9–10

"How beautiful is the place": Psalm 84:1–4 paraphrase

"all their incompleteness made whole": 1 Corinthians 13:10, 12 paraphrase of THE MESSAGE

"the love of the King reaching": See Psalm 36:5

"they would always find refuge": See Psalm 91:1

"walking the paths of this love": See Ephesians 5:2

"They would always praise the King": See Hebrews 13:15–16

"He would always go with them": See Matthew 28:20; Hebrews 13:21

Acknowledgments

· ·

Working on this book, I have been reminded over and over that we do not walk alone. I have been nourished on my journey by the wisdom of many, including Eugene Peterson, Paul Miller, and Tim Keller. I'm also grateful for each person who came alongside me, sharing their time and talents, to help bring this book into the world.

I especially want to thank Bob Allums, a true Barnabas, for his unfailing vision and support for this book. Elaine Pierce and Jenny Russon gave invaluable early readings of the manuscript as the story took shape. I'm grateful to the members of Rabat International Church for their fellowship and encouragement along the way. My editor at River North, Deb Keiser, was a devoted shepherd during the publication process. I'm also truly indebted to Andy Scheer, who masterfully edited the manuscript.

I owe a great deal to my parents, Warren and Ann Himmelberger, whose marriage has been a reassuring example of faithfulness and love throughout my life.

I'm deeply thankful for Elizabeth and Caitlin, my daughters and friends extraordinaire, for whom I first wrote this story. Later they eagerly joined the editorial adventure, offering perceptive feedback and wonderful insights all along the way.

Most of all, I am thankful for Jack, who has shared every step of this journey with me. Without his sacrificial love, grace, and unending encouragement, this book could not have been written.

FICTION FROM MOODY PUBLISHERS

River North Fiction is here to provide quality fiction that will refresh and encourage you in your daily walk with God. We want to help readers know, love, and serve JESUS through the power of story.

Connect with us at www.rivernorthfiction.com

- Blog
- Newsletter
- Free Giveaways

- Behind the scenes look at writing fiction and publishing
- Book Club

MOODY
PUBLISHERS

www.MoodyPublishers.com